V. E. N. O. M.

In Venenum Potentia

TY MITCHELL

V. E. N. O. M.

Signed,
Special Agent Ethan Parker

Printed in the United States of America
ISBN 978-1-7335436-0-6
Red Rope Press
PSC 7 Box 139
APO, AE 09104
www.RedRopePress.com

V. E. N. O. M.

If you loved this book and would love to receive FREE short stories from the V.E.N.O.M. universe—and updates about the sequel to this book—please join our mailing list at www. tymitchellbook.com

To my children Julian and Elena.
Anything is possible if you put God first.

If the people cannot trust their government to do the job for which it exists- to protect and promote their common welfare- all else is lost.

-President Barack Obama

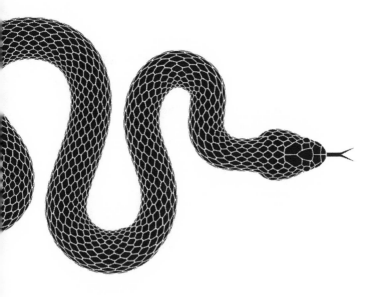

1.

Catskills, New York

The nighttime mountains seemed frozen in time, their wooded terrain as brutal as it was scenic. One wrong step in the darkness could turn a lost soul into the feast of the forest.

A string of snow-covered houses clung to the forest's edge, lifeless Christmas lights still hanging from the gutters, holiday spirit now little more than a memory. The home closest to the trees was old but sturdy, with a brick chimney and purlin rooftop. Dim light seeped from a second-story window. Three black cars were parked outside; two SUVs and a sedan.

Inside the house, the sound of laughing children echoed off dated wallpaper and wood trim whose once-bright paint had chipped away like smoker's lung. In the bedroom, a single light bulb hung from the ceiling. Two pushed-together twin beds and a dusty nightstand were the room's only furnishings.

A group of young Chinese children lay on their stomachs atop the mattresses, watching in rapt attention as Jun Li read their favorite folk story: *The Tale of Lok Lee and the Dwarf*. It was a story they'd all heard many times before yet longed to hear again. Their attention was unwavering as Jun Li's active voice captured their imaginations.

Jun Li was the complete opposite of what the listeners had expected. His hair was jet black and shoulder length. He wore a black leather jacket, crisp jeans and polished shoes. The children marveled at him because he was somewhat like a fairytale himself. They felt like they could close their eyes, make a wish, and magically become him.

Jun Li glanced up as he turned the page, smiling at the purity he'd felt as a child. Then he checked his watch and felt a lump in his throat. His audience was clearly expecting more, but he marked the page and closed the book. "I think that is enough for tonight," he said.

The children all whined together like a symphony.

"Can't you read just a little more, Jun Li?" asked the youngest .

Jun Li shook his head. "I can't. It's getting late, and you have to go back to sleep. I shouldn't have awakened you all in the first place."

The children did as they were told and climbed under the patchy comforter that covered the double-bed. But the oldest, a thirteen-year-old boy, stepped to the floor and headed for the door.

Jun Li stepped in front of him. "Where do you think you're going?"

"I have to go to the bathroom," the boy said.

Jun Li studied the boy's face. "Koa, is it?"

The boy gave Jun Li a suspicious look.

"I heard one of your brothers say it earlier," said Jun Li.

"Mr. Pei says I should go by my American name, John."

Jun Li grabbed Koa by the back of the neck and looked him dead in the eyes. "Koa is a strong name for a strong young man. Do you understand?"

Koa nodded.

Jun Li stepped aside. "All right, Koa, you may go, but

don't be gone for too long. You're the leader of this group, which means you lead by example."

Koa smiled with confidence—which was rare for him; his teeth overlapped, and he kept smiles to a minimum.

Jun Li turned toward the other children as Koa left for the bathroom. "As for the rest of you…sleep. We'll finish the story when you wake up."

Jun Li gave each of them a kiss on the foreheads. They said their goodnights and tucked themselves in. Jun Li pulled the ratty string connected to the light bulb and left the room.

In the hall, he waited for Koa to go into the bathroom and close the door. He stretched his neck, then proceeded down the creaky staircase.

The living room was nothing special, with modest furniture and a small wooden table for tea. The only things that gave the space any personality were the many black-and-white photos.

Jun Li noticed two cups filled with steaming tea. "I see that you were not able to finish your tea," he said. "My apologies." He turned to the old Chinese couple, bound and gagged in facing chairs. They kept their focus on each other, never breaking eye contact. Their clothes had been torn during their earlier struggle with the five henchmen standing over them.

Jun Li's footsteps triggered a panic in the old woman, and her breathing quickened. Her bloodshot eyes grew wide, pleading for her husband to do something. But there was nothing he could do but watch with the eye that wasn't swollen shut.

Jun Li stroked the woman's face while looking at the old man. "Those are some special children you have upstairs. Why don't you allow them to live by their birth names and speak in their native tongue? Are you trying so hard to forget your past that you would deprive our future of its heritage? Or are *they* making you do that?"

Jun Li ripped the gag from the old man's mouth. The man took a moment to catch his breath through swollen lips still dappled with blood. Finally he whispered, "Those kids…they are not your future."

Jun Li took a sip of tea. "Ban Tian Yao—not readily available here in the States. Who's getting it for you? The Americans?"

The old man raised his head up and said in Mandarin, "I don't know why you came into my home with such disrespect. Your reasoning is beneath me. But there's still hope for you, lost boy. I will be generous and give you a chance to leave unharmed. I suggest you take it."

Jun Li's face tightened into a snarl as he snatched the teapot and dangled it over the old woman's head. "You're not in a position to be giving chances. Those days are over. Now give me what I came for."

The old man scoffed, then winced at the sting in his cheeks. "You always were the ant that tried to push the mountain. If you possessed so much power, you wouldn't know what to do with it."

Jun Li smirked. The sight made the old man hold his breath and feel his heartbeat.

"There's only one way to find out," Jun Li said. He tilted the teapot and poured the steaming liquid onto the old woman's lap. Her screams pierced the gag and filled the room.

"Jun Li!" the old man yelled over her screams. He moved as far as his restraints would allow. His throat closed at the sight of his wife shaking from her hands to her tender red thighs.

"I hear that Ban Tain Yao is a great remedy for dry scalps," Jun Li said. He grabbed the back of the old woman's neck and held her head down on her lap. The old man's lips quivered.

Jun Li grew tired of his silence and signaled for one of his men to go upstairs.

"Wait," the old man finally said. "Please, don't. I'll take you to it but please, don't hurt my family."

Jun Li grinned and eased his grip on the old woman's fragile neck. He placed the teapot down and spoke to his henchmen in Mandarin. "You three take him to the car. You two, stay here and watch her."

As they carried the old man outside, Jun Li kneeled in front of the old woman. He tilted her head up so their eyes could meet. He took a second to observe her. She might have been beautiful in her youth, but the years had not been kind to her. "Don't take this personally," he said in Mandarin. "Everything I do is in the name of my country." He let her head drop and then stood.

One of the henchmen went upstairs, while the other pulled out a nine-inch blade behind the old woman. Jun Li walked outside, where the old man was pinned against an SUV. "There was a time when honor meant something," the old man said. "When your enemy plotted to kill you but still respected you enough to let you know he was the one trying to do so. You think this is going to bring honor back to what we had?" The old man shook his head. "This will only weaken you. Betraying your own makes you a coward. But it's not too late to make this right. We can stay with the original plan if—"

The henchman walked out cleaning his blade with a piece of the old woman's dress, then threw the bloody cloth on the ground.

Jun Li halted arm's-length from the old man. He loathed the man's horrified face. A part of him still respected the man. "This is me making it right, old friend," he said.

The old man ground his teeth and slipped a three-inch blade from his sleeve. He slashed the throat of the nearest henchman, who crashed to his knees. His blood flowed freely, soaking into the snow. A second henchman received four quick stabs to the abdomen, and joined the first on the ground. The old man sliced through the remaining henchmen with little effort. Jun Li stood still, admiring the old man's skill. He thought about the many lessons the old man had given him when he was younger. But this was a different time, and Jun Li was ready to prove himself.

After cutting down the last henchman, the old man wasted no time coming for Jun Li. The snow crunched under his feet as he sprinted for Jun Li.

Jun Li didn't move a muscle. The old man tried many times to cut the smirk off Jun Li's face. But Jun Li dodged with ease, calculating each move. He noticed something different in the old man. His swings had less power now, and his movements were not as sharp.

The old man propelled a stab, but Jun Li caught the blow by the wrist. The bloody blade shook inches from his face. Jun Li took a moment to stare at a ring on the old man's finger. It was a gold Chinese Cobra with green emeralds for eyes. Jun Li's ice block hands compressed the old man's wrist, making him fall to his knees.

"I remember you telling me the story of the Naja Atra when I was a child," Jun Li told him. "That used to mean something to me. *You* used to mean something to me. But I will restore what you have lost. The new V.E.N.O.M is here, and I am its leader."

Jun Li delivered a crushing blow to the old man, making his vision go black. Silence returned to the forest, and the clock was now ticking.

2.

Brooklyn, New York

Jake lay in the dark, eyes staring at the ceiling. It wasn't the sirens that kept him up, or the loud neighbors. This was a typical night for him. His body was numb, mind empty. Getting a good night's sleep was a luxury he couldn't afford, and when he did manage to sleep, the nightmares would remind him why he stayed awake.

His studio apartment was a little bigger than a closet; not much to it but a bed and his punching bag. The only part of his apartment that had an ounce of effort in it was a memorial to his late wife and daughter: a single shelf hanging from the wall. There was a picture of them together, old jewelry, drawings and handwritten letters. But the centerpiece of it all was a gray stuffed toy rabbit that was sullied from its ears to its ankles. Jake's daughter dragged it everywhere she went. The fur was rigid and smelled of ashes, but he would never wash it. Jake walked past this monument every day and thought about what he'd lost.

He looked over at his clock: 2:37 a.m. *One of my better nights,* he thought. He grabbed an amber vial, downed two pills without any water and rose to his feet. A calendar with a smiley face hung above his bed, with sixty-two days crossed out. Looking at it made his mouth dry, but seeing the marked-out days kept him motivated.

In the bathroom, he had to crouch down to see his face in the round mirror. He kept his body at a slim build, but he's been in better shape. His dark brown eyes had violet bags under them. His beard was scruffy and sprinkled with gray stubble. His hair was shoddy, as if showering was something done on those rare occasions when he remembered the need.

In the corner of his apartment, Jake pummeled on his punching bag like his life was in jeopardy. The leather was worn from the months of frustration and guilt forced upon it. He gave the bag one last hook, then stopped to catch his breath. His left hand slid out of the glove as he flexed it. Third-degree burn wounds ran from the beds of his fingers to just below his wrist, but it had healed well.

He went to the dresser and picked up the amber pharmacy vial, but to his disappointment it was empty. He rummaged through his things looking for more, but came up short. A heavy sigh deflated his body as he checked the clock: only 4:30 a.m.

* * *

"I'm sorry sir, but your prescription cannot be filled," the pharmacy technician said.

She was a young blonde with sky-blue eyes. The top of her head reached the bottom of Jake's chest. When she spoke, she cleared her throat between sentences. Jake figured it was a nervous tick, and he was only amplifying it with his appearance.

He stared at her for a moment with an empty glare, but he didn't mean to. He was mesmerized by her beautiful eyes, but he quickly snapped back to reality when he felt those same eyes judging him.

"I'm sorry, what did you say?" he asked.

"Your prescription. It can't be filled," she said, this time with annoyance in her voice.

"If the insurance won't go through, then I'll pay for it myself and get reimbursed later." Jake reached in his pocket.

"It's not the insurance. Your next refill isn't for another seventeen days."

Jake scoffed. "That can't be right. I just got these pills the other day."

"If you mean two weeks ago, then yes, you received them the other day. Now you have to wait another two weeks or get written approval from your physician. Then I'll be happy to fill it for you"

Jake surveyed the store to make sure no one was standing behind him. The floor plan was open, with little islands of merchandise to create aisles.

His face balled up at the options. "It's just that… I'm in and out of the office all week, and I don't have time to make an appointment. I'm really in pain. Are you sure there's nothing we can do here to—" Jake placed his burned hand on the countertop near hers, and she immediately backed away. He picked up on her fear and ran his hand through his hair.

The pharmacy technician tried to manufacture a smile, but her eyes told her true feelings. "I could probably call somebody for you if you want," she said. The offer was more for her peace of mind than Jake's needs.

"No. No, that's all right," Jake said through a bitter smile. "It's probably best if we do it your way. Paper trail and all. Can you tell me where the nasal spray is?"

"The left back wall. Last shelf."

"Thank you," Jake mouthed. He hauled himself to the back wall, shoulders slumped. It was one thing to seem desperate, but in front of a pretty young girl…only made it worse. Once he got to the destination, he stood there for a minute with his eyes closed. *What have you let yourself become?* he asked himself.

He opened his eyes and picked up the first sinus and cold medicine he saw. When he turned around his body tightened. His eyes locked in on a man dressed in black with a hood over his head. Usually Jake wouldn't think twice about this, but he could see the pharmacy technician shaking from where he was standing, and tears crept down her rosy cheeks.

The hooded man stayed fixed in his stance and aggressively whispered his demands as the young technician filled a bag up with different prescriptions. Jake walked light on his feet. He got to an angle where he could see something substantial bulging from the man's sleeve. It could be a gun or a roll of paper towels. Jake didn't want to risk being wrong.

It's too early for this, Jake thought. *I should have left when I had the chance.*

Jake made eye contact with the young technician. Her helpless look pulled on his conscience. He took a deep breath and stepped forward, until he was next to the hooded man. "Hey, are these the ones that make you drowsy?" Jake asked, trying to get the technician's attention. "Because if they are, then I can't take them. I have to be at work in an hour."

The hooded man turned his head an inch, but his shades made it hard to tell which way he was looking. "Why don't you wait in line like everyone else, *Chancho*?"

Jake studied everything about him. His Hispanic accent. His weight and height. His bouncing leg. This man was on edge. Jake had to tread lightly.

"I'm sorry. This'll only take a second. Plus, I was here first, so technically—"

As Jake stepped forward, the hooded man pulled out an 11-inch double-barreled derringer. The pharmacy technician's eyes grew wide as her breathing got shorter.

Jake took a few steps back with his hands up. "Hey, calm down, okay? I just wanna show you something." He unzipped his leather jacket, exposing the police badge clasped on his waistband. He now had a full-frontal view of the hooded man. He had tattoos climbing out of his collar and sleeves. From the poor quality, he guessed they'd been done in prison. "Okay, now that we know who we both are, let's talk about this," Jake said.

"Ain't nothing to talk about, *Chancho*. You should have never tried to get into my business. Hey, don't move!" he exclaimed, swinging the derringer at the other customers.

"Everyone stay calm and get on the ground," Jake said. "You're right. I shouldn't have gotten in your business. I was two minutes away from walking out the door, but pride held me back. Don't make that same mistake." Jake shifted his gaze to the technician. "What's your name?"

"Laura," she said with a crackled voice.

"Okay, Laura. Everything is going to be fine. I just need you to take that bag and give it to our friend here. Can you do that?"

Laura's trembling hand grabbed the black plastic bag and eased it to the hooded man. He snatched the bag and backtracked toward the door. "Don't try anything funny. Everyone wants to go home today, right?" Once his back touched the door, he kicked it open and bolted down the block.

"Are you okay?" Jake asked Laura. She nodded but could barely look up. "Call the police, now." Jake ran to the door and glanced out before he made his full-on pursuit.

The hooded man barged through people in the Brooklyn neighborhood as Jake closed in behind him. He tried to lose Jake in the small crowd by slipping into a narrow one-way street behind a chain of restaurants. Not one person was in sight, just delivery trucks and dumpsters. The sun couldn't reach over the building, so the street was shaded. The hooded man looked back as he ran, but saw no one behind him. He slowed down to a brisk walk and laughed to himself. His laugh ended in a grimace as a callused fist leveled him right where he stood. Jake hovered over him as he shook the pain from his left hand. He disarmed the hooded man and took the derringer apart. "No shells. You're a lot dumber than you act." Jake picked up the hooded man, threw him against the wall face first and cuffed him. "I don't punch in until nine o'clock. Right now, it's approximately 8:48 am. So, you already got me in a bad mood."

"Fuck you, *Chancho*! You wouldn't be so tough if you hadn't sucker punched me."

Jake pulled the black plastic bag from the hooded man's crotch. He looked inside and saw only top-shelf opioids clustered together in various sized bottles. There was a tingle on his tongue as he took a hard swallow and stuffed the bag in the right breast pocket of his jacket.

"You robbed that place for pills? You couldn't get your fix anywhere else?"

"I ain't no junkie, *Chancho*. The scripts in that bag is

worth 100 times more on the streets than whatever they could hold in those registers."

"Yeah? And what about your freedom? Is it worth more than that too?"

"What are you my guidance counselor now?"

Jake continued to search the hooded man. "You called me Chancho. What gang are you affiliated with? MS-13? Los Zetas? Marieltoes?

"I ain't in no gang, officer."

"Oh, it's officer now?"

"Yeah. And like I said, I ain't in no gang."

"You just like to get the tattoos of the gangs you're not a part of, right?"

"Are you gonna book me or square up? Because I swear I'd make you my little white bitch. I got a couple of them already just like that snowflake in the pharmacy."

The hooded man puckered his swollen lips over his shoulder. Jake smiled then stepped back. "I'm gonna do you one better…I'm gonna let you go."

The hooded man looked over his shoulder in confusion. "Say what, fool?"

"You're free to go. Let Murphy's law decide your fate."

"What's the catch?"

"No catch. Just saving myself from a headache. See, if I take you in, then you're going to jail. It'll be an open and shut case, and you'll get sentenced to some ridiculous amount of time only to be reunited with your friends on the inside. Meanwhile, there's gonna be ten more weeds just like you ready to take your place. And what do I get outta the deal? A mountain of paperwork? Court dates taking up half my day? All so you can make parole and come home to influence a younger generation because your stint in the hole somehow gives you cachet? No way, Jose, that's not for me."

"My name's Carlos, homie."

"Whatever. I say we skip the judicial bullshit and handle this at the lowest level possible. I take your gun and the stuff you stole. The rest is on you. Deal?"

"That gun ain't even mine."

"Too bad. Those are my conditions. You said so yourself, 'everybody wants to go home.' Does that include you?"

Carlos sighed then nodded.

"Good. Keep facing the wall." Jake uncuffed him.

"My bad about all that stuff I said earlier. You're actually a pretty cool gringo."

Jake said nothing.

"You still there, man?"

Silence.

"I said are you still—" Before Carlos could turn around, Jake locked in a choke hold and dragged the hooded man behind the dumpster. He wrapped his legs around his waist as he constricted his forearm across Carlos' windpipe. His face turned burgundy, and his eyes stretched past the sockets until he fell unconscious.

Jake took a moment to catch his breath and compose himself. He checked Carlos' pulse. Still alive. Once the drugs were fully secured in his breast pocket, Jake walked towards the main street. His phone rang, and he waited for a few rings after he saw who was calling.

"This is Jake."

"Jake. What are you doing?" the voice asked.

That's a weird way to start a conversation, Jake thought as he looked around. "I was on my way in. Why?"

"Don't worry about coming in today. At least not until

this evening. I got something I want you to check out ASAP. Double homicide and possible mass kidnapping."

"All right, where is it?"

"Right outside Catskill. CPD is expecting you."

"Catskill? Lieutenant—Catskill is upstate. That's almost three hours away by train. Why are we working a case up there?"

"The suspects have a nationwide APB on them, but the powers-that-be want to crack down in the Tri-State area first. We got tasked to support CPD like everyone else. I figured since you spent some time up there for your... recuperation leave, you'd be the best man to send."

"There's gotta be someone else that can do this," Jake said through a sigh. "I'm literally ten minutes from the station."

"There's plenty of people that can do it. But I want you on the ground for this one. Listen, Jake, I always felt like you came back a little too soon, especially with the holidays just passing. But you say you're all right and the doctors cleared you, so my opinions don't mean much of nothing. I just thought that maybe if you go back up there—"

"Okay. I'll go."

"Good. This is going to be a low-threat task. Just go up there, flash your badge and bring back whatever information you find. By the time you get here, the case, along with your findings, will be handed over to higher authorities. Can you handle that?"

Jake rubbed the back of his neck. He knew he didn't have much of a choice, so he clenched his jaw and breathed through his nose, "You'll have a report tonight."

He hung up the phone and jammed it into his pocket. The next sight had him stuck in his tracks. Laura was pointing him out to an older man who was short in stature and balding at the top of the head. She tried to flag Jake down, but he pretended not to see her and signaled for a taxi.

"Excuse me," Laura said over the crowd. "Excuse me!" She reached Jake with the older man right behind her. "Hey, remember me? I was in the pharmacy that was robbed not too long ago. This is my boss, Rick."

"How are you?" Rick asked as he reached out for a handshake.

"Fine. Thank you," Jake said, shaking his hand.

"So, did you catch the son of a bitch?" Rick's sudden change in attitude surprised Jake.

"No, he got away, unfortunately." He waved his arm, careful not ruffle the plastic bag.

Rick reached out for Jake's right arm and asked, "Well, what are we supposed to do?"

Jake dodged the gesture and readjusted the plastic bag in his jacket from the outside of his coat. "You should call the police and file a report. They can officially start an investigation."

"But you are the police."

A cab pulled up, and Jake already had one foot inside before it could come to a full stop. "Actually, I'm a detective. Homicide. It's not my area."

"So, you're not going to do anything?" Laura asked.

"It's not my area," Jake said more softly.

"Some detective you are."

Laura's attitude stopped Jake from entering the cab. He looked her up and down, then looked to Rick. "If I were you, Rick, I would start from the inside out. That's usually how these things go."

"What do you mean?" Rick asked.

"I highly doubt the perp knew the best time to come into the store, when high-value meds were out on display begging to be taken. He might have had help. Oh, and by the way, you're looking for a Hispanic male, early twenties. He has a thing for snowflakes."

Rick's neck snapped toward Laura as she looked away.

"Is that enough detecting for you?" Jake asked as he entered the cab.

3.∎

Miami, Florida

It was the peak of winter in most places, but Miami's beaches told a different story. While New York was enduring the harsh climate, Miami wasn't even thinking about it. The Miami Herald building was in Doral, Florida, right off the coast. Inside, rows of desks were filled with people. Everyone was either on the phone, having meetings, or typing a mile a minute, determined to make a deadline.

Everyone except Zasha Avery. She just sat at her cherry mahogany desk in her executive black leather chair, observing as everyone else clawed their way over each other to break the next big story. A part of her was over the whole media bit, but she understood the grind.

She kept her strawberry blonde hair wrapped in a tight bun. Her skin was delicate and tanned from the Miami sun, which caused her freckles to blend well together. At thirty-one, she was the youngest Pulitzer Prize winner for investigative journalism, for her coverage of Cuban affairs. She let her talents be known by having her most cherished award as the centerpiece of her desk, with a gold nameplate right behind it. Out the corner of her coral-green eyes, she spotted Walter Sanner, the senior editor for the investigations department.

Walter was a tall, slender man with the scowling face of a pit bull, and wore thick-framed glasses. He had a limp that came from knee surgery earlier in the year, and walked with a cane. Everyone made a path as Walter hobbled straight to his office without saying anything to anyone.

Zasha knocked twice before she opened the door and peeked inside. Her smile reached wall to wall, brightening up the room better than any sun could.

"I'm not here," Walter said without looking up.

"That's funny because I clearly see you, Walter," Zasha said, still forcing a smile. "You sure you're in the right department? The funnies are downstairs."

"You know the morning routine, Zasha. People aren't allowed to talk to me until after my third cup of coffee."

"I know, and I'm sorry, but this is very important." She closed the door behind her and tip-toed to the nearest seat.

Walter knew it was going to be something he didn't like because of the tingle in his knee. "You got two minutes."

"I know it seems like I'm pestering you with this, but I wanted to know if you'd had a chance to look over my proposal?"

Walter took a beige folder stuffed with papers from under a pile of other folders, and plopped it on his desk. "I did. And it's good. Really good." Zasha's shoulders sprouted from the compliment. "Too bad we can't approve it."

"What? Why?"

"Short answer—we simply don't have the resources to pull off this kind of project."

She scoffed. "And the long answer?"

Walter rubbed his brows as he stared at Zasha with his beady eyes. "Okay, the long answer is, we don't have the resources to build a six-man investigation team to go to D.C. and report on politics. Mainly because that's not our job."

"Dirty politics. We're here to unearth corruption and report the truth to the people. Rise above the fake news."

"We're here to report what's going on in the city, and anything that has a direct link to the Hispanic community. We have plenty of local political scandal that you can investigate here. You want to do this passion project, go start a blog on Facebook."

"But this is our chance to make a difference."

"Have you worked in politics? You'll see how different it really is."

"I'm trying to push us forward as a news outlet, Walt. The political climate in this country is a shambles, and the news outlets are right behind it. My sources are solid, and I feel like I could run the table if we jump on this now. We're only as big as Miami. I could change that."

Walter cleared his throat and took off his glasses. "Zasha, I know that you're an amazing journalist with a collection of accolades for your work, including a Pulitzer that can attest to that, but if you ever undermine my department or me with your snooty attitude, you will be out of that door faster than you can blink."

Walter's attitude gave Zasha an unfamiliar chill on the back of her neck. "Where's this coming from? Did I do something wrong?"

"How could you? You're a leading example of how a journalist should be. You're fearless, unbiased, and you have a real hunger that never went away even after all your success. I couldn't ask for anything else. In fact, I wouldn't."

"But?"

"But I do wonder about your tactics at times. I know that there are some people, including myself, who don't appreciate the fact that you have these *shadow sources*. And I personally take offense that you shove that advantage under everyone's nose every chance you get."

"So, you're questioning my journalistic integrity?"

"No. But how you get your leads… That's a different story."

"You're not going to greenlight a project because you don't trust my sources?"

"I'm not going to greenlight *your* project because you're only a team player when it benefits you. And as bad as you want to seem selfless, everyone knows it's just a ploy to push your career forward. Stick to the local news or find opportunities elsewhere." Walter ended the conversation by opening his laptop.

* * *

Zasha strolled along the wall in her office, studying each of her awards. They were lined up perfectly in order of size. Some of them were as recent as last year; however, her drift down memory lane did nothing to lighten her spirits.

At that moment, Zasha's assistant entered the office. She was more of an intern than anything else, but stayed with her most of the time. "Ms. Avery?" the assistant said in a soft voice. "You have a call from Brian on line one."

Zasha rolled her eyes and let out a heavy sigh. "Tell him I'll call him back."

"I did, but this is like his fifth time calling. It seems important."

"It always is with him. I'll answer in here." As the assistant left, Zasha went to her desk to pick up the phone.

"Hello Brian," she said with a sarcastic cheer in her voice. "Usually you're on your tenth call by this hour."

"I'm sorry for the string of calls, but I've been super-busy trying to break this story all morning, and I need a favor."

"What, did the snow geese not migrate to that part of New York yet?"

"Very funny, but for your information, I got something big...A double murder."

"Congratulations."

"For what?"

"I know that type of thing doesn't happen often in your part of town."

"That's a bit morbid don't you think?"

"So is wasting my time. What do you want, Brian?"

"Well, like you said, this type of thing doesn't happen in Catskill often. So, I'm calling for a consultation."

"No, Brian, I can't. I am swamped to no end over here. No offense, but I don't have time to deal with small-time stuff right now."

"I understand, but just do me this one favor. Look at the pictures I sent to your email an hour ago and tell me what you think."

Zasha choked the phone as she did a muted scream into it. After a few seconds, she loosened her grip and took a deep breath. "Okay, I will be a team player and give you five minutes. After that, I have to go."

She logged into her computer and scrolled through hundreds of emails before she got to Brian's. She opened the files and flicked through the pictures. "Okay, what am I looking at?

"The crime scene. The photos were taken a few hours ago."

Zasha slowed down the clicks as each picture got more gruesome. One picture showed the bloodstains of an old woman, smeared all over the floor. Another showed the body covered with a white sheet.

"Oh my God," Zasha said. "The police let you take these in an active crime scene?"

"Not exactly. My source on the task force gave me copies."

"You mean your deputy cousin."

"Not over the phone lines, Zasha!"

Zasha continued to click and paused on one picture. There were two men with sunglasses and NSA jackets caught walking from the house. She zoomed in on the face of one of the men, but the picture was too blurry.

"What is this?" she asked.

"What? What are you looking at?"

Zasha narrowed in to get a better look. "JPEG 18. Are those NSA agents leaving the crime scene?"

"Oh yeah, sorry, I didn't mean to send that one. I took that picture when we first got there. All the other ones are legit photos taken by the police."

"Why would the NSA be there?"

"I'm not sure."

"And where were your guys?"

"They were outside waiting for these agents to finish. Weird, right?"

"Yeah, weird." She focused more on the picture.

"But what's even weirder is what my cousin, I mean, my source told me. They got reinforcements coming in from all over the state to investigate the scene and take their findings back to wherever they came from. He overheard them saying there's going to be a nationwide manhunt for whoever did this."

"Who the hell did they kill in that house?"

"I don't know, but the crazy part is…I don't think anyone does."

"What do you mean?"

"Well, first of all, I was worried about not being able to break the story in time because of the NSA, but get this, there's no coverage of this story…anywhere."

"Give it some time. Anything can happen in a New York minute, no matter how far upstate you are."

"Okay, how about this, I did some research and found county records that showed the house was seized by the bank and had no occupants for years. However, when speaking with the neighbors, they claimed there was an older Chinese couple who stayed there with several kids."

Zasha pressed her lips together as she shook her head. "You know, this story would make a great piece with The Conspiracy Daily. Have you checked for freelance work?"

"I know it sounds crazy, but I haven't even gotten to the good stuff yet. The police report officially recorded this as a double homicide. Two bodies left the scene, but only one was checked in at the town morgue."

Zasha's ears perked up. "Which one didn't show up?"

"The Chinese male. There are no records of him whatsoever. It's almost like…he doesn't exist. You add that plus the NSA and the county records showing no one was supposed to be living there in the first place… I think I'm on to something. Maybe the government is trying to cover up a high-profile person in witness protection who got whacked or something. Look, I know I might be reaching on this, but if I'm right…this could be a game changer for me."

"Game changer," Zasha said, unaware whether Brain heard her. She looked over to the corner of her desk, at a picture of herself as a teen with her two younger sisters. She was so pale back then, and her hair was a mess.

Brian continued to talk, but Zasha only caught the end of it.

"…that's why I feel like your help would make a huge diff—"

"—Your five minutes are up." She hung up the phone.

* * *

Zasha walked into Walter's office while he read on his iPad.

"You know, persistence killed the cat," he said, without looking up.

"I thought curiosity killed the cat."

"Yeah, well, I had a cat who kept trying to break into my condo to eat my birds. I called animal control, and they took it to a shelter. I'm pretty sure they put it down."

"Heartwarming. Listen, I was thinking about what you said, and I think I'm going to take your advice."

"That's great except I didn't give you any advice."

"Sure you did. I just had to read between the lines."

Walter placed the iPad on his desk and gave her his full attention. "What are you up to, Zasha?"

"I'm taking a back seat. This whole time I've been stressing about catching myself and didn't even realize that I've been jeopardizing the morale of the team. Everyone's a star here. They deserve a chance to shine."

Walter bit the corner of his lower lip. He narrowed his eyes as if her real motive was right behind her. "What's your angle?"

"No angles. I just want to take some time off to recharge."

Walter scoffed into a chuckle. "I haven't had a day off since I started working here twenty-five years ago."

"I'm stressed, Walt. I need some time away from this place."

"We're all stressed. It comes with the job. Didn't you read that in your contract?"

"This environment is becoming unhealthy. I don't think I can work in these conditions any longer."

"I once watched you sleep in your office for a month trying to break a story. You expect me to believe the nonsense coming out of your mouth right now?"

"No. But that's what I'm going to tell HR if I have to. And I really don't want to do that."

Walter took his glasses off and leaned back in his chair. His scowl became tight, and the hairs on his arm rose.

"All I need is two weeks."

Walter let out a sigh. "Fine, I'll give you ten days, and you still have to turn in your pieces by deadline."

"I'll take it," Zasha said as she turned to bolt for the door.

"Hold it!" She slowly turned around, waiting for what he had to say. "What are you going to be doing for the next ten days?"

"Does it matter?"

"It does if you want to leave."

Zasha painted a bitter smile on her face. "Well if you must know, I'm taking a trip to New York."

"What's in New York?"

"My sister."

"You don't have a sister in New York," he said through a chuckle.

"She's flying in for the weekend."

"From where?"

"Canada."

"Couldn't she just drive?"

"She's on the far side."

"What's she doing in Canada?"

"Minding her business. But I'm sure if I call her, she wouldn't mind explaining this whole thing to you. Then you can explain to her why you're hounding me." Zasha pulled out her phone and pushed one button, letting it ring on speakerphone.

Walter rocked back and forth in his chair as he looked her up and down. "That won't be necessary."

"Are you sure?"

"Yes. Hang up." Zasha hung up and put the phone away quickly. "And I apologize for prying. You're right, this place is cracking down on all of us."

"It's okay. I just want my time off."

"Fine. But you better watch yourself. I got eyes in New York. If I find out you're doing some unauthorized investigation on the company's dime, you might as well invest in real estate there because there's no way you're coming back to Miami to work."

"I'll email you my features in a couple of days."

Zasha turned around, and this time Walter let her leave.

She texted Brian: *Give me the info of the next cop coming to town.*

As she walked back to her office, she waved her assistant over. "Hey, I'm going to be gone for ten days. I want you to reschedule all my appointments for the following week and sort my emails while I'm gone. Only forward me the important ones."

"Okay. Where are you going?"

"New York."

"Wow, that's exciting. You finally going to see Brian?"

"God no. The last thing I need is someone following me around every second I move."

"Oh. Well, if you have time, I think you should visit him."

"Why would I do that?"

"Because, and don't take this the wrong way, you don't really hang out with friends or family here. I know he can be a little bit of a clinger, but at least he calls and checks up on you. That's more than what most people get."

Sometimes the truth stung, and Zasha wasn't immune to it. "Just make sure you forward me those emails."

4.

The inside of the Catskill Village Police Department was much smaller than what Jake was used to. Only a few officers roamed the halls, as the rest were on patrol. Everyone else he saw was civilian. Jake sat on a worn bench, waiting for someone to help him. The idea of how wholesome this place was crossed his mind, and he imagined himself working here. A small town with the occasional teenage trouble or alcohol-related accident at the local bar. The thought put a brief a smile on his face, until he spotted one of the secretaries pointing him out to an officer.

This officer's belly hung over his waistband, but the rest of his body was skinny. He sported a high and tight haircut with a muscle mustache. The officer studied Jake up and down as he walked toward him.

"You Penny?" the officer asked.

"Detective Penny, yes," Jake said. As much as he was burned out from the job, Jake still had enough pride to be called by his proper title. The two grabbed each other's hands, gave one firm shake, then released. Their eyes never left each other.

"Right. Well, I'm Sergeant Wincenciak. I'm supposed to be taking you down to the crime scene and whatnot. You're the fourth guy today, so we should make this quick before my lunch. If you wait outside, I can pull the car around—"

"Actually, I was hoping to get a quick debrief before we moved out to the location," Jake said as he pulled out a pen and pad.

Sergeant Wincenciak chuckled to himself. "All right, here's your debrief. A Chinaman and his wife were murdered. Anything else?"

"What were their names?"

Sergeant Wincenciak cleared his throat from anything rude he might have said. "Wei Pei was the name of the husband. And Barbara was the name of the wife. Go figure."

"And what was the cause of death?"

"The wife died from a slit throat. Wei Pei was found outside the house with no visible trauma. There was a lot of blood in the snow, but we don't think it came from Wei Pei."

"Is there an ETIC on the autopsy?"

"We'll know in about week from now. Sorry, we don't have the fancy technology like the city. But there was one thing we could clearly see…Wei Pei's left ring finger was chopped clean off, then cauterized soon after."

"What about the kidnapping?"

"We can't tell for sure. There could have been three kids, there could have been nine. The one that we do have isn't telling us jack shit."

Jake stopped writing. "You have a witness? Here?"

"Sure do."

"No one mentioned anything about a witness."

"That's because we didn't release that information. Those fancy agents thought they were gonna come up here and take our case. Not one of them checked the bathroom, but our deputy did. I guess taking a piss paid off."

"Do you mind if I speak with the witness?"

* * *

Jake walked into the interrogation room without a sound. The room had nothing but a steel table and two chairs at each end. In one of those chairs sat Koa. He stared blankly into space, with sandbags under his eyes, fighting the urge to sleep. The Knicks jersey given to him by CPD was too big, and his sweatpants were soiled. Jake sat at the table and took in a look he knew all-too-well. The look of being lost, feeling helpless, and having nothing to live for.

"Hi," Jake said. "My name is Detective Penny, but you can call me Jake. I came a long way to talk to you. I'm here to help you. I wanna try and reunite you with your family, but before I can do any of that, I just want you to know something…" He leaned in and whispered, "It's not your fault."

Koa's bottom lip quivered as tears built up in his eyes. His pain mutated into anger at the sight of Jake's face. He clenched his fist and burned his sights on Jake.

"Just tell me what you know," Jake continued.

Koa never blinked. He breathed heavily through his nose as his lips curled into his mouth. "He promised he was going to take us to the parade in the city. It's the year of the pig. Pretty unlucky."

"Do you know who would want to hurt your guardian?" Jake asked.

"Of course," Koa whispered. "It was you." A single tear ran down his face.

Jake took a hard swallow. "Are you saying the men who did this look like me?"

Koa shook his head while more tears raced down his face. "You did this. You did it. I know you did this. He told me it was you." Koa's voice echoed in the small room as he bashed his head with a fist repeatedly, saying the same thing over and over.

Jake stared, words caught in his throat. Before he could say anything, Sergeant Wincenciak rushed in with one of his deputies to see what was going on. Jake could feel his head get heavy as he turned around. Sergeant Wincenciak's mouth was moving, but nothing was coming out. Jake became dizzy trying to focus on what was going on.

"Jesus Christ, get the kid outta here," Sergeant Wincenciak said to the deputy.

The deputy grabbed Koa and closed the door behind them. Sergeant Wincenciak snatched Jake up by the arms and tossed him to the wall. Jake didn't seem to notice. In fact, it was more of him allowing himself to be thrown to the wall as opposed to Sergeant Wincenciak's own strength.

"What the hell are you doing?"

Jake only heard pieces of the question. The silence brought him back to reality. "I just asked him some questions. Obviously, he's still in shock."

"Don't you patronize me, *Detective*. Now let's get one thing very clear so there's no confusion from here on out, this is my investigation. You're here to collect information and go back to wherever the hell you came from. You tracking?"

Jake wanted to tell him off, but he knew it wasn't worth it. He shrugged free from his soft grip and placed his notepad in his pocket. "It's your show, Boss. I'm just here to do a job."

Sergeant Wincenciak sighed and rolled his shoulders. "Meet me outside in five minutes."

As Sergeant Wincenciak slammed the door behind him, Jake took a deep breath and massaged his eyes.

* * *

Sergeant Wincenciak unlocked the house door and led the way to the crime scene. The air had a raw, metallic aroma that made Jake intake small gasps of breath. In the living room, everything was turned upside down and wrapped in yellow caution tape. Jake could see the bloodstains dried into the rusted wood floors.

"This is where most of the damage happened," Sergeant Wincenciak said. "They killed the wife there, took the husband outside to whack him, and took the kids."

"Did they take anything else?" Jake asked.

"I don't think this family had much."

Jake took cautious steps as he observed the room.

"You've been here before, haven't you?" Sergeant Wincenciak asked.

"What?"

"Your lieutenant said you spent some time up here. Were you here with family?"

"No."

Sergeant Wincenciak brushed off Jake's cold response and continued to talk, but Jake drowned his voice out. Instead, he took note of everything that was out of place. The abundance of picture frames with no photos. The teacups that were barely used. The drops of tea dried into the floor. No forced entry on the door. Something wasn't quite right.

"Hey," Sergeant Wincenciak yelled for the third time, "you alive over there?"

"Yeah. Did you say something?"

"I was trying to apologize for earlier. This is a family town you know. We haven't seen anything like this before, and we're all a little freaked out."

"It's understandable. No harm, no foul. So, I'm guessing you've had some experience with this. Prior military?"

"Yeah, how'd you know?"

"Your jargon. You used the word tracking, you understood what ETIC meant. The haircut. It's all military."

"You damn right. Four years. Air Force. You?"

"Eight years. Army Ranger."

"Oh, that's cool. My job was services, but we were in the war zone just like everyone else."

Jake chuckled to himself. "I'm sure you were."

Sergeant Wincenciak looked away to hide his happy smile. "It's good to talk to another veteran. Makes this exchange a whole lot easier. You wanna see where we found the kid?" he asked, already walking up the stairs.

"Sure." Jake tried to follow, but his coat got caught on a nail sticking out the wall as he turned. He cursed as he yanked on his jacket, trying not to tear it. After a couple of tugs, the wall seemed to be winning the battle. He grabbed his coat and made one strong pull tearing a piece of the wall out. He glanced inside the opening and noticed a row of plastic bags going down to the middle of the wall. As he tore the rest of the wall apart, Sergeant Wincenciak came rushing down with his eyes wide.

"Whoa, whoa, whoa, what the hell are you doing?! This is an active crime scene!"

"There's something behind this wall. I just need one

big…pull." On the last word, Jake broke free from the wall and out fell six slabs wrapped in dense plastic. They'd been in the wall for some time because the dirt and dust were ingrained in the fibers of the plastic. Jake and Sergeant Wincenciak stared at each other for a moment in silence. Then Jake pulled out a pocket knife and grabbed one of the slabs.

"Wait, what are you doing?" Sergeant Wincenciak asked.

Jake narrowed his eyes at him. "I'm opening the package."

"But you can't do that. We have to call someone."

"If you don't feel comfortable, you can leave."

Sergeant Wincenciak looked towards the door then back at Jake. "No. I'll stay. In case you need back up or something. But if anyone asks, this was all your idea."

Jake penetrated the corroded plastic with the blade and sliced it open. Out fell a bundle of cash, mostly hundreds and fifties. Sergeant Wincenciak's eyes grew even wider.

"Maybe we should call someone now," Jake said.

"Detective Penny," Sergeant Wincenciak said with his eyes still on the money, "remember what we talked about back at the station?" His eyes migrated over to Jake who had already put away his pocket knife.

"Right," Jake said, walking to the door. "It's still your show."

5.

Lieutenant Trent Simons looked over Jake's report as Jake sat straight up in his chair across from him. Lieutenant Simons' office smelled of his cologne—a smooth fragrance with a trace of lavender. It wasn't too loud yet just enough to let anyone know whose office it was when they stepped in. Despite his charming baby face, Lieutenant Simons was pushing into his mid-forties. His salt-and-pepper hair was full and slicked to the side, and his light eyes added to his young appearance.

After every other sentence, Lieutenant Simons looked up and sputtered. Once he finished, he took off his glasses and plopped the report on his desk, staring Jake down. He had a way of reading people, but Jake's poker face was tight.

"You sure this is what happened?" he asked.

Jake nodded.

"Uh-huh. I just find it odd that five agencies and a squadron of police officers from all over the Tri-State area searched that place dry and found nothing. But when you go, somehow it's this Sergeant Wincenciak that stumbles across—" Lieutenant Simons opened the report to get the exact numbers. "—Three million dollars in unmarked cash, six different passports for this Wei Pei individual, a ton of documents written in Mandarin, and…a kid?"

Jake sat back with his arms folded and took a moment before he spoke. "For the record, they found the kid before I got there."

"It still doesn't make any sense."

"Sergeant Wincenciak was a bloodhound. He's very passionate about his work, and I was impressed with his relentless attack on the investigation."

Lieutenant Simons scoffed. "Cut the crap, Jake. He was a prick, and you know it. Hell, I knew it within five minutes of talking to the guy over the phone. The only reason I'm questioning this is that if this turns out to be more than some random act of murder, it could be big for you."

Jake knew how much this could catapult his career back to where it was, but he didn't want that. The only thing on his mind was getting home and taking the package out of his left breast pocket. "It was an easy miss. I went up there looking for information, not evidence."

Lieutenant Simons held the report for a second longer hoping Jake would add something more. When he didn't, Lieutenant Simons closed the report and placed it in his desk. "Okay, but a bust like this could have set someone up for the long haul. Maybe even a higher position in the future." He glanced over at his service dress uniform hanging on the coat rack pressed and ready to go at any moment's notice.

"I'm sure Sergeant Wincenciak will take full advantage," Jake said.

Lieutenant Simons sighed. "Well, as promised, the case will be taken by higher authorities. I'll give your report to Chief in the morning, and he can add it with the rest of the slush pile." Jake rose to leave, but Lieutenant Simons said, "Hey, wait a minute." He paused looking for the words to say. "How are things going with you?"

"Fine," Jake said, sitting back down.

"I didn't send you all the way up there just for work, you know? I was hoping you would have stayed longer to clear your head. No one would look at you any different if you needed more time off."

"I'm fine, Trent." Jake rarely called his superiors by their first name, but they had a closer relationship. This was his way of driving his point home.

Lieutenant Simons didn't want to push the issue any further than he already had, so he nodded. "You know what…why don't we go somewhere? The Nets are playing tonight, and we can watch the game at Bruno's over some Cokes."

Jake chuckled. "Cokes? That sounds like fun." His smile was cut by a sudden reminder. "But I actually can't tonight. I got this thing."

"Thing? What thing?"

"This thing with some people. I made plans last week. We'll do it another time. I promise."

"Hey, no problem. I'm just glad to see you interacting with human beings again. I'm here if you need anything, Jake. We've been friends for a long time. You don't have to go through this alone."

Jake cleared his throat. "I appreciate that."

"So, I'll see you tomorrow then?"

"Actually I'm off tomorrow, but I'll see you around."

"All right. Take care of yourself."

* * *

Jake sat in a semi-circle with twelve other men and women. They all met once a week in this room with four white walls and nothing on them. The laminated wood flooring had scratches on it from daytime activities, probably from after-school programs. Jake hated the idea of innocence and immorality being harbored in the same room.

In the center of the semicircle was a student desk, officially dubbed *The Hot Seat*. A man sat there and told his story. He sweated through his clothes and stumbled over every other word, and all eyes were on him. The desk had a banner hanging in front of it that read: WELCOME NIGHT WARRIOR AA GROUP.

The man in *The Hot Seat* came to the meeting late, and this was the price—speaking in front of a bunch of strangers about his week. Once he finished, everyone stood and clapped. Some people gave him a hug on his way back to his seat. The leader of the group, Sally, came from outside the circle to speak. She was in her mid-fifties, and wore a brown curly wig. She wore the same t-shirt every week. It read: I AM A SURVIVOR.

"Thank you, Colin," Sally said as she directed him to his seat. "Would anyone else like to share before we start our exercises?" No one was eager to volunteer. Sally scanned the room and landed on Jake. "Ray, how 'bout you? You've been awfully quiet these past couple of meetings, and you always motivate us with your journey."

Jake knew he needed help, but was too prideful to give his real name. The name he picked belonged to his favorite baseball player, Ray Washburn. Jake had gotten the idea to attend the meetings from a forgotten ad posted at work. Being here didn't make him feel any better. It just reaffirmed that he wasn't the only person in the world with problems. "I don't have much to say this week," he said.

"I've been in the program long enough to know that someone like you always has something to say."

"Come on, brother," one of the members said. "It's always love here."

Jake took a deep breath and made his way to *The Hot Seat* with applause to back him up. Once he got settled, Sally took her seat. The silence made the focus on Jake even more prevalent. For a moment, he felt like he was back in the Catskill with nothing but time to think.

"Hello, my name is Ray, and I'm sixty-three days sober."

A single clap broke the silence, and a wave of applause followed. Jake was the unofficial leader of the group. People believed in themselves because of him.

"But I don't feel sixty-three days sober," Jake said through the claps. The silence returned. "I have nightmares, so I don't sleep. Things from my past keep…clawing at me. Reminding me of what happened." Jake rubbed his thumb under his ring finger while he gathered his thoughts. It used to be a way to make sure he had his wedding ring on before he left the house; now it was a nervous tick in stressful situations. "Alcohol was a way to suppress the memories and forget for a few hours. But, uh… I have to stay on the path and beat this."

"What are your dreams about?" Sally asked.

Jake adjusted in *The Hot Seat*. "I have a loaded gun to my head, and I pull the trigger, but nothing happens. I just keep dreaming. Then I hear my family calling, but I can't find them. The more I run to be with them, the farther they get. I just wanna know why they had to leave and I had to stay."

Sally noticed everyone dragging from Jake's story and rose to her feet. "You know what, I think it's time we start our exercises. Everyone, give Ray a hand of applause for always sharing and being a true model of staying strong."

Everyone clapped, but Jake didn't feel it was warranted.

The meeting came to an end, and everyone said their goodbyes. Jake was the first one to the door as usual.

"Ray," Sally said before he could leave. Jake waited as she approached him. "I'm glad you came this week. I know being consistent can be rough."

"Thank you."

She studied Jake for a moment. His eyes were dried out. His lips chapped and his tongue purple. "It was getting kinda bleak when you were up there. Is everything okay?"

"Yeah. I just zoned out a little bit."

"Our past doesn't define our future, Ray. Part of the recovery process is letting go. It can be the hardest part, but it's well worth it in the end."

"What if holding on is the only thing keeping me from going completely over the edge?"

Sally folded her arms and stepped a little closer. "I'm here to talk whenever you need it," she said quietly.

Jake looked into her worn face and knew she had been through a lot. But as much as she'd been through, he knew she wouldn't understand. "Yeah I know," he said, bouncing his leg and looking toward the exit.

"These people look up to you," Sally said. "You give them hope. You're the only one that has some form of stability given the circumstances. You still got your job. You're healthy for the most part. Heck, you're sixty-three days sober. Dave is a distant second at seventeen days. I would hate to see these guys watch their hero fall due to lack of communication."

"I don't mean to be rude, but I'm no one's hero. I'm in

here like the rest of these people, just trying to figure it out. I'm the last person they need to look to for hope."

Sally broke eye contact and cleared her throat. "Well, like it or not, you are the hope for *these people*. I just wish you'd see your worth before it's too late."

* * *

A cab dropped Jake off at a corner in his neighborhood. The driver wouldn't dare drive all the way. Jake lived in the Crown Heights neighborhood of Brooklyn. His building was six stories high, and on the ground floor was a mini market where people loitered outside. One of the loiterers knew Jake and tagged along with him to his building.

"Hey Detective Penny," the loiterer said with open arms. "How's my favorite cop who's not shooting black people today?"

"I'm fine, Johan. No black people dead on my account."

"Hey man, what did I say about using my government name? It's Jay in the streets."

"And what did I tell you about hanging out in front of this store. The owner's already complained twice about you and your friends being out here."

"I'm just trying to protect the community. Making sure no outsiders come into our neighborhood to rip my people off, y'know?"

Jake chuckled. "If that were true, you would become a cop. Then you would be able to make a real difference in the community. Maybe even your pockets, too."

Jake looked over to a young boy, no older than twelve, hanging with the loiterers. He walked over to the boy and kneeled to his level.

"What are you doing out here?" Jake asked.

"I'm just hanging out," the boy said.

"You got what I asked for?"

"Yeah. I do." The boy pulled out a piece of folded paper and handed it to Jake. Jake unfolded the paper and scanned the page.

"It's good. Except you got a B minus in Grammar. That's too close to a C."

"It's you *have* a B minus, and that teacher doesn't like me."

Jake took out a few dollars. The boy tried to take it, but Jake snatched it away. "Go home. I don't wanna see you out here again."

The boy took the money and went home.

"Hey, that was cool, man," Jay said. "That was really cool, but we need to talk about this job you're supposed to be getting me…"

As Jay rambled on, Jake focused on something that couldn't be real. A Chinese boy with an oversized Knicks jersey and sweatpants hopped into a vehicle down the block.

Jake walked towards the car, completely ignoring Jay. The closer he got to the car, the more he zeroed in on the boy's face. He couldn't quite identify him behind the tinted windows. By the time he got close enough, the car had driven right past him.

No, it couldn't have been, Jake thought.

* * *

The hours that followed had Jake's heads spinning. His sixty-three-day streak was washed down from the bottom of a whiskey bottle. He wiped fresh tears from his eyes as he downed a few painkillers.

The gray rabbit was in the trash can and doused in whiskey. He lit a match and watched the fire sputter over one of his most precious memories of his daughter. All he had to do was drop it in, and the past would be gone. But the match burned out before he could decide. A sigh of relief left his chest.

He dropped the match and bottle of whiskey, and reached under his pillow to pull out a stainless steel Sig-Sauer P226. The cold steel pressed against his temple, sending a jolt through his body. The tears stopped, and his breathing slowed. His hand shook, but his grip was tight. He closed his eyes and pulled the trigger, only to hear a click from the hammer. He released a deep breath and opened his swollen eyes. A small piece of him died. He took the stuffed rabbit from the trash can and wrung it out . His back crashed on the bed, pistol by his side, stuffed rabbit in his hand as he passed out.

6.

The late afternoon sun felt like a warm blanket covering Jake's face as he snoozed. That slumber was interrupted by his phone vibrating against something substantial. When he opened his eyes, he couldn't move. He tried to produce saliva as he rose to his feet, but quickly aborted the effort when the crushing weight on his forehead forced him to fall back down. His body tumbled out of bed, and the vibrating phone became more of a jackhammer in his ear. Once he located it, he reached and answered on the final buzz.

"Hello?" he answered with a frog in his throat.

"Jesus Christ, Jake, where have you been?" Lieutenant Simons asked. "I've been trying to reach you all day."

Jake took a deep breath with his palm pressed against his forehead. It helped with the beating sensation, but not by much.

"I told you I was off-duty today," he said.

"Yeah, well, it looks like you're going to have to pull a double. There's someone here who wants to talk to you about your report."

"Report? What report?"

"The report you wrote yesterday for Catskill . They have questions."

Jake fully opened his eyes as he climbed to his feet.

"Who's asking?"

"Some guy from the NSA. It's probably a routine thing they're doing with all the reporting officers."

"Can't you just tell him what I told you?"

"I tried. He said he wants to speak with the detective who wrote the report personally."

Jake took a long sigh away from the phone. *So much for passing it on to the higher authorities,* he thought.

"Okay, give me forty-five minutes, and I'll be there."

"You got fifteen. Get your ass down here now."

* * *

Jake strolled into the precinct, half-conscious, without acknowledging anyone. He had on dark shades to block any light from blinding him, and the same clothes as yesterday. Lieutenant Simons approached him from his office, but was kicked in the face ten feet out by a pungent aroma that made his eyes blink double-time. He looked around to see if anyone else noticed, then quickly pulled Jake to one side. "What the hell are you doing, Jake?" he asked with a sobering stare. "Please don't tell me you've been drinking."

Jake dropped his head looking for an answer. Unfortunately, nothing came up.

"Do you not remember our agreement? Hmm? You get off the booze and I'll bring you back to work. Was that not what we agreed upon?"

"Yes, it was, but—"

"I have a reputation, you know. I vouched for you to come back to the higher-ups and now we have a goddamn NSA agent here to talk to you and you can barely walk."

"Trent, I'm sorry."

"This is beyond irresponsible. It's reckless. And now you're putting my job in jeopardy. I know you're still hurting, but this type of behavior isn't gonna ease your pain, and it definitely isn't gonna bring Lia and Andrea back."

Jake snatched his shades off and stared Lieutenant Simons down. The fact that he would bring his deceased wife and daughter into this brought rage from the pit of his stomach to the center of his bloodshot eyes.

Lieutenant Simons knew he had crossed the line, so he focused on the task at hand. He reached into his pants pocket and pulled out a few pieces of gum. "Take this. Drink some water and pull yourself together. We're waiting."

* * *

Jake entered Lieutenant Simons' office without a sound. There was something different about the room. The smooth lavender cologne of Lieutenant Simons was overpowered by a new musk. Jake would catch hints of the lavender every now and then, but this new fragrance had a chokehold on his nostrils. He looked past Lieutenant Simons to see a man facing the window. He was dressed in a crisp navy blue suit that fell perfectly on his broad shoulders. He didn't turn around right away, even though he knew someone had entered the room.

"We're sorry to keep you waiting," Lieutenant Simons said. "But here's the detective you wanted to see. Jake, this is Special Agent Ethan Parker. Agent Parker, this is Detective Penny."

Parker turned around with a gracious smile that lit up the room. Everything about him was sharp. His hair was blond and cut to a low bald fade. His light blue eyes were clear of any stress. He wore a skinny blue tie with a silver tie clip to keep it in place. Even his nails were freshly manicured.

He walked towards Jake with his hand extended. "It's nice to finally meet you, Detective," Parker said, shaking his hand. He was just a hair taller than Jake, so they met eye to eye. "Now that you're here, we can get right to business."

"Absolutely," Lieutenant Simons said. "We're ready to help you in any way that we can."

Parker cut his gaze to Lieutenant Simons, then back to Jake. "Actually you've already been a tremendous help, Lieutenant, but I think I got it covered from here. We'll call you as soon as we need your expertise."

Lieutenant Simons scoffed as he adjusted his belt. "I'm sorry, maybe I misunderstood, but you told me that you wanted to go over the details of the Wei Pei case."

"Yes. With the detective who wrote the report."

"But this is my office."

"Good for you. The view is amazing by the way." This time Parker's eyes stayed on Lieutenant Simons. He wasn't going to ask a second time. Once Lieutenant Simons left the office, Parker said, "Please, have a seat, Detective."

Jake sat in the same chair he had last night, while Parker sat on the front edge of the desk.

"What's this about?" Jake asked.

"Just a standard debriefing about what you saw yesterday. We have reasons to believe that this case is connected to another case the NSA is working on. I'm just turning over every stone before I move forward."

"Well, like the Lieutenant said, I'm willing to help in any way I can."

"Excellent. So, approximately what time did you arrive

at the scene?"

"A little bit after 11:30 a.m."

"Anything stand out to you when you got there?"

"It was like any crime scene. I tried looking for anything out of the ordinary to help piece together what happened."

"Is that how you found the evidence behind the wall?"

A rush of adrenaline ran through Jake's chest and came out in a nervous chuckle. "Um, actually, it was Sergeant Wincenciak who found the evidence. I was just an observer."

"Really?" Parker asked as he fingered through some papers. "Because I have a signed statement from Sergeant Wincenciak saying that you found the evidence. Says here you pulled the wall apart and cut the bag open with a personal knife. Next thing you know, out came Christmas."

Jake's heart dropped to his stomach. He could feel the sweat squeezing from his armpit.

Why would he tell the truth, he asked himself.

Jake didn't know what to say next, so he kept quiet.

His anxiety tickled Parker. "Don't worry, you're not the first cop to lie on an official statement, and you certainly won't be the last. At least you weren't trying to hide anything incriminating."

"But something is wrong. Otherwise, you wouldn't be here."

"That is, unfortunately, true. Your discovery put our nation's security at risk, and now we have to put everything in order. Part of that is finding out who the hell you are. There are about ten NSA agents back at headquarters going through every inch of your life through their computers. Phone records. Internet History. Credit card statements. All from the past fifteen years."

The air was so thick that Jake couldn't breathe. All this

information was hard to take in with a scrambled brain. He didn't know if he should be outraged or puke all over Parker's brown leather shoes. After a few seconds, Parker burst out laughing.

"It's a joke, Detective. You know, because we're the NSA and we're always violating people's privacy. Jeez, lighten up."

Jake finally exhaled. A cool breeze traveled up his sweaty back to remind him that he was still alive.

"Can I call you Jake? Maybe it'll ease some of this tension."

"Sure."

Parker's voice became serious when he said, "But all jokes aside, you did start something that has to be finished."

"It sounds like I need to get a lawyer."

"You don't need to do anything except tell the exact truth from here on out." Parker's smile disappeared, and this seemed to be the first time Jake saw his true face. "What I'm about to tell you can never leave this room. It can never be repeated outside of us, and make no mistake, this is not me asking you to participate; rather, I'm informing you that you've already begun." Parker didn't blink a single time while talking. "Do you understand what I just said to you?"

Jake paused for a moment. "I do...but honestly this sounds like something that's way above my pay grade and I think I would feel more comfortable if Lieutenant Simons was here with us."

Parker's stone face chiseled a bitter smile. "Really? Well, I wouldn't want you to be uncomfortable." Parker stood up and pointed a charcoal black M1911 .45 ACP with an aluminum silencer attached to it right between Jake's eyes.

Jake froze, but the sweat from his forehead dripped

down. His heart stretched in his chest.

"Is this a joke?" Jake asked.

"Unfortunately for you this is the complete opposite."

"You are pointing a weapon with deadly intent at an officer in a police station. Are you *fucking* insane?"

"I bet I could shoot you right now in the middle of your own police station and walk out of here without any problems. What do you think my chances are?"

"I'm not a betting man."

Parker snatched Jake's gun from his holster. "We all have our vices. Otherwise, you wouldn't have walked in here drunk as a skunk. Now, I would like to carry on this conversation without this…incentive…to keep you comfortable, but you must promise me two things. One, that you will take this conversation seriously. And two, you won't do anything stupid. You picking up what I'm putting down?"

Jake nodded.

"Good." Parker holstered his weapon and kept Jake's gun by his side. "Now that we got that out of the way, we can get back on track. Yesterday you went to a crime scene in the Catskill Mountains. What did you see?"

"Why is this a matter of national security?" Jake asked through a dry heave.

"Answer my questions first, and then we'll get to yours."

Jake took one last deep breath. "I found the money behind the wall. The passports and documents came after more digging."

"Did you see anything unusual?"

"Besides the little bank inside the wall?"

"Yes, Detective, besides the little bank in the wall."

"The place was a mess. If I had to guess, I'd say our

suspects were looking for something. Possibly the money."

Parker went into deep thought. "What about the boy? You talked to him, right?"

"I tried, but he freaked out, and the deputy took him away."

"Anything else?"

Jake shook his head.

"You're telling me that's all that happened?"

"I'm telling you that's all I know."

"Last question. Why did you lie on your police report?"

"I didn't want this case to be dumped into my lap because of someone else's oversight."

Parker adjusted his suit and cleared his throat. "Like I said, this doesn't leave the room." He paused for a few seconds, wondering where he should begin. "The male victim, in this case, has been presented to the public as a man by the name of Wei Pei. That name will be on his tombstone and the very few people who did know of his existence will mourn over that person. But in the shadows of the world, he was known as Liang Do Shen. The leader and organizer of the most vicious mercenary group in the world… V.E.N.O.M…at least, once upon a time ago."

"I'm sorry, who is this?"

"The Veiled and Exclusive Nation of Organized Mercenaries. Do Shen single-handedly built this organization and it was the most powerful of its kind. It was split into two sides: the government officials, lawyers, doctors, everyday pencil pushers, they were the private mercenaries. Regular people doing things not only to push the V.E.N.O.M. agenda but to be a part of an anonymous network that could access unlimited resources. Probably 99% of those people were relatively harmless.

Then there was the one percent. The spies, assassins…

the guns for hire. These people were highly dangerous and virtually untraceable. Do Shen enlisted these specialists from all over the world to carry out covert operations for any country willing to pay the price. He had no allies. No partners. Pay the tab, and he could make just about anything happen."

"Like what?"

"You name it: assassinations, espionage, political corruption, arms deals, the occasional overthrowing of a government. Picture the best of the best recruits from intelligence agencies all over the world, militaries, rogue agents and many more all working for one man."

"You mean people like you."

Parker smiled at the jab. "America didn't always do things the diplomatic way. I must admit, that part of our history I'm not too proud of and will never truly get over. But it happened. I'm sure one day we'll face our ugly truths, but until then we have to deal with what's in front of us right now."

"What about the international laws? They were made to prevent this type of thing from happening."

"Yes, but V.E.N.O.M. was like NATO for Do Shen. Those very same laws protected him along with his organization. Protocol One of the Geneva Convention, Article forty-seven says, 'A mercenary shall not have the right to be a combatant or a prisoner of war.'"

Jake shook his head. "What does that mean?"

"It means that for a short period of time V.E.N.O.M. was untouchable. Do Shen ruled the world from the shadows. Eventually, we smartened up and found a way to cut his power."

"How?"

"President Bush put into law the Military Commissions

Act of 2006, also known as HR-6166. That law authorized trial by military commission for violations of the law of war and for *other purposes*. V.E.N.O.M. was that other purpose. Before he knew it, Do Shen's empire had collapsed. The organization disbanded and nations began to distance themselves from him. He didn't have a string to pull or a number to call, but before things got really bad for him, he was able to strike a deal with the U.S.: give up complete power, and in exchange, he would be protected on U.S. soil."

"Well, good thing we held up our end of the bargain."

Parker chuckled. "Throughout the years there were rumors that he kept a little collateral for himself. Just in case that opportunity to be on top ever came back."

"What kind of collateral?"

"That information is classified. Your concern should be focused on your role in all of this."

"What do you want from me?"

"Do Shen was assassinated, but he died as Wei Pei. That is, of course, until you found that mountain of evidence that exposed who he really was. So, in retrospect, you started everything that's about to happen."

"And what's about to happen?"

"War, Jake. Every ex-Venom now knows where to come to find what we're looking for."

"This… collateral?" Parker answered with a cold stare. "Can't you put out a most wanted list or something? I guarantee they wouldn't be able to walk the streets if you did."

"It's not that simple. After V.E.N.O.M. disbanded, the mercenaries integrated back into society and obtained new identities. We don't know what they look like, where they're coming from, or if they even still exist. All we know is if what they're looking for gets into their hands, it can be damaging on a global level."

"So, again, what do you need me to do?"

"Your job. As of now, you are the lead detective on the Wei Pei case. It's picked up too much steam just to leave it alone so while you investigate, I'll be doing my own work behind the scenes through you. You work the case until Do Shen is in the ground. That's three days from now. Once that happens, you can close it. You'll get a decoration for serving your country, a nice little pay bump, and an all-expense paid trip to a location of your choosing. All you have to do is keep it quiet for three days."

"And if I refuse?"

Parker chuckled. "You don't want to make this difficult for yourself, Jake. This is a rare opportunity to do some real good in the world. To stop an organization like V.E.N.O.M. from resurfacing would mean more than anything you could ever put on your resume. From this point on, nothing else matters. Besides, I already told you…you started this yesterday. Welcome aboard."

Parker extended his hand, not sure what he'd get back. Jake stared at the gesture with his nose wrinkled. He stood and walked toward the door without even an attempt to reconcile.

Before Jake could open the door, Parker said, "Jake…I would hate for you to be on the wrong end of this. I know you didn't ask for any of this, but refusing will only make your situation worse. Who knows what we'll find in your past."

Parker winked, then tossed his gun back to him.

* * *

Jake exited the office, and the air seemed a bit fresher. He bolted toward the exit but was blocked by Lieutenant Simons. "Whoa, whoa, whoa, whoa, where do you think you're going?"

Jake's thoughts raced so fast that he couldn't formulate a sentence. For all he knew it could have been a dream. "I have to go home and rest."

"Good, I agree. And you'll have plenty of time for that because as of now you're suspended."

"What?"

"You need more time, Jake. You're not ready to be here. And that's my mistake, not yours. I'll deal with Agent Parker from now on. In the meantime, I don't want to see you anywhere near here. If you give me a call in a few weeks, we can see—"

Jake walked away before he could finish. His thirst was stronger than ever before.

7.

Jake scrambled through his apartment, looking for something to get his mind off things. He stopped the ransack to look at the memorial. The good memories of the past made him second guess what he was doing. He turned the photo to face the wall and continued to rummage through his belongings until a series of heavy knocks came from the door.

Jake opened the door and saw Zasha standing there with her perky smile. She was wearing a red winter cap, black and red scarf, black mittens and a black pea coat with the tag still on it. New York weather was unfamiliar territory to her. "Hi, I'm sorry to bother you, but I'm looking for a Detective Penny." A light shiver came after her sentence.

Jake took a moment to gather himself. "That's me," he said as he looked past her.

"Great! Listen, I know this is completely unprofessional, and you could probably lock me up for this, but I was wondering if you could give me an exclusive on this story that I'm running."

"I don't have any exclusives." Jake tried to close the door, but Zasha blocked the attempt with her foot.

"You are the lead detective on the Wei Pei case, right?"

He opened the door and screened Zasha a little more closely. "How do you know that?"

"I have my sources. They also said you found a major piece to the puzzle in the case."

"Sounds like you can get your exclusive from whoever you're talking to."

Jake tried to close the door again, but this time Zasha placed her whole body in the way. "Look, I know you don't owe me anything, and I am completely out of line for even coming to your private residence, but if you won't do this for me, then do it to help the victims of this tragedy. Set the narrative on something that's hardly being reported on as it is."

Jake thought for a second. He remembered that whether he liked it or not, he was now the face of the case. Maybe this could be his way of jumping in front of it and having some control over the situation. Then Koa's broken face flashed in his mind. He didn't need a second longer to think. "There's a diner on Washington Ave called Arty's. It's about five blocks from here. We can talk there in twenty minutes."

"Thank you so much. This is going to be a big help for me…and for the victims of course. So, I'll see you there or—" Jake closed the door in her face. "Okay, I'll just meet you there then," she said through the door.

* * *

Arty's Diner was a staple in the community. It had been in business since the 50's and had priceless relics all over the walls to tell its story. The owner, Arty, was a fourth-generation heir to the establishment. He was a balding white male with liver spots all over his arms and head. Even though he owned the place, he was never too proud to wait tables. Jake was a regular and was taken good care of for his loyalty. Jake and Zasha sat in Jake's favorite booth, next to the front window.

"Here you go," Arty said. "One latte macchiato for the dame and one Party Arty for Jakey Boy."

The Party Arty was a coffee-flavored blend of liquor and whipped cream, a perfect mixture for a daytime drinker.

"Thanks, Art," Jake said.

"Anytime, my boy. And by the way, it's about time you brought a nice piece in here." Arty tried to whisper, but Zasha heard him clear as day as he winked and walked away.

Her jaw dropped, but there was a playful smile behind it. "I didn't know I was going to become your *piece* if we came here."

Jake smiled, but only to cover his embarrassment. "I'm sorry. Subtlety is not Arty's forte." He took a swallow of his drink, and it gave him the shakes. After not drinking them for sixty-three days, he had forgotten about that extra kick. "Before we start talking about anything, you must know that there are some things I can't release to the press."

"Of course," Zasha said as she dug through the layers of clothing to grab her phone. "Any information you can give would be fantastic."

"Okay, but again, it's gonna be a lot of boring police talk and dead-end clues."

She smiled as she leaned forward. "We can talk about whatever you want." She hit the record button on her phone and Jake started.

Jake was on his fourth Party Arty, and Zasha loosened up with a Long Island Ice Tea. By now the dinner crowd had filled the place, and they were both laughing more than talking over the utensils scraping on plates and the mixed chatter.

"I don't think you understand the full scope of the premise," Jake said, finishing off his Party Arty.

"Well, apparently, I don't," Zasha said. "Would you like to expound for the record?" Her smile reached all the way to her earlobes. The shade of red lipstick she chose made her lips look plump and soft as rose petals.

"Yes, I would. And you can put this on the front page so there won't be any confusion." Jake raised his glass to signal Arty for another drink. He cleared his throat and looked at Zasha with a straight face. "The whole thing takes place in the land of Equestria populated by varieties of ponies, including variants of Pegasus and unicorns, along with a number of other sentient and non-sentient creatures. Anyway, the main pony is Twilight Sparkle. She's like the Lebron James of studying friendship, love, and everything fun."

Before Jake could get out another word, Zasha burst into tears from laughing.

"Are you gonna let me finish?" Jake asked.

"I'm sorry, I just never thought I would be in New York City talking to a man about his obsession with My Little Pony."

Arty brought over another drink. "Anything else for you, sweetheart?"

"No, I'm fine, thank you." Zasha's smile warmed Arty's cheeks. He looked at Jake as he walked away and gave him a proud stare. "Anyway, back to this obsession."

Jake took a sip of his new drink, then wiped his mouth. "It's not an obsession; it's a way of life. At least that's what my daughter would say. She made me watch every single episode at least three or four times when she was little."

"That's sweet."

"I'll remember the words to that show before I remember my wedding vows on any given day. I think that makes me an expert or something."

"I agree. In a court of law, you would be the My Little Pony subject matter expert. That's a heavy title." Jake had a hearty laugh from his gut. Something that hasn't been done in a long time. "You should smile more. It looks good you, in a weird way."

"In a weird way?"

"Yeah. One side stretches a little farther than the other. It's cute."

It was true, the right side of Jake's mouth stretched farther than the left when he smiled. It had always been like that since he was a kid. He remembered getting picked on for it in school. The other kids would call him Crooked-Mouth, but the name never stuck. Jake made sure of that.

"So, what about now?"

"What do you mean?"

"The show. Do you and your daughter still watch it or is she on to something else?"

The question brought Jake back to his grim reality. He stared into his glass as it all came back to him. "No. We don't."

"Uh-oh. Maybe she's moving on from Little Ponies to little boys."

Jake rubbed his ring finger with his thumb. "She... passed away fourteen months ago."

Zasha's smile disappeared. She put her hands over her mouth, but her cheeks were flushed. "I am so sorry. I had no idea."

Jake never looked up from his glass. "It's okay. I mean, how could you?"

"And your wife?"

He replied by sucking down the rest of his Party Arty. When he finished, his eyes crept up from the table to meet hers.

"You know, I lost family too, my sisters. I know it can be a challenging thing to deal with, and sometimes you can feel helpless and alone but when you think about it—"

Zasha grabbed for his hand, but he pulled away. She studied his burnt hand before he put it under the table.

"So, Florida?" Jake asked. "That must have been a long trip, right?"

Jake's sudden change of subject turned Zasha off, but she understood. His eyes begged her to move on. "Right," she said finally. "The Wei Pei case. Um, it's more of a passion project. As I said, my family was taken away from me when I was young, so I instantly connected."

"Surely murders and kidnappings are happening all over Florida. You didn't have to come to New York to make a connection."

"That's fair, but…I needed a change. A colleague of mine told me about this opportunity, and I couldn't pass it up."

"You sound like a true advocate for the victims."

"They're included in the opportunity, sure."

Jake took a deep breath as he rubbed the back of his neck.

"What?" Zasha asked.

"Nothing. You're not the only one who's thinking about boosting their career off this, so, no judgment from me."

"And you're not?" Zasha asked.

"No."

"Then why do it?"

"Because it's my job," Jake said.

"I know, but what do you really want from this?"

Jake thought about that as she tried to break through to him with her eyes. It almost worked. Instead of falling for the trap, he looked at his ringing phone. The number was blocked, but he knew he had to answer it.

"This is Penny." He listened to the voice on the other end, then looked at his watch. "Okay, I can do that, but it might be faster if you pick me up from somewhere. No, I don't drive." He listened to the response. "Okay. I'll see you there." He hung up and noticed Zasha staring at his phone. "I'm sorry about that," he said. "Work."

"No problem. I have to get going as well."

"I wish I could be more helpful, but as I said, the details were cut and dried ."

"I had a wonderful time. I got to eat at the world-famous Arty's Diner. Plus, I got some amazing insight into My Little Pony."

Jake cracked a smile, but it was short-lived.

"Listen, I'm staying in New York for a little while longer. If you want to meet up and talk about developing details, or just in general, I'll be around."

Jake pondered the invite. It had been a while since he'd enjoyed the company of another person, especially a woman. "Sure. I don't see why not."

Zasha pulled out an eggshell-colored business card with a bold elephant font and wrote her number one the back. "I'm staying at the Waldorf Astoria for another week. You should stop by."

"That's a pretty nice setup."

"When in Rome, right?" She handed him the business card. "If you have time, maybe you can show me where to get an authentic New York pizza. I would love to try one."

She gave Jake a flirtatious smile, but he was more interested in the business card. What he read triggered his interest.

"Averyanov. That's your real last name?" he asked.

Zasha pressed her lips tight and scratched her head. "Uh, yeah. It's Siberian . On my grandfather's side."

"Why don't you just introduce yourself like this?"

"I don't know. I shortened it in college to kind of fit in and never got around to changing it back."

Jake placed the card in his wallet and made his way toward the exit. "Sometimes being someone else is the best option," he said with his back to her.

"You should say that to your wife and kid."

Jake's chest tightened as he turned around with his face on fire. "What did you say?"

Zasha was still smiling. "I said, you say that, but this is the life we live."

Jake's anger was extinguished when he heard what she truly said. He was a little buzzed, so maybe the words got twisted together. Either way, he gathered himself and parted ways with a friendly nod.

8.

The Greenwich funeral home was a quiet, somber place right outside of Jamaica, Queens. The pea-green floor was vacuumed without a single piece of fiber out of place. There was a room with rows of pews leading up to a stage with a handcrafted podium that had the home's crest carved into it. A family was being shown around in the room while another family walked past Jake into an office.

Jake imagined himself in a coffin right below the podium, with no one there to see him off. That thought eased his mind a bit, until Parker walked in his line of vision.

"You freaked out?" Parker asked.

Jake snapped out of his daze, upset that Parker would interrupt his tranquil moment. "What?"

"The funeral home. Sometimes people can't stand to be in one because it's like brushing shoulders with death itself."

"I'm fine," Jake said, walking away.

Before he could get far, the funeral home director came over to greet them both. He was a small man with a receding hairline. He wore a black silk suit with a red bowtie. "Hello, gentlemen. My name is Adam Greenwich. I'm the director of the home. One of my staff said that you would like to speak with me?"

Parker signaled with his eyes for Jake to take the lead.

"Yes, my name is Detective Penny, and this is Agent Parker. We have a few questions about a particular funeral arrangement that may have come through here as recently as yesterday."

"I'll be more than happy to help, but legally I can only divulge so much information."

"Any cooperation would be a great help at this point, Mr. Greenwich," Parker said.

Adam studied them both with his body angled away. "Do you guys have badges or something?"

They both took out their credentials and handed them over. Adam scanned them carefully, as if he understood every detail. Once he was done inspecting them, he tried to hand both credentials to Jake, but Parker quickly snatched his own. "Follow me to my office."

* * *

Adam's office had two walls filled with books and one dedicated to pictures of his staff and family. As morbid as it was, he was proud of his family business because it was something he could call his own. While Adam jammed every key on his keyboard, Jake could feel Parker's eyes on him. He wondered if Parker could smell the remnants of the Party Arty soaking through his pores.

Every few seconds, Adam would stop and shake his head. "I'm sorry guys, but I'm having a hard time finding an open account on this…Wei Pei, you said? Maybe the family went to a different funeral home."

"We have a very reliable source who said the arrangements were made here," Parker said. "He has to be in your system somewhere."

The door opened, and a female staff member entered the office. "Mr. Greenwich, the Perez family is here for their appointment."

"Thank you, Tonya. Tell them I'll be there in ten minutes."

The staff member nodded and turned for the door, but Parker stopped her and said, "Excuse me, ma'am, you wouldn't have happened to have a Chinese family come in this week for a man by the name of Wei Pei, would you?"

"Sorry, I was off for the past three days, I wouldn't know."

"I'm telling you, I don't think he came through here," Adam said.

"Have you checked the closed accounts?" Tonya asked. "It's a long shot, but he could have been put in there by mistake."

Adam gave her a smile to mask his annoyance. "Thank you, Tonya. I don't know why I didn't think of that." He continued to type as she left the office. Once he finished, he stared in amazement at the computer screen. "Well, what do you know, she was right. The Wei Pei account is indeed closed."

"What does that mean?" Jake asked.

"It means he should already be in the ground. We don't close accounts until the day after the funeral, but I check all accounts before they close and I don't remember this one." Adam scrolled down and whistled when he got to the bottom. "This guy's family spared no expense when it came to his burial. They forked out two-hundred and fifty grand for the arrangement."

"Who paid for it?" Jake asked.

Adam did some more power typing, causing Jake to

clench his jaw. "It doesn't say. It all came through from an anonymous donor."

"You're telling me someone can drop that kind of cash and not even leave a name?" Parker asked.

"Technically, yes. Most of the families who come here can barely afford a floral arrangement, let alone the full burial service. So, we provide a program where the loved ones can collect donations to pay for the funeral. Donors can choose to be known or stay anonymous. Either way, as long the check clears, we don't really concern ourselves with who is making the payment."

"There has to be some record of someone making the arrangements," Parker said.

Adam rose from his computer and rushed towards a small filing cabinet resting under a mounted TV. He pulled out a thick file and went through its contents. He whipped out a single sheet and handed to Parker. "Here. We have a wet signature from someone. His name is…Thomas Gaily. It looks like he signed all the necessary documents, but that doesn't mean he was the donor. It just means he took responsibility for making the service happen. If anyone would have an idea about the actual donor, it would be him."

9.

Jake and Parker walked up the grand limestone entry of a New Jersey mansion. They stopped to stare at a red 2018 Lamborghini parked out front. It looked as if it had been built from scratch in that very spot, and never touched again.

"How many years do you think you'd have to work to afford something like this?" Parker asked.

"I'd probably have to sell my soul, then refinance it in the afterlife just to make a down payment," Jake said.

"Exactly."

Parker rang the doorbell. A few seconds later, the door was answered by a petite Hispanic maid. She looked troubled to see Jake and Parker towering over her.

"*Hola*," Parker said. "We're-looking-for-Mr.-Gaily. Is-he-home?"

The Hispanic maid closed the door without saying a word.

"Smooth," Jake said, rolling his eyes.

"What?"

"You just insulted that woman."

"I did not. I was trying to be sensitive."

"You have a funny way of being sensitive."

The door swung open, and Mr. Gaily appeared. He was a heavyset man with a large round nose. "Can I help you gentlemen with something?" he asked. His accent came from the thickest part of Brooklyn.

Jake opened his mouth to speak, but Parker jumped in. "Good evening Mr. Gaily. Sorry to interrupt you, but we were wondering if you could answer a few questions for us."

"And who are you?"

"Where are my manners?" Parker said as he pulled out his credentials. "I'm Special Agent Ethan Parker, and this here is Detective Penny. We would really appreciate it if you could be of assistance with an ongoing investigation."

"Did something happen?"

"No, no, we just have a few standard questions, then we can get out of your hair."

Mr. Gaily looked back for a moment to check on his chattering family having dinner. Then he stepped outside and closed the door with just a crack of light behind him. The wind chill caught him off guard, so he bundled up. "Okay, make it fast."

"Where is your place of employment?"

"Wall Street. I'm a senior advisor for BlackRock."

"And you work how many hours a week, roughly?"

"'Bout sixty."

"That's not too stressful for you?"

"I fish. That's enough to keep the crazies away."

"Must be nice. I hear that fishing is a great way to clear your mind. You must be doing a lot of that after a death in the family."

Mr. Gaily's face turned white. His eyes bounced back and forth from Parker to Jake until he settled on Parker. "What kind of investigation you say you were working on?"

"I never did say. But back to your deceased family member—"

"I don't have no deceased family members."

"Are you sure?" Parker asked as he pulled out some papers. "Because I have a bunch of documents here with your signature stating you paid two-hundred and fifty thousand dollars to send someone off. They must have been near and dear to you."

Mr. Gaily took a hard swallow as he glanced at his signature. "I ain't paid for nothing."

"So, this isn't you?"

Mr. Gaily shook his head with his lip poked out. "I don't know what to tell you, boys."

"Then I'm sure you won't mind coming down to Greenwich Funeral Home so the staff can say we have the wrong guy. Clear up all this confusion."

"And I'm sure you won't mind pulling your pants down and sitting on a popsicle. I ain't going nowhere without my lawyer."

Parker grinned as he looked to Jake, who was far less amused. "Fair enough. I guess we have to take matters into our own hands here then."

"And what the fuck is that supposed to me—"

A loud buzz followed by a blue flash seized Mr. Gaily's body and he came crashing down at Parker's feet. Parker exposed a small shock baton in the right sleeve of his jacket.

Jake rushed to Mr. Gaily's aid. "Jesus Christ, Parker! What the hell did you do?!"

Parker lifted Mr. Gaily by his underarms. "Grab his feet and help me take him to the garage."

He can't be serious, Jake thought.

Jake didn't move a muscle. "This is illegal. I don't want any part of it."

"When are you going to realize that you've been a part of this since yesterday when you found all that evidence? Now, either you help me carry this blob to the garage or stay here and explain to the maid why her boss is unconscious." Parker jerked his head toward the front door. Jake turned around to see the maid just inside, staring out in shock.

Parker looked at her and held a finger to his lips. She bowed her head and rushed away.

"Grab him," Parker said.

* * *

The garage could hold up to six cars, but only two occupied it. The place mimicked a luxury car showroom, with bright halogen lamps in the ceiling and fresh marble floors. On the walls were pictures of Mr. Gaily fishing. But most importantly, it was detached from the house, which was perfect for Parker.

Mr. Gaily's wrists and ankles were zip-tied to a chair. He saw blurry figures standing in front of him as he came to. His wounded voice called for help, but a dirty cloth muffled his attempts.

"Finally," Parker said. "I thought you would never wake up. The voltage wasn't even that high. Now, where were we? Ah, yes, we were discussing your involvement with a funeral arrangement." Parker yanked out the cloth from Mr. Gaily's mouth. A bit of saliva poured out before he could talk.

"You guys are *fucking* nuts! As soon as I get out of this, the both of you's are gonna be drifting in a river somewhere."

Jake pulled Parker to the side with a firm grip. "What the hell are we really doing here?" he whispered. "This isn't the way to do things. This isn't the way *I* do things."

"Okay," Parker sighed. "If it makes you feel any better, you can go watch the door. Give me ten minutes."

"Parker—"

"Go. Everything will be fine here. If this asshole doesn't give me the information I need, then I'll send the subpoenas down his throat. But right now, time is of the essence. Ten minutes."

Jake dragged his feet toward the door and kept watch.

"Hey! Hey-hey-hey-hey, where are you going?" Mr. Gaily said. "Don't leave me here with this maniac!"

Parker took off his suit jacket and folded it neatly over a chair. He then rolled up his sleeves while he stretched his neck. "I was starting to think he would never leave. If I'm being honest here, I completely understand why you didn't want to say anything. My interim partner can be a bit of a hardass at times. But now that he's gone feel free to open up as much as you want. Just about this funeral business though, because we only have ten minutes."

"For the last time, I don't know what you're talking about."

Parker's sigh was a bit raspier this time. He turned his attention to the mantel hanging from the wall with fishing equipment. "You said you were a fisher, right?" Parker walked over to the mantel.

"At least twice a week," Mr. Gaily said.

"Do you take your kids?"

"No, they're not interested."

"That's a shame. I used to fish with my old man when I was a kid. He would take me to Lake Frederick in White

Post, Virginia. One of the best fishing spots I've ever been to. But I absolutely hated going to Lake Frederick because it was about seven hours away from where we lived which was Norton, Virginia. You ever been to Norton, Virginia? Don't go. It's a mud hole."

As Parker was talking, he rigged a fishing line into a hook and made sure the knot was firmly tied . Mr. Gaily's lips quivered as he followed Parker with his eyes.

"Anyway, we would leave the afternoon before so we could be there by nightfall and cast off at the crack of dawn. And forget about getting a hotel room. My father was too cheap to spare the luxury. So, we would stay in this hot, musty '83 Ford Sierra until it was time to get on the water. The last time we went I must've been exhausted because I fell asleep on the boat while holding all the bait," Parker said through a chuckle. "My father must have called my name a few times because by the time I heard it he was yelling. His voice scared me so much that I dropped all the bait in the water. Now, Lake Frederick is known for its Largemouth Bass, and I remember an army of them coming to devour every last piece of my father's bait. He was pissed. In fact, he was so pissed that he tried to make me get the bait back…with my mouth. I spent at least two minutes under water before he would let me back on the boat. I woke up sometime later to the smell of his boots cooking in the sun and being soaked in the back seat of his car while he was in a bar." Parker gazed at the hook as it shimmered in the light. "Needless to say, I didn't care for fishing too much after that."

Mr. Gaily scoffed. "Sucks for you."

Parker chuckled. "Yep. Sucked for me, indeed."

He twirled the hook between his index finger and his

thumb then pounced on Mr. Gaily, forcing him to hold his mouth open. The hook punctured his bottom lip, and he screamed so loud that his eyes went crisscross in his head. Once the hook pierced all the way through his flesh, blood poured from Mr. Gaily's mouth and onto Parker's hands.

Parker took the reel and gently pulled it so there was no slack. He then tied the other end to the open door of one of Mr. Gaily's cars. "Now, Tommy, can I call you Tommy? I'm gonna call you Tommy. Now I believe you had something to tell me about this funeral service you paid for."

Parker brought his ear inches away from Mr. Gaily's ensanguinating mouth, but all that came out were whimpers and cries. "What was that? I can't quite make out what you're saying." Mr. Gaily continued to ramble on through his whimpers. "Come on Tommy, I know you can do better than that." Parker plucked a note off the reel. That shocked Mr. Gaily back into reality and what he's gotten himself into. Parker crept closer to the door and pushed it back and forth causing Mr. Gaily's lip to stretch out.

"No, no, no, no, okay! I'll talk," Mr. Gaily said with a slur. "I'll talk, Jesus Christ, just don't close that door.

Parker rushed toward Mr. Gaily. "I'm all ears."

Mr. Gaily caught his breath. "I didn't pay for the funeral. Somebody gave me the money with specific instructions."

"Who?"

"I don't know."

Parker tugged on the reel, and Mr. Gaily winced in pain. "That's not good enough, Tommy. I need a name."

"I don't know the prick's name, all right?! All I know is he was an Asian guy who I met in Atlantic City."

"That doesn't make sense, Tommy. Why you? Why trust a stranger with a quarter of a million dollars?" Parker asked as he tightened his grip on the reel.

"I don't know, but he knew things about me," he said through the pain.

"So what, I know things about you. That doesn't mean that I'm gonna give you that type of money."

"He knew personal things about me. He knew where I worked. He knew about my family. He knew where my girlfriend lived. And he knew that I was in deep with a loan shark who has ties to the Borgata. That's where we met. He and his men brought me to his VIP section. The conversation was fifteen minutes, tops!"

"He was blackmailing you?

"No. He said… if I did what I was told exactly the way he said it, he would wipe my debt clean: 1.8 million!"

"And you believed him?"

"I thought he was a crazy son of a bitch, but then I thought, what do I have to lose? I did what he told me exactly how he wanted it. Within 24 hours I was out of the hole. No questions asked. I swear, I never saw him again."

Parker released his grip. "I'm sure those instructions included keeping your mouth shut about this?" The fear in Mr. Gaily's eyes told Parker all he needed to know. "Okay, here's what you're gonna do. Take some time off work. Two weeks minimum. You're going to buy two sets of tickets in two different parts of the world for you and your family leaving within the next 48 hours. Tell no one about this. The day before you fly out, you hit the road. Go someplace far.   Remote. Make sure you have enough cash to last you for a few weeks, you understand? No paper trail." Mr. Gaily nodded like a battery was in his neck. "Lay low for as long as you can." Parker ripped the hook out quick then cut the zip ties loose. "Again, don't mention to a single soul what you did or what happened here tonight."

Mr. Gaily tended to his wound with a towel Parker handed him. "How will I know when it's safe?"

"If you're still alive next week, then that's a good start."

Parker cleaned his hands and grabbed his jacket right before he walked out. Outside, Jake was standing there with a stone face, fists clenched. Parker walked past him unruffled, which made Jake wonder what he'd gotten himself into.

V.E.N.O.M.

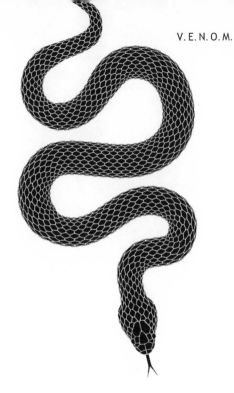

10.

Parker drove a 1968 Mustang Bullitt that had a stealth-black exterior and tinted windows. The inside was the personification of Parker himself: clean, pressed and symmetrical. He zipped through light traffic on the way to Atlantic City.

Jake kept his eyes straight, not moving a muscle.

"You got something to say to me, Jake?" Parker asked.

"Don't start with me right now," Jake replied. "You really don't wanna go down that road."

"I think I do. Right now, your face is tighter than a schoolgirl who got stood up on prom night. If we're gonna be walking around the Borgata asking questions, then our chemistry has to be on-point."

Jake zeroed in on Parker's face. "Was our chemistry on-point when you aimed your gun at my face? Or how about what you did back at Gaily's? Were we a team then?"

"Considering the circumstances, I think you're blowing this a little out of proportion."

"Considering the circumstances, I think you're a piece of shit. You do whatever it is that you do on your own, but when you involve me, that's when I draw the line."

"Do my tactics… bother you, Jake?"

"You tortured a civilian," Jake said over the engine. "You tortured a civilian for information and made me an accessory after the fact."

"Oh please, I didn't torture that guy. I used an aggressive interrogation method to withdraw vital information from a suspect who was impeding an ongoing investigation that just so happens to have our national security in limbo."

"Right. In other words, just another decoration to go across your chest. Well, you can save your little recommendation for me because I want no part of it."

"You know what? You need to get over your high horse, all right? If you had half the energy then that you do now, you would have stopped me. At the very least said something instead of me dragging it out of you like this."

"It wouldn't have made a difference, and you know it."

"Why not? You're not just some civilian with an iPhone ready to sell a story to the media. Are you?"

"This isn't about me. This is about you and your tightrope walk with the law. Sometimes I don't even know which side you're on."

"But we know which side you're on, don't we? So why didn't you step in ?"

Jake's jaw tightened as he looked out the window.

"Detective Penny, as a man of the law, why didn't you intervene when the law was being broken?"

Jake thought back to when he'd stolen drugs from a gang member just the day prior. His principles were laced with hypocrisy and they had no business coming out of his mouth, so he stayed quiet.

"I'll tell you why you didn't do anything," Parker continued. "It's because you knew it was necessary. You and I both know we're not dealing with anything less than extraordinary. We have to do what we came to do by any means necessary. Ethics and morals are for the buddy cops. We're in a different world now, so I suggest you start assimilating."

* * *

The head of security—Gee—escorted Jake and Parker through the security room of The Borgata. The walls were plastered with fifty-inch LED screens and smaller monitors. Lined up below them were watchers in matching black uniforms, spying on every gambler with hyper attention.

"So, you want video footage of our private VIP section, three days ago around 9 p.m.?" Gee asked. He had a long pointy nose with subtle acne on his cheeks.

"Yes sir, preferably inside the lounge to get a better understanding of what we're dealing with," Parker said.

"That's gonna be a no-go. The clients pay for their privacy and, even if that wasn't the case, I can't. No cameras in the lounges."

"So you have blind spots in the casino?" Parker asked. "What kind of security are you running here?"

"Like I said, customers pay for their privacy. Plus, in order to reserve a lounge, you have to have a special relationship with the casino. We wouldn't insult our best customers by watching them."

"Okay, just show me what you can."

"And that is where your problems continue to grow. See, I can't just *give* footage away. I could lose my job. If you're here for an official investigation, then there's a procedure to follow along with a healthy amount of paperwork. But, if there were some incentive for me, maybe we could streamline that process." Gee's grimy smile irritated Parker.

Parker took a few steps forward into his personal space and lowered his voice. "Are you interfering with an ongoing investigation? Because the last guy can tell you that's not a good idea."

"What happened to the last guy?"

Parker paused. "He went on to a better place."

Gee scoffed. "Cute, but your threats hold no weight here. If you want to look at that footage now, you have to go through me."

Jake rubbed his ring finger with his thumb as he wondered how Parker was going to muscle his way through this one.

A smile slowly crept onto Parker's face. Gee stood confidently. "Well then, I guess we'll just have to serve a subpoena."

Gee shrugged his shoulders. "Do what you must. It'll take months for it to stick without a viable reason why you need that footage."

"Oh, the subpoena isn't for the footage. It's for the snooty loan shark that doubles as the head of security of the casino he's ripping off."

Gee's face turned white as a nervous chuckle trembled from his mouth. "What are you talking about? I'm not a loan shark."

"That's not what the subpoenas will say. I'm with the NSA, Gee. I'm sure we can find a lot of embarrassing things on your computer, along with records of you skimming off the top of the casino's profits to loan to these high rollers while also using company resources to enforce power. Investigators will say the scheme was ingenious. The crook looking for himself never gets caught."

"But it's not true," Gee said with a cracked voice. "It'll never stick in court."

Parker's laugh erupted from his gut as he doubled over to catch his breath. "I'm not trying to send you to jail," he said between laughs. "I'm just planting the seed, my boy.

Because you will lose your job and the casino's going to pay heavy legal fees to avoid scandal. They may collapse, they may not, but the main thing to focus on is you. After a lengthy trial, you will be found not guilty, rightfully so, but by that time, it'll be too late. The people who really run this place will have it in their mind that you were stealing from them while simultaneously ruining their reputation. They'll want to take care of you. And the way I hear they handle business, you'll be begging for prison. You picking up what I'm putting down?"

"This is extortion. I can report you right now."

"Go ahead! Get the ball rolling on the story. Saves me from having to plant any evidence."

Gee tried to stand straight, but his shivering body wouldn't allow his spine to straighten out. "Who are you?"

"Think of your deepest, darkest fear in the whole world. The one that keeps you up at night... I'm its creator," Parker whispered. "Just show us the footage, Gee. You don't want to see me create."

Gee gulped and looked to Jake for guidance, but Jake gave him nothing. "Right this way, sir." As Gee led the way, Parker looked over to Jake and gave him a wink. A tingling feeling raised the hairs on the back of Jake's neck.

Gee took them to a lone monitor off to the side. "We digitally store our footage by each shift, thousands of hours all on a mega drive. After thirty days, we send the files to a database in New Mexico." Gee picked a file and fast-forwarded through the footage. "Tell me when."

Parker leaned in closer. "Stop right there...rewind thirty seconds, then play." Gee did exactly that, and they all observed. "All right, there's Tommy-boy. He's walking with the security and...they go into lounge number two around

9:20 p.m. Fast-forward until they leave."

Gee did so until Parker aggressively tapped him to stop. At around the 9:37 p.m. mark, they saw Mr. Gaily leave the lounge alone. Soon after, the two men who escorted him in came out, followed by a small man.

"Stop right there," Parker said. "Him. We need to find out who he is."

"I can pull up payment records to see who rented out the lounge for that night. If you don't mind waiting, of course."

"That would be great, Gee. We appreciate it."

Gee held his position until Parker waved him off.

* * *

Parker scanned the area as he pulled up in Jake's neighborhood. The whole community watched as this mystery car came to a stop in front of them.

"Nice neighborhood," Parker said.

"It's even better when you don't look like the nervous white guy."

"I'm not nervous. More alert than anything." A ping lit up Parker's phone. "Okay, my guy just sent me some intel on our mystery man. The reservation for the lounge was under the name Frank Coe, which is hilarious by the way. It took some digging, but they were able to link *Mr. Coe* to a property in West Virginia. The property is being rented out to a Chang Ho Yuen. I'm willing to bet everything they're the same person. If we hurry now we can—"

Parker looked over and noticed Jake trying to control his shaking hands. His thumb tapped on the steering wheel until he came up with a solution. "If we hurry now, we can get enough sleep to be fresh for the road tomorrow."

"We're driving?" Jake asked.

"Yeah, I feel it's best to stay off the grid. I'll pick you up here at nine o'clock. And Jake…be ready to go. No late nights."

Jake opened the door to leave.

"One more thing," Parker said before he could step out. Jake rolled his eyes and closed the door, not looking in Parker's direction. "I don't do this often, but when I'm wrong, I like to take accountability. So, I apologize for the position I put you in back at Thomas Gaily's place. You have my word that I will never put you in a situation that would have you go against your character again. We cool?"

Jake nodded then exited the car.

V.E.N.O.M.

11.

The next morning, the sun peeked through the clouds and illuminated the Waldorf Astoria. Jake stood on the corner adjacent to the hotel, gazing at Zasha's business card as a herd of pedestrians moved through the crosswalk.

What am I doing here? He thought.

He put the card in his pocket and walked in the opposite direction. Even if he did see her, he wouldn't know what to say. But before he could turn the corner, Zasha walked out of the hotel and spotted him.

"Detective Penny," she called out, and dashed through the intersection before the traffic light could turn green. "What are you doing on this side of town so early, Detective?"

"I was in the neighborhood and thought I'd stop by to see how you were adjusting."

"I'm adjusting just fine. I mean, I could use a little more sun, but other than that, I'm good. Have there been any new developments since we last spoke?"

"No. Like I said, I was just in the neighborhood and thought I'd stop by."

Zasha gave him a suspicious smile. "Well, since you were just in the neighborhood, why don't you take me out for breakfast? I was on my way to a sandwich shop I found online."

The cold air dried Jake's mouth. He took a swallow and

cleared his throat. "I would, but I can't. I have to move on a lead in an hour."

"Really?" she asked, ears perking up.

Jake confirmed with a nod.

"Okay, well at least you have a good reason for blowing me off."

"I would never blow you off."

Zasha smiled as she tried to cover her rosy cheeks from the wind. "I mean, it wouldn't be professional." Jake said.

"If you find anything, will you be able to give me an exclusive?"

"We'll see."

"I'll let you get to it then. Good luck." She seemed to float as she backtracked into the crowd. Her smile was a magnet that pulled Jake in, but he managed to resist for now.

As Zasha went through her bag to take out her phone, she realized she didn't have her room key.

She walked through the lobby and up to the front desk. "Hey, George, I left my room key in my room like a klutz. You think I could get another one before I head out?"

"Of course, ma'am. Let me finish with this guest first, and I'll be right with you."

"Take your time." Zasha stepped away from the counter to create space for others. All the while, a musk slithered to her nose over the breakfast food.

"Business or pleasure?" a smooth voice from behind her.

She turned around to see Parker's hypnotizing smile. Her eyes screened him up and down as she clutched her purse against her chest. "Excuse me?"

"Are you here for business or pleasure?"

She made sure to take in last-minute observations.

"Pleasure," she finally said.

"Kinda weird to vacation in New York this time of year. Most people go to places like...Miami."

"I think it's weird that a complete stranger would question my vacationing decisions."

Parker chuckled as he leaned on the counter. "I didn't mean to pry. I just find it fascinating to meet tourists like myself from different places. My trip was a mixture of business and pleasure. I originally came for a conference. Then my wife wanted to stay an extra couple of days, so we did. They say this is where all the New York movies are made."

Zasha released her purse from her chest. "Yeah, something like that."

"The city is bigger than I imagined. You here alone?"

Zasha slammed her purse on the counter and shook her hair loose. "Okay, let's cut the crap. We both know what this is."

Parker's eyes narrowed as his head tilted back. "We do?"

"Yeah, we do. And you tell your *wife* that I don't care how many eyes he has in New York. If I catch you or any of his puppets following me again, there will be hell to pay. You understand me?"

Parker took a second to register what she'd said. "Question, why is my wife a man?"

"Do-you-understand-me?"

A smirk etched itself into Parker's face, bringing out his strong jawline. "Sure. I'm sorry I even bothered you."

"Good. You're dismissed."

The desk clerk came back and handed Parker a piece of paper. "You enjoy your vacation, ma'am," Parker said to Zasha.

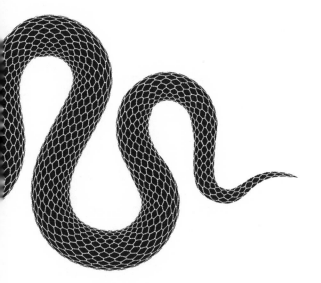

12.

Bluefield, West Virginia

Parker pulled up to a humble home in a wooded area. The entire landscape looked like something inside a flea market snow-globe. A sudden thought of regret for not wearing more layers filled Jake's mind. The southern cold was a bit different than city cold. He and Parker plowed their way up to the front door.

"Let me do all the talking this time," Parker said. "You just back me up." He knocked three times.

"So just keep doing what I've been doing this whole time then," Jake said.

"Exactly."

A quick glance from the inside of the curtains caught Parker's attention. "Excuse me? Mr. Yuen? I saw you at the window. My name is Special Agent Parker, and this is Detective Penny. We wanted to ask you a few questions."

They both waited for a response.

"I don't have any time," Mr. Yuen said through the door.

"This will only take a moment of your time, sir," Parker said. "You could really be a great help to us."

"I don't know anything about nothing. I work and come home. That's it."

"That's fine, Mr. Yuen, but your lack of cooperation

could be detrimental to the success of an open investigation. You wouldn't want to hinder that process in any way now, would you?" Parker rubbed his hands together fast enough to make a fire, then pulled out his gun. He put his weight on his back leg and braced himself to kick the door down, but Jake jumped in front of him. Parker rolled his eyes and holstered his weapon, giving Jake a chance to use a more diplomatic approach.

Jake took a moment to find his words. "Mr. Yuen? This is Detective Jacob Penny. Listen, we just wanna take a few minutes of your time to discuss an old friend of yours. Does the name Wei Pei ring a bell?"

Silence followed Jake's question. Parker stared at Jake without blinking, his right leg bouncing and itching to kick something down.

"I don't know a Wei Pei," Mr. Yuen finally said.

"If you don't know a Wei Pei, maybe you can help us out with the real person, Liang Do Shen."

Parker quickly reached for Jake's ear. "What the hell are you doing?" he whispered.

"I'm trying to get him to talk. Beating around the bush isn't getting us anywhere and going in guns blazing isn't the smartest option either."

"It may be our only option now that our intentions are known. We have no idea what this guy is capable of. He could be planning an attack on us right now, and we're standing here vulnerable to—"

One lock clicked open, another bolt slid back, and a final lock turned until the door creaked open to reveal a gray-haired fossil of a Chinese man who could barely stand. Jake tried to peek into the house, but Mr. Yuen hardly let any light in.

"Mr. Yuen, thank you for taking the time to—"

"What do you think you know about Liang Do Shen, young man?" he interrupted.

Jake looked to Parker, who urged him to continue. "I don't know much about him. But I do know that you two are connected somehow."

Heavy footsteps from upstairs had snow falling from the roof and onto Parker's shoulder. He looked up and followed the steps with his eyes. "Are you alone, Mr. Yuen?" Parker asked as he focused on the footsteps.

"My wife," he said quickly. Parker wasn't convinced, but he kept his reservations to himself. "How does this work?" Mr. Yuen continued. "You take me a few miles up the road and shoot me in the back of the head. Make it look like suicide. You people are good at stuff like that."

"We're the good guys, Mr. Yuen," Parker said. "We're trying to put this thing to rest."

Mr. Yuen scoffed. "There is no rest. Once an evil deed is done, it lives forever. I can't even bury my friend without the U.S. government trying to rip apart whatever dignity he has left."

"So, you did give Thomas Gaily the money?" Parker asked.

"Only to avoid people like you."

"We have to take you in for further questioning," Jake said.

Mr. Yuen stepped outside with barely any clothes on. "Do as you wish."

"Actually, that won't be necessary," Parker said. "For now. We'll get the proper paperwork and pay you a visit later. Come on Jake."

"Everyone has to answer for their debts," Mr. Yuen

called out. "Yours may be coming sooner than later." He slammed the door shut and secured each lock in reverse order.

Jake's eyes blinked rapidly as he followed Parker back to the car. "Now you wanna go by the book? We should take this guy in. He just admitted to being associated with Do Shen."

"Agreed, but he was too quick to surrender, which means he has something bigger to hide. I'll have my people draft a high-level subpoena for him and his wife, Bigfoot. That way, we can see what's in the house. In the meantime, we'll sit on him and make sure he doesn't try to skip town."

As they walked back to the car, Jake kept his eyes on the house.

13.

The next several hours had Jake and Parker stationed down the road from Mr. Yuen's house, behind a broken-down pickup truck. Nightfall became the perfect backdrop for the Mustang, and the built-up snow gave the disguise of belonging to the otherwise flamboyant vehicle.

Jake cracked open a soda and guzzled it. He thought of the ways he could slip rum inside without Parker noticing. But he ultimately settled for the PG drink.

"That stuff'll kill you, you know?" Parker said.

"As opposed to standing next to you? I'll take my chances," Jake said through a burp.

Parker chuckled. "Come on, you can't tell me a step into the unknown isn't more exciting than handling cold cases."

"A man like me doesn't need much excitement in his life. More peaceful sleep maybe."

"You sound like the people in my hometown. No excitement. Just common folks living their common lives with the occasional religious experience. I call them the bucket people. Just a bunch of crabs not going anywhere. The irony in that is none of the crabs actually want to leave the bucket because once they're free, there are no more crabs to pull down. They lose their purpose."

Jake felt compelled to defend the idea of being common because he too came from a small town—in Harper,

Kansas. It wasn't much, but some of his best memories were from there—and some of his worst. "There's nothing wrong with settling for what you know. Some people would envy that lifestyle. God, I know I do."

"Are you a religious man, Jake?" Parker asked, staring out the window. "Did your mama put you in the choir, take you to church four times a week and give the last of her paycheck to the congregation in hopes of having a better life for you?"

Jake rubbed his ring finger as he took a deep breath. "No, I'm not a religious person. But I don't have to agree with it to understand it. Some people need hope in this world with everything that goes on, and you being here makes that more of a fact than blind faith."

Parker scoffed into a laugh. "I think it's a bunch of B.S. Fearing the unknown and praying to some supreme being to make your life better. I believe in me. I got where I am today because of me. I control my future."

Jake had a response, but he kept it to himself. There was no use in going back and forth with a person like Parker. Silence was the appropriate response.

"You know, I met God before," Parker said, turning his attention toward Jake. "He's not that great of a guy actually."

"I really don't want to hear about your near-death experience."

"No, it's nothing like that. When I was a kid, I would have trouble sleeping. I'd fidget in my bed, make little noises, just restless the whole night. Until one evening this strong bear claw of a hand came cutting through the darkness and placed itself on the right side of my face like a pillow. I remember a sweet smell coming from him, but I couldn't quite pinpoint it. It was the most masculine thing I'd ever felt in my life. My heart would race every time it came near me, but after a while, I got used to it. I even grabbed his hairy forearm to hold onto like my favorite toy. That hand stayed with me until I went to sleep. I can still remember his thumb caressing my cheek. When I woke up, I told my mother about it, and she told me that it was God coming down to protect his angel." The thought of his mother brought a sparkle to his eyes, and he smiled.

"From then on, every time I had trouble sleeping, sure enough the *hand of God* came down and calmed me to sleep. Then one night, I was going through my normal sleepless phase, and the hand of God came right on schedule. Only this time, it was a full moon that night, so my room was more lit than usual. As God approached me, I could see his eyes contrasting in the moonlight. At first, I was shocked to see that God had soulless ice-blue eyes with a scar going through his left eyebrow. But then it didn't take long for me to figure out it was my old man. The scar was from when my mother clocked him with a lamp to keep him from beating me to death. Come to find out, he didn't have the most soothing touch either. He worked a lot with his hands, so they were calloused. Instead he used a cloth formed around his hand and would dab chloroform into it to put me to sleep. And then it hit me. It all finally made sense. The pastors always preached for people to be God-fearing; it'll save your soul. But really it was because God was my father, and he struck fear in me like no other human could every day of my life. That is, of course, until he passed away. Heart attack. I watched God get buried like the rest of us, and I told myself I would never fear anyone like that again."

Parker was a product of his environment, and Jake could resonate with him on some level. Parker didn't leave much room for him to respond, so Jake left it at that. Silence seemed to be the thing that bound them together.

A black-and-white squad car cruised by them and stopped in front of Mr. Yuen's house.

"Right on schedule," Parker said, watching.

There was a beat before two officers exited the car and walked toward the door.

"Maybe we should back them up," Jake said.

"No. Let's see how this plays out. Yuen's probably gonna send them packing anyway." Parker looked over at Jake, who was focused on Mr. Yuen's house. "I never told anybody that story, Jake. Saying it out loud to someone really puts it in perspective for me."

Jake nodded. Parker returned the gesture.

14.

"What do you want?" Mr. Yuen said through the door.

The two officers, one of Asian descent and one American, stood on the frosted porch, looking confused. "Sorry to bother you, sir," the American officer said. "But we're responding to a call made earlier to come and check on this house. "

"I didn't call the police," Mr. Yuen said.

"Well someone did, and now we can't leave until we make sure everything is okay in the house. "

After a few seconds, Mr. Yuen unlocked each lock rapidly and opened the door. "I didn't call the police," Mr. Yuen said, his voice firm.

"We understand, sir. We just need to do a standard check, and we'll be on our way. May we enter?" the American officer asked as he stepped forward. Mr. Yuen placed his hand on the officer's chest and lodged his body in the doorway.

"Only one. Him." He signaled for the Asian cop to come inside.

The American Cop sighed as he rolled his eyes. "Make it quick," he said to the Asian cop.

* * *

The Asian cop followed Mr. Yuen through his living room. There were black-and-white photos everywhere. The layout was simple: a sofa, a coffee table and a little TV in the corner that hadn't been turned on in ages.

"What is your name?" Mr. Yuen asked.

"Nguyen. Officer Nguyen, sir." The young officer had no trace of a foreign accent.

"Would you like some tea, Officer Nguyen?"

"No thank you. I'll just do my checks and be out of your hair."

Officer Nguyen glanced over to the kitchen to see an older woman, Mrs. Yuen, whispering to someone, but the wall blocked the other person. She stared straight up at the ceiling as she talked in Chinese to the shadow. Her voice was panicked and her body rigid. Before Officer Nguyen could get close enough, she quickly slid the door closed.

"Where are you from, Officer?" Mr. Yuen asked from behind.

Officer Nguyen's attention went back and forth between Mr. Yuen to the kitchen. "Bluefield. Born and raised."

"No, no, no, I mean the origin of your family. Where is it?"

"Well, I'm second-gen Chinese American, so I don't know too much about the origin of my family. Is your wife from China?"

Mr. Yuen looked towards the kitchen then back to Officer Nguyen. "Yes," he finally said. "We both are."

"You don't find too many people like us in this neck of the woods," Officer Nguyen said. "That's why you chose me to come in here, right?" Mr. Yuen didn't say anything. "I'm not judging. I get the same response from white people when they see me at the door. It's just good to speak with someone you have something in common with, you know? I'm sure your wife would feel the same. Do you mind if I say hi to her?"

"I'm afraid that's not possible. She doesn't speak English. Trying to communicate would only embarrass her."

"She shouldn't feel too bad. I can't speak a lick of Chinese."

Mr. Yuen's eyes lit up. "Really? Not one word?"

Officer Nguyen shook his head.

Mr. Yuen tapped his fingers over his lips, then an idea struck his index finger erect. A light chuckle mixed with a cough escaped his mouth.

"What's so funny?"

"We have a saying for people like you where I come from."

"People like me, huh?" Officer Nguyen said through a smile. It was more of him being professional than friendly, but he was prepared to be offended.

"Yes. Would you like to hear it?"

"Sure. Why not?"

Mr. Yuen licked his lips. "The saying goes, 'if you are who I think you are, then your last breath will be in this house,'" he said in Mandarin.

They both stared at each other without moving a muscle. Officer Nguyen's expressionless face mirrored Mr. Yuen's. His hand rested on the handle of his all-black Beretta. His hand had always been there, but Mr. Yuen just now took notice.

Officer Nguyen cracked a gentle smile that allowed Mr. Yuen to let out a breath. "Are you going to tell me what it means?"

Mr. Yuen watched Officer Nguyen's hands, which were

now resting on his hip. "Yes, after I get the tea and bring my wife for you to meet. I'll be back in a moment." He walked into the kitchen and slid the door closed behind him.

Officer Nguyen peeked out from the peach curtains and saw his partner had gone back to the car. He switched the radio on his shoulder off and took off his coat. "Hey, if that offer for tea is still on the table, I would like to take you up on—"

An axe came flying through the air within inches of Officer Nguyen's nose. He looked back to see Mr. Yuen charging at him with his war cry rising with every step. Before Officer Nguyen could place his footing, Mr. Yuen struck him with a swarm of punches to the face and kicks to the chest. This once fragile old man had rejuvenated himself into the robust fighter he once was. Officer Nguyen absorbed the blows until he caught one of Mr. Yuen's punches. He threw a right hook and his knuckles aligned perfectly with Mr. Yuen's jaw, forcing him to fall to his knees.

Officer Nguyen's arm slithered around Mr. Yuen's neck and compressed his windpipe. "Do you feel that old man?" he asked in Mandarin. "That's the feeling of your life slipping away from you. That precious last breath that we all take for granted. Just tell us where he hid it and I promise not to slit your wife's throat in front of you."

Blood drained from Mr. Yuen's mouth as he gasped for air. His nails scratched through the wood floors trying to reach for something, but to no avail. Officer Nguyen tightened his grip, but a swift blow to the head made him release his hold. His face landed on the feet of a titan disguised as a human being. He was a six-foot-nine black man with muscles carved into his t-shirt. Officer Nguyen tried to rise to his feet but was met with a gun to the face.

"Take him to the back, Chinelo," Mr. Yuen said between breaths. "And make sure no one sees either one of you."

"What about the officer in the front?" Chinelo asked. His accent came from Nigeria.

Mr. Yuen took a moment to catch his breath. "I'll take care of him."

"But he is an innocent man," Chinelo said. "He could have a family."

"We don't have a choice. They have found us."

"We could leave undetected. Take *him* with us and dispose of him later."

"We don't have time for that. They will eventually track us down before we can—"

Everyone's attention was suddenly drawn to the hard knocks coming from the door.

"Hey Nguyen, you almost done in there?" the American Cop asked. "We still got two hours left on shift, and I want to finish our rounds."

Before anyone could think of their next move, Officer Nguyen knocked the gun out of Chinelo's hand and took cover behind the sofa.

As Chinelo chased down the handgun, Officer Nguyen unholstered his weapon and shot Chinelo in the right shoulder.

Mr. Yuen ran towards the dinner table and flipped it over to retrieve a Daewoo USAS-12 attached under it. He let off a few rounds, ripping the living room apart with each shot.

"Nguyen! What the hell is going on in there?!" the American Cop screamed from the other side of the door.

Officer Nguyen returned fire then ducked back down.

"They got me pinned down in here," he said. "There's two of them. One in the dining room to your left. The other—"

Mr. Yuen let off more rounds.

"I'm calling for back up!" the American cop said.

Officer Nguyen could hear his partner's footsteps sprinting to the car. He glanced over the sofa to check his position. Chinelo and Mr. Yuen were nowhere in sight.

The house fell dark, and everything shapeshifted in the shadows.

Officer Nguyen grabbed his flashlight and crossed it over his shooting wrist. His heavy breathing was beating against his blown eardrum. He stopped breathing every few seconds to pick up any sounds in the silence, but nothing would give. Staying there waiting for backup was not an option, so he backtracked towards the kitchen.

When he opened the kitchen door, he came face-to-face with Mrs. Yuen. The sight of a gun took her breath away as she stood there frozen. Officer Nguyen took a step forward, and her silence was broken into sporadic Mandarin and pointing.

"Ma'am, I'm going to need for you to be quiet," he said over her chatter. "I'll get you out of here, but we need to find your husband." She grabbed Officer Nguyen closer while she yelled uncontrollably. "Everything is going to be okay, ma'am. I just need you to—"

He stopped to take a better look at Mrs. Yuen. Her innocent eyes became black with hate. There was a dagger in her hand, puncturing his lung. A dribble of blood ran from Officer Nguyen's mouth down his chin.

Mrs. Yuen took her bloody hand, placed it on Officer Nguyen's neck, and pressed her lips to his ear. "I take pleasure in knowing you will burn in hell," she whispered in Mandarin.

Officer Nguyen fixed his lips to curse at her, but his words garbled in the blood he coughed up. His face turned red as he watched her trembling smile spread across her face. He shot her in the chest. Her petite body plastered to the wall, then collapsed to the floor. Mr. Yuen saw everything from a distance.

Officer Nguyen turned his attention toward Mr. Yuen and coughed up more blood through a faint laugh. "It's over old man," he said. "It looks like *your* last breath will be in this house." He stumbled as he struggled to stay upright.

Mr. Yuen let a single tear slide down his cheek, then pulled out a long knife. The blade shimmered in the moonlight glinting through the window. "At least now we truly have something in common," he said in Mandarin. He charged at Officer Nguyen full speed, rage in his eyes.

Officer Nguyen's gun felt like a dumbbell as he aimed it. He let off one shot. Then another. Then another. All of them connected, but Mr. Yuen's body was numb. Officer Nguyen continued to fire aimlessly, but Mr. Yuen tackled him to the ground and stabbed him in the stomach repeatedly until he didn't have enough energy to raise the knife again. Mr. Yuen's body collapsed on top of Officer Nguyen, and with his last breath he reached out to his wife to touch her fingertips.

Chinelo rose from the shadows and observed the scene. His emotions traveled from his soul and cultivated his racing heart. It devastated him to see an old friend like this. He pulled Mr. Yuen's body off Officer Nguyen and placed him next to his wife, then prayed over their bodies. The mourning didn't last long, as flashing blue-and-red lights from outside filled the house. Escaping undetected was no longer an option.

15.

A squadron of cop cars stood in front of Mr. Yuen's house. Neighbors were blocked as they walked outside to see what all the commotion was about while every cop in sight had a weapon drawn. Parker casually walked through the crowd with Jake close behind him, until they were stopped by the officer in charge.

"Whoa, whoa, whoa, where the hell do you think you're going?" the officer in charge asked. He was an older man, but his hair was dyed jet black.

"Good evening Officer..." Parker closed in on the name tag, "Coleman. I'm Special Agent Parker, and this is my partner Detective Penny. We have reason to believe that a suspect we're looking for is being held in this house and we have direct orders to bring him out...alive."

"Direct orders from whom?" Officer Coleman asked.

"The proper paperwork will be brought here shortly. It'll answer any questions you may have."

"I'm gonna need to see some credentials from you boys."

"Certainly."

Both Parker and Jake pulled out their badges. Officer Coleman observed them closely, still not convinced of their intentions. "What the hell is the NSA and NYPD doing in my back yard?"

"Our jobs, Officer Colman," Parker said as he snatched their badges back. "Now, if you can hold your men off for a few more minutes—"

"The thing is, Special Agent Whoever-You-Are, we have an officer trapped inside that house and we don't know his status. Without that paperwork, I'm not waiting another second to find out."

"I assure you if that officer inside is still alive, then it would be in his best interests for us to wait. You don't know what you're up against."

"I'm sure in the NSA leaving a man behind for the sake of the mission is standard behavior, but that's not how we do things in my county."

Coleman and Parker's egos clashed as they stared each other down. Parker's smirk did nothing but aggravate Officer Coleman and his grueling snarl.

A deputy came up behind Coleman. "Sir, the men are in position. What do you wanna do?"

Eyes still on Parker, Officer Coleman said, "If they don't come out in the next thirty seconds, we press."

"Someone's coming out!" a voice called out. Chinelo walked out the front door with his head down and his arms by his side.

"Don't take another step, asshole," Officer Coleman said through a bullhorn. "Let me see your hands."

Chinelo slowly raised his hands above his head. The higher they went, the more they looked like tree branches swaying in the wind. For a moment, everyone was caught watching his size increase with amazement.

"Take him down," Officer Coleman said.

 Two cops placed themselves on Chinelo's sides as he stood like a statue. The officer on the left had to jump to grab his wrist, but in one swift motion, Chinelo grabbed the cop, took his gun, then shot the other cop and held the first hostage.

"Let him go," Officer Coleman said. Chinelo crouched down behind the hostage cop and backtracked into the house. "Don't move! If you go inside the house, we're coming for you. It's that simple."

Two black SUVs pulled up behind all the cop cars. A small man with glasses named Jarrett ran frantically to Parker, a crisp envelope in one hand. "Here you go, sir," Jarrett said, out of breath.

Parker snatched the envelope and removed its contents. "It took you long enough." He walked in the middle of the standoff with his hands in the air. "Okay, everyone calm down. I have what we've all been waiting for right here in my hand."

"Someone get this yahoo out of here," Officer Coleman said.

"Before you do that, I want you to hear this. Under direct order from General William Hayden, the director of the National Security Agency, I have a high-level arrest warrant for anyone in that house, that will supersede any ranking authority in the state of West Virginia. That includes the state governor. Again, it also states that the persons must remain alive while being transferred into my custody. It's all here."

Officer Coleman snatched the paper from Parker and skimmed it quickly. "This is bullshit! There's no way I'm letting him walk away after all this. I have a man shot right in front of us, one taken hostage and another one waiting inside, goddamn it."

Parker stepped into Officer Colman's personal space.

He settled his voice and said, "If this massive human being was the only thing to walk through that door, then the officer inside is dead. Another one will be dead on your watch if he doesn't receive medical treatment soon. Now, I'm taking the suspect into my custody. And if you or any of your men try to stop me, it will be the last mistake of your professional career. You picking up what I'm putting down?"

Officer Colman's face tightened as he lowered his gun. Parker turned his back and walked up to Chinelo, coming face-to-face with the big man. The hostage cop's face trembled under Chinelo's bloody hands, gun pressed into his neck.

"If you wanna get out of this alive, then you'll let him go and come with me," Parker said.

"It is too late," Chinelo whimpered. "I will never be safe."

"You're right. I cannot guarantee your safety for the long term. But I can guarantee a higher-percentage chance of seeing tomorrow if you're with me rather than a bunch of mountain cops. You know they're never goin g to stop, and killing you only protects them. Come with me. You owe it to Yuen."

Parker's logic had Chinelo loosen his grip on the hostage cop. Once the hostage cop broke free, the fleet of officers rushed in, but Parker stopped them with a single hand raised.

"You," Parker said to a random officer. "Handcuff him then step away." The officer looked over to Coleman who reluctantly nodded. The officer pulled out his cuffs and secured them on Chinelo's wrists in front of him. Jarrett stepped up to Chinelo and placed a charcoal burlap bag over his head. Parker nodded his head, and a couple of suited men escorted Chinelo to one of the SUVs.

"No one goes in or comes out of this house," Parker whispered to Jarret. "I want a full scrub down of the scene and a report on any findings within two hours. When you're done, have my car taken back to New York. Detective Penny and I will ride with the big fella so we can personally make sure he gets to the nearest black site."

"Right away, sir," Jarrett said.

Chinelo's walk to the SUV parted the sea of officers as they looked on with bottled emotions. Jake took in all the confused faces as they stared at him. Morale was dead, and there was nothing Officer Coleman could do. When Coleman made eye contact with Parker, pride straightened his spine. Parker winked with a smile, right before stepping into the SUV.

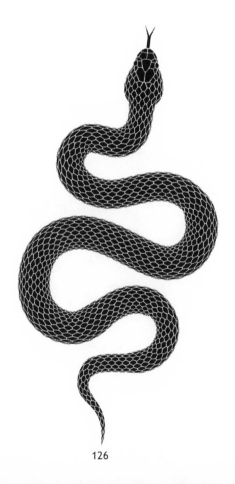

16.

As the SUV hauled down the empty highway to the nearest black site, Jake tried everything to conceal his shaky hands. His fingertips were numb to the touch, and his sobering thoughts caused a headache.

Jake, Chinelo, and Parker sat in that order while two suited men with shotguns sat across from them. Parker was too busy making arrangements over the phone, while Chinelo sat like an empty vessel with his hands cuffed in his lap. One of the suited men stared at Jake without ever turning his eyes.

Jake almost fell victim to the staring contest, until he brushed shoulders with Chinelo. There was an energy about that which made Jake think about what he was doing. He tried to gaze through the mesh burlap bag, but he couldn't see anything.

Parker finished his phone conversation, seeming pleased. "Okay, the nearest black site is an hour away, and the coordinates are being transmitted to our GPS. Tell the driver if he can get there in forty-five, the first round is on me."

One of the suited men tapped the plexiglass, and the SUV sped up.

Parker had a way of reading people, especially in stressful situations. The silence told him more than any words ever could. "Is this you boy's first convoy?" he asked the suited men. They both looked at each other, then nodded almost in unison.

"I can tell. You're a little uptight. You see my partner here? Cool as a fan. This isn't his first rodeo." Parker looked over at Jake and winked.

He was right. Jake had been on more dangerous convoys when he was in Afghanistan. He asked himself if Parker knew that because of his temperament, or because he'd read about him in some file. If only Parker could see his hands, then the real story would be revealed.

Jake's train of thought was derailed when high beams from a following car gleamed through the tinted windows. The two suited men rose to alert status.

"Calm down fellas," Parker said. "It could be someone trying to pass. Give it a few seconds. They should be on their way." Suspicion crept up Parker's neck when he saw the car wasn't passing. "Tell the driver to speed it up a little more."

One of the suited men knocked on the plexiglass window, and it rolled down to show two more men up front.

"We got a suspicious vehicle behind us. Why don't you push the gas, so we can—"

A collision to the bumper had everyone rattled in their seats. The driver pressed the pedal to the floor, but the car behind stayed close and continued to crash into the bumper. Shots from the chasing car ricocheted off the bulletproofed SUV.

"Get us out of here," Parker yelled.

The collision from the chasing car had the whole SUV shaking, but somehow Chinelo was able to keep his composure. The driver swerved through the empty highway, trying to avoid the attack. He checked his rearview mirror for a split second to locate the car, but when his eyes returned to the road, he came face-to-face with an adult buck watching his life come to an end. The next thing Jake knew, his body was tumbling within the SUV, but his seatbelt kept him from going too far.

Jake could hear himself breathing, but everything was pitch black. He opened his eyes to blurry vision and distorted gunshots ringing in the distance. The smell of smoke, gas, and metal choked him to the point where he had to turn his head to the open window. The SUV was upside-down, with broken glass everywhere. One of the suited men died slumped in his seat. The other was shot down right outside Jake's window.

Jake crawled out of the SUV, shards of glass scraping through his clothes, and there was no more gunfire. He looked down the road to see a woman and child holding hand s in front of a burning car. He couldn't see their faces, but he could tell it was his wife and daughter from their silhouettes.

"L-Lea?" His eyes glowed in disbelief as he limped towards the flames. "Andrea ? Is that you, baby?" His body geared up to run, until something like a hook grabbed his shoulder and snatched him down behind the turned-over SUV.

"Are you trying to get yourself killed?" Parker yelled over the gunfire.

Jake looked around, trying to remember where he was. The sounds of war echoed in his ears again, and his heart pounded against his chest. Looking down at his hand, he noticed the black burlap bag on the ground, followed by a trail of blood on the snow. It led to a large figure running into the darkness. Jake pulled his weapon and started his pursuit.

"Jake! Stand down!" Parker said, but Jake was already on the hunt.

* * *

Chinelo zipped through the dimly lit woods, trying to keep his balance, but the dense snow bogged down his every step. He took a moment to catch his breath, and adjusted his injured shoulder to take some pressure off it. He didn't know where he was going, but he was determined to get far away from the crash site. Before he could have another dash, Jake issued a warning shot that went right past his ear. The thought of booking it ran across Chinelo's mind. It was dark. Jake had just come out of a car accident. The odds of his accuracy being drastically decreased favored Chinelo, but he decided on a more tactful approach.

"Don't move," Jake said. "Let me see your hands, now!"

Chinelo raised his cuffed hands like a sunrise.

"Turn around."

Chinelo did a 180. His face was covered in streaks of dried blood, and he had a few scratches on his neck. The air was brisk enough to see their breaths settling in the atmosphere as they exhaled.

"You're coming back with me," Jake said.

Chinelo chuckled, gathered the phlegm built up in his nose, spat out the blood-infused concoction to the side and said, "Trust is a sacred thing. It is all two strangers have in the middle of the woods. If I were you, I wouldn't trust anyone in that car."

"That says a lot, since you were in the car too."

"You should believe me when I say that it will be best for both of us…if you let me go," he said between breaths. Chinelo took a step forward, but Jake raised his gun in response.

"That's not gonna happen."

"You do not trust him. I can see it in your eyes. It is in your voice when you speak to him. Why not go with your instinct?"

The forest grew silent, which was no good for someone like Jake with a lingering suspicion. It wasn't often that he had to look up to someone to meet their eyes, but being in this situation made his nerves sharp. He'd taken down big guys before, some with ease, but Chinelo was a different story. Even though he had the upper hand, he still wanted to be cautious.

"Walk slowly in front of me where I can see your hands. We're going back." Chinelo did as he was told but stopped to stare at Jake. "Don't do anything stupid. You're cuffed, and you're injured. I will leave you where you stand."

"You heard what your boss said. You have to bring me back alive."

"*They* have to bring you back alive. I could give two shits how you come back."

"Very well then. We will do it your way."

Chinelo trotted towards Jake, and before he knew it, Chinelo had grabbed his wrists and turned out of the line of fire. Jake let off a few shots before Chinelo broke the gun free and tossed it into the forest.

Jake took a few steps back as Chinelo approached him and, as quick as a blink, a roundhouse kick swooshed inches from his face. Chinelo's legs were so long that he didn't leave his pivot foot. Jake slipped but quickly gathered himself. Chinelo faked a charge then reset his fighting stance, which was him standing straight up.

Jake tried to anticipate Chinelo's next move but decided not to wait and grabbed him by the waist, slamming him into powdery snow. Chinelo used his legs to his advantage, and immobilized Jake by wrapping them around his legs.

Chinelo locked his fingers to make one big fist and bashed Jake on the top of his head.

Jake blocked the blows with his left hand and countered with hard jabs to the abdomen to loosen Chinelo's vice grip.

The two broke free and squared off in their readied fighting stances. Head-to-head, there was no way Jake could compete. He figured it was best to stay on offense instead of waiting for an attack. He swung in combination, but only struck the cold air.

Chinelo created separation by kicking Jake in the chest and into a tree. He charged at Jake, but Jake rolled out of the way and took Chinelo's knee out at an angle. This was Jake's time to take advantage. His frozen knuckles stung a little more than usual on   Chinelo's cheeks.

Chinelo caught up to the combination and blocked one of the punches, then head-butted Jake, leaving him to see colorful spots in the darkness.

Chinelo stumbled to his feet, then roundhouse-kicked Jake in the face, dropping him like a pile of rocks. He picked up a boulder nearby and stood over Jake. His adrenaline had him huffing as he held the boulder over his head, ready to smash Jake's face. Jake closed his eyes, feeling defeated, and accepted his fate. Chinelo saw the surrender and his temper subsided. His breathing returned to normal, and he could feel the weight of the boulder pinging on his shoulder. He lifted the boulder high above his head and threw it down with all his strength. After a few quiet seconds, Jake opened his eyes and saw the boulder right next to his head. He looked up and Chinelo had vanished into the darkness.

17.

Jake sulked on his bed while he washed down his painkillers with vodka. His face was being held together by bandages, and his chest felt like it was cracked in half every time he inhaled. He could still feel Chinelo's stone foot pounding across his face. Fighting like that required some specialized training. As the painkillers took effect, his mind started to wander.

Why give me such a beating just to let me live, he asked himself.

It would have been in Chinelo's best interests to kill Jake, but the fact that he was lying in his bed slowly killing himself was something he couldn't wrap his head around. Then he took note of what Chinelo had said about not trusting Parker.

Is it that obvious? he asked himself. *And if so, could Parker tell?*

Before he knew it, all the pain in his body was gone. He thought maybe he'd be ready for a second round with Chinelo, but that was just the drugs talking. As he turned into a different resting position, his wallet dropped to the floor and the contents fell out, snapping him out of his near-slumber. There was a debit card, a picture of his Lea and Andrea, a couple of wrinkled dollars, and Zasha's business card. He picked up the business card and twirled it through his fingers.

Jake opened the door to see Zasha's rosy cheeks under her winter coat. Her smile crumbled when she saw his face. She wanted to look away, but the damage held her attention.

"Jesus Christ," she said, her mouth barely closed. "What happened to you?"

"Long day at the office," Jake said. Even though it hurt like hell, he managed to give her his signature crooked smile.

Zasha stepped into the apartment, but never took her eyes off him. "Maybe it's time for a vacation."

"You're preaching to the choir. Can I take your coat?"

"Sure." Jake took the coat but realized he had no place for it, so he hung it on the corner of his closet door. Zasha examined his soulless apartment with a steady eye. She solemnly stayed in her apartment due to her schedule, but at least she understood how to make it seem like she had a life. This was a step above solitary confinement. She stopped by the memorial, and locked in on the picture of Lea and Andrea .

"Your family's beautiful."

"Thank you."

"What were their names?"

Jake's throat locked up as he walked past her. With his back to her, he said, "Lea was my wife, and Andrea was our little princess."

"I like how you put this all together. Something to remember them by and—"

"I am glad you were able to make it on such short notice. Maybe we should jump right into what I need." Jake had mastered the art of deflection from months of people trying to give their condolences. The way he saw it, if it wasn't going to bring his family back, he didn't need to talk about.

"Right. So, to what do I owe the pleasure of this invite?"

He cleared his throat and faced her. "I might need something from you, and it's gonna sound a little bizarre."

She studied Jake up and down before a smirk appeared on her face. The thought of the tables turning tickled her. "What's in it for me?"

"Don't you want to know what it is first?"

"We'll get to that. First, I need to know if the payoff is worth my time."

"You have connections. They led you to this case. They led you to me."

"I cannot confirm or deny this assumption."

"Let's just say, off the record, you do."

"Nothing is off the record with a member of law enforcement."

"It is with me… I wanna use your connection."

"Why?"

"I need to find someone."

Zasha clicked her tongue behind her teeth as she shook her head. "That's going to cost you, Detective. Depending on who it is, you might not be able to pay the bill. That is, of course, if I even have such a connection."

"I probably can't pay the bill, but I know someone who can. He'll accommodate the person you work for and make sure you're set up for success with the story. But it has to be done now."

Zasha folded her arms and shifted her weight to her left foot. "Excuse me?"

"I don't want you to get your hands dirty. If you link me with the guy that helps you find people, you will get whatever you want, and your name will be left out of this."

Zasha scoffed. Her mouth soured, as if trying to hold back any bad words from coming out. Jake picked up on the mood change and ran back what he'd said in his head.

"Maybe coming here was a mistake. I should go." She clutched her purse and headed for the door. She opened it, but Jake was right behind her to close it.

"Please," he said. "I'm sorry if I offended you in any way, but I need your help. I have to try something. A lot of people could get hurt if we don't find this guy."

Zasha sighed as she rolled her eyes. "I work alone. There's nothing you have that I want.

"What if had something that you need?"

"And what do I need, Detective?"

Jake thought for a moment then said, "I know a great pizzeria in downtown Brooklyn. Best in the borough."

Zasha chuckled. "Really? Your bargaining chip is a date?"

Jake blushed under his bruises, but she couldn't tell. Suddenly a sharp pain struck his chest, but it wasn't from his injuries. "No, that's not what I meant," he said. "I just assumed it would be a good idea—"

Zasha laughed under her breath. "I'm joking." She took a moment to look into Jake's eyes—one black. She couldn't figure out why, but there was an intrigue in him that sparked her interest. She approved with a smile that worried Jake a little.

"Does this mean you'll do it?" he asked.

"I need details about the case. Full and exclusive access. I get to interview you and whoever you catch. And I get a hard copy of this investigation all the way, from the very beginning. Those are my terms. Take it or leave it."

Jake was one-hundred percent sure that he couldn't deliver on any of those demands, especially since he didn't have full access himself.   He hated that he had to lie to her, but he had no other choice. He hoped she'd understand. "Done."

They shook hands, and Jake was a little surprised at how strong her grip was. Zasha took her laptop from her bag. "Do you have wi-fi?"

"No."

"Good. Turn your phone off and take out the battery." She threw him the bag. "There's a UHF jammer in there. I need you to take it out, turn it on and place it near your highest window." She pulled out a USB stick and plugged it into her laptop.

"What's that?"

"It's a reverse hotspot. It allows me to be online while technically being offline, which is great because I won't be affected by the jammer. It also acts as a VPN just as an extra precaution."

"An extra precaution for what?"

Zasha closed her laptop and took a deep breath. "I'm sorry, Detective, but if you want me to do this, then you're going to have to stop being a cop for a few hours. I am a two-time Pulitzer Prize winner in a field where men, historically, reign supreme. The one thing I've learned is, to write your name in history, sometimes you must use the dirt from under your fingernails. Now, who are we looking for?" She cracked her fingers, ready to set a record for speed-typing.

Jake took a second to process everything, but quickly realized she was waiting for him. "That's the thing... I don't know exactly."

"Tell me what you do know."

"He's Nigerian. Late thirties. Approximately six-foot-nine. Last seen near Green Valley, West Virginia, about twenty hours ago."

"That's it?"

"Yeah."

Zasha stretched her neck as she got settled on the bed. "You sure do know how to make a girl work for a living. Put the jammer up, and I'll call you over when I have something."

"If you want, I could probably bring up a chair from somewhere."

"No, the bed is fine. I actually prefer it here." Her lips parted as she followed Jake with her eyes to the window. She took a long look, then got right to work.

After hours of research, Zasha was still zeroed in on her laptop. Her hair was in a ponytail and her shoes were off. She would adjust her neck and shoulders, but then immediately get back to typing and scrolling. She was so focused that she didn't notice Jake scanning her features. The freckles on her arms. The tiny black heart tattooed behind her left ear. The mole on the back of her neck that she made sure to cover with her hair. Jake wondered if she was self-conscious about it, or if that was a spot only people who were close to her knew about.

She let out a long exhale and lay flat on the bed with her eyes closed. Her brain was cooked.

Jake approached optimistically. "Do you have something?"

She half opened her eyes. Jake was hypnotized by her slightest glance, but he shook loose from her spell in time to listen to her speak.

"I don't know," she said.

"What do you mean, you don't know?"

"I mean, you're asking me to find unsalted water in an ocean. I have a couple of possibilities, but nothing firm."

"Well, let's hear them."

"I'm telling you, these are far-fetched theories."

"I don't care. Tell me."

"Fine. An APB was put out on a suspect that fits your description over twenty-four hours ago in Green Valley." She tapped on the bed for Jake to sit next to her. He sat down at arm's length, but she inched close enough for their legs to touch. Her perfume sent chills through his body.

"Two hours after it was posted, it was taken down," she continued. "There was a sighting of a person who fit your description in Pineville, West Virginia, which is a little over an hour away from Green Valley. That person was taking a bus from there to here."

"New York? Why would he be coming to New York?" Jake asked.

"We don't know if it was actually him. This is all circumstantial. I hacked into the security feed at the train station, but I couldn't see his face."

"You did what?"

"Remember, you're not a cop right now."

Jake shook his head.

"But I did ask myself the same question…if it is him, why come to New York? You said when he got away all he had were the clothes on his back and a bullet wound, right?"

"He needs something before he can disappear for good. Which means he could be meeting someone."

"What do you think he needs?"

Jake thought about that collateral Parker had mentioned before. "I'm not sure. What time would he get here?"

"He would have been here four hours ago. And since this is our best option, given the circumstances, I decided to continue down the rabbit hole of him coming to New York, and looked into departing international flights within the next forty-eight hours, tickets sold to people with Nigerian passports. Of course, he could have any nation's passport, but if he's trying to flee the country, it might be easier to get through customs if he goes home. I have a match for eighty-seven African males leaving the country for Africa, but again this guy could be going anywhere in the world.

"Let's just assume he's going home. We can't check every flight."

"Most of those flights are coming out of JFK, but what caught my eye were the few leaving from LaGuardia. Those flights stop in Atlanta first, then they're off to their final destinations."

"Why does that stand out to you?" Jake asked.

"I'm just thinking abstractly, but…if I wanted to get out of the country, I would want to be seen as little as possible, right? So, he comes to New York, collects whatever he came to get, books a flight out of LaGuardia, a non-international airport, where the security isn't as strict and all he has to do is get through customs in Atlanta .

"Why risk the connecting flight and not go directly from JFK?" Jake asked. "Sure, the security is tighter, but once he's through customs, he has nothing to worry about."

"Sometimes the best hiding places are in plain sight. Atlanta is the largest international airport in the country. He would blend right in. Add on the fact that technically no one is looking for this guy in the first place and it kind of makes sense. At least that's how I would do it." Jake took a moment to put it all together.

"And that, folks, concludes this week's episode of *Finding the Impossible*," Zasha said. "Tune in next week, when we'll try to find a safety pin in the Mariana Trench."

"Very funny, but if we find this guy, it'll be a game changer."

Zasha took a beat before asking, "Why is it so important to find this person anyway?"

"Does it matter?"

"No. But when I start putting the pieces together, questions do arise. I mean, obviously, this isn't a state or federal manhunt, otherwise he would be all over the news. But somehow a local city cop has been tasked with bringing this *high threat* criminal down."

"Detective."

"Excuse me. Detective. Maybe it's the journalist in me that wants to dig for the truth, but something isn't adding up here."

She was smart. Maybe too smart. Jake thought about her ripping a bogus story apart if she could piece this together with the little information she had.

"What time is that flight out of LaGuardia?"

"At 9:15," Zasha said. "You're not actually thinking about going, are you?"

Jake looked at the clock. He had roughly five hours. "Yeah, why not?"

"Well aside from ninety-nine percent of this theory being speculation mixed with imagination and a dash of bullshit, the odds of you actually finding this person are slim to none."

"I agree. But if this guy is trying to leave the country, then he has to hole up somewhere before his flight. Check all surrounding hotels for check-ins as recent as yesterday with check-outs tomorrow."

Zasha typed away on her laptop, and was shocked at what she saw. "Hmmm. I accessed all hotel databases within a twenty-five-mile radius of LaGuardia. Check-in yesterday and check-out for the next two days. Filtered the list of last names to African males and…we have one. Checked in today at the LaGuardia Plaza Hotel. The hotel notes say the guest requested an airport shuttle at 7:30 tonight." They both looked at each other, astounded. Could they have found the needle in the haystack? "I'm coming with you," Zasha announced.

"No, you're not."

"You're going to need back up."

"And that's not gonna be you."

"I can help."

Jake grabbed Zasha by the arms, tight enough to hold her in place, and stared directly into her eyes. "You're not coming." He let her go once he realized she was static in his grip.

"Were you always this…passionate, Detective?"

"Were you always a hacker?"

She chuckled. "I guess we both led different lives in the past."

"Like you said, this could be nothing. But I'm not gonna jeopardize your safety for it. I'll let you know what happens. You can stay here if you want."

Zasha looked around the apartment, tilting her head from side to side. "No thanks. I should probably get going anyway."

Jake realized his place wasn't fit for a woman to stay alone. Asking her seemed like a weak attempt to close a somewhat awkward exchange.

"Right. I'll keep you posted."

18.

Chinelo found himself in the Element Lounge of the LaGuardia Plaza Hotel, enjoying a steak and his favorite drink: rum and coke with one ice cube. He didn't usually drink, but this night was an exception. This was the taste of his freedom closing in with each passing minute. He'd cleaned up nice for the occasion, wearing a blazer with a white collar shirt. His hair was down to a buzz cut, and his beard neatly trimmed. The waiter brought over another rum and coke and asked if could he bring anything else. Chinelo shook his head no, and was left alone. There were a few patrons in the lounge, mostly suits enjoying happy hour. He took a sip of his drink and let the liquid coat his throat. He smiled and set the glass down.

"Usually when a man wants to confront another man, they do so face-to-face," Chinelo said, seemingly to himself.

Jake exited the booth behind Chinelo and sat across from him. Their eyes clashed over the charade of peace in their smiles.

"You are more skilled than you appear, cop."

"Detective," Jake said with a snarky grin.

"Detective. How is your face?"

"It's as good as any face would be after taking a beating. Nothing a drink can't fix."

"Well, allow me to oblige you." Chinelo signaled the

waiter for another rum and coke. The waiter brought the drink immediately.

Jake tossed the straw, downed the drink in two gulps and let out a refreshing sigh. "That's good."

"I am glad you approved. Shall I have another fetched for you?"

"We're good for now. Thanks."

Chinelo waited before speaking. He wanted to play out all the scenarios in his head. "So, what can I do for you?" he finally asked.

"For starters, you can keep your hands where I can see them, away from the knife. Then you can slowly exit the table with your back facing me, and we can leave together."

"So soon?"

"I told you I was bringing you in."

"I have not even finished my meal. Where I come from it is not proper to waste a fine plate like this."

Jake cocked his gun under the table. "I guess you'll have to be unproper for today."

Chinelo chuckled as he picked up his fork and knife and cut a piece of steak to devour. He took another sip of his drink, then wiped his mouth with a napkin. "I must admit…you are a persistent one. Maybe to a deadly fault. Are you here alone, Detective?"

Jake paused, hoping his shifting eyes didn't give him away. "No. I got a whole fleet of guys waiting for you outside, and they're itching to say hello."

"That is good. That is really good, except you are forgetting one thing." Chinelo flashed his hands out in front of Jake's face. They were almost the size of his head. "I am not handcuffed this time. Which means it will not take more than a second for me to snap your neck. And make no mistake, if you try to stop me this time, I will show no mercy."

"There's something you oughtta know about me as well. I had a couple of drinks before coming over here, so that pretty much evens the playing field."

Chinelo relaxed his hands flat on the table. "Tell me something, do you think that by capturing me it is going to change anything?"

"It'll put a little dent in your plan."

Chinelo scoffed. "Does it look like I have a plan? I am here because of you and your people." His voice was hushed but aggressive.

"You're here because of who you are."

"And who am I?" he asked in his regular voice. "What did I really do? Think about that for one second. What mastermind plan am I trying to execute from my home country?"

Jake tried to put the pieces together, but it was a little tricky without all the information. "You had a straight shot to Atlanta from West Virginia. Why'd you come to New York?"

Chinelo studied Jake's face. His eyes lit up when a realization popped into his head. "No, this cannot be. You do not know what you are fighting for, do you?" The thought of Jake being vulnerable tickled him. "You are fighting a war in the dark and do not know which side is going to shoot you in the back of the head. I misjudged you, Detective. You are more of a fool than I thought." Chinelo took another sip of his drink.

"Then tell me what they're looking for. If you're truly innocent, then we can work something out."

"It does not work like this. None of us are innocent.

We all have sins that we must pay for. Secrets that we do not want brought to light. It is not about how long you can run from them, but will you be alive long enough to face them." Chinelo looked over his right shoulder for a second then back to Jake. "Remember when I told you the only thing between two strangers in the woods was trust? Now is the moment to implement that theory."

"Why should I trust you?"

"I should be asking myself the same question. You are the only liar at this table." Chinelo's eyes dug deep into Jake. "You came here alone."

"No, I didn't—"

"Look through me, Detective. The truth is right behind me." Jake focused his line of sight into Chinelo's face. "Now look over my right shoulder. Five Asian gentlemen are sitting at the table in the corner, but there's only one drink on the table. They are pretending to take pictures of themselves with their mobile device, but the camera is conveniently pointed directly at us. They are sending status updates and would not be able to do that if you weren't here alone."

Through his peripheral, Jake spotted the five Asian men sitting at the table. His throat almost closed after he gulped. "They could be anybody."

"Or, they could be the hit squad sent here to kill me. Well, us now that they see you sitting here having a drink with me. But it does not have to be that way. We can work together. I can get you out of here safely, and you can let me go."

"That's not gonna happen."

"Do you understand what is at stake here?" Chinelo asked in a firm voice. "We have to work together if you want to stay alive."

Jake gripped his gun tighter to keep it from slipping in his sweaty palm. The urgency to make a decision was mounting his brain. "I can't let you go."

Chinelo took a deep breath through his nose and sat up straight. "Then I guess we will pick up where we left off in Green Valley *after* we deal with them."

Jake's eyes bounced back and forth from Chinelo to the Asian men in the corner. Then, a familiar voice called out, "Detective Penny?"

Chinelo's eyes traveled to the voice, and a smile crept on his face. Jake looked out of the corner of his eye, it wasn't who he thought it was. Zasha walked toward the table with her perky smile. "I thought that was you," she said.

"What are you doing here?" Jake asked with a crackle in his voice.

"Oh, I was just in the neighborhood."

Jake knew she was trying to be funny, but this wasn't a laughing matter. "You were in the neighborhood at a hotel?"

"Exactly." She looked to Chinelo and extended her hand. "Hi, Zasha Avery."

Chinelo took her hand and gave it a gentle peck. "Pleasure. Would you care to join us, Mrs. Avery?"

"It's Miss and thank you. I would love to." She bunched in with Jake, forcing him to inch over.

"Actually," Jake said, " my friend and I were in the middle of business, so maybe it's best if we meet up later."

"Nonsense," Chinelo said. "I would never let *business* get in the way of being in the presence of a beautiful woman."

Zasha's cheeks became flushed. "Wow, I like him."

"Yeah, he's a real charmer," Jake said through his teeth.

"It's just, I don't want you to feel like you have to stay on my account."

"Do not worry," Chinelo said. "It is not like someone is putting a gun to her and making her stay." Chinelo smiled as the sweat from Jake's neck soaked through his collar. "Can I offer you anything to drink, my dear?"

"I'll have what you're having."

Chinelo signaled for another drink, and the bartender rushed it over.

Zasha took a sip of her rum and coke. She cringed once it touched her tongue, but took another sip anyway. "So, you're a friend of Detective Penny. How long have you two known each other?"

"Not very long," Chinelo said. "But our work brings us together."

"What kind of work do you do?"

"I do a lot of things, but I mainly focus on freelance work. For the right price, I can make just about anything happen."

"You know, I think you've overstayed your welcome, Zasha," Jake said.

"What? Why? Do you feel that way?" she asked to Chinelo.

Chinelo shrugged. "Not at all."

"See, he doesn't have a problem so what's yours?" Zasha asked.

"I don't like unannounced visits. I think of all people you would understand that."

"I was in the neighborhood," she said, her tone low.

Jake gathered his thoughts before he said the wrong thing. Between the Asian men in the corner, Zasha's safety, and Chinelo's hand inching closer and closer to the steak knife, he didn't know what his next move should be. "I'm this close to closing this business deal. You being here is a danger for that deal and other outside sources."

"I beg to differ, Detective," Chinelo said. "In fact, I think things are about to open up for renegotiation."

Jake saw a figure from the corner table walking towards them but couldn't make out the face. His breathing slowed down. His leg bounced like a jackhammer under the table.

Meanwhile, Chinelo was as calm as a summer breeze. His face turned into an unblinking stone. It was on Jake to make a move.

One of the Asian men stopped at the table, and no one moved. "Excuse me," the Asian man started. He had no trace of a foreign accent, and he couldn't have been more than twenty-one years old. "Sorry to bother you guys, but I was wondering if you could take a picture of my friends and me. One of the guys just found out he's going to be a father."

Jake acknowledged the Asian man with subtle eye contact. He looked to Chinelo, whose raised brows encouraged him to make a decision. Zasha looked around, wondering if anyone was going to answer him .

"It'll only take a few seconds," the Asian man continued. "I have my camera if—"

As he reached in his jacket pocket, Jake sprang up from his seat with his weapon drawn. "Let me see your hands, now!"

The few people in the bar ran out screaming. Chinelo raised his hands, pretending to be shocked.

"What the hell are you doing?" Zasha asked.

"Yes, what are you doing, my friend?" Chinelo asked with confusion in his voice.

"All right, everybody shut up," Jake said.

The Asian man threw his hands up, holding his cell phone. "Look, man, I just came over here for a picture. I don't want any trouble. Please."

"Just shut up and keep your hands where I can see them," Jake said.

The Asian man had tears streaming down his face, looking for an explanation from Zasha or Chinelo. He looked over to his table, where everyone stood still. Doubt began to knock at Jake's door as he felt everyone's eyes burning on him. "Please. I have a family," the Asian man said. "You can understand this, can't you? Let me go home to see my daughter."

Jake's heart jumped up and down in his chest. Then he came to the realization that this could have been a ruse from the beginning, so Chinelo wouldn't have to leave in handcuffs. The possibilities had Jake's head on a swivel, perhaps looking for a solution. Before he could make any decisions, hotel security entered the lounge.

"Freeze!" the hotel security guard said.

As Jake turned his attention toward the command, the Asian Man grabbed Jake's gun and turned the barrel downward. Chinelo punched Jake in the face and stabbed the Asian man in the chest with his steak knife before running toward the exit.

Jake's gun fell to the floor, but he quickly recovered it, bringing Zasha down under the table with him for cover.

The remaining Asian men at the corner table all pulled out automatic weapons and shot wildly throughout the bar, killing the security guard. The bullets rained nonstop, dissecting every fabric that created the lounge.

The Asian men stopped to reload, and Jake took the

moment to fire back, causing them to scatter. He hit two of the Asian men while leading Zasha behind the bar.

The Asian men started firing again before they could make it to the exit. Outside the lounge, Jake could see Chinelo towering over the panicked crowd, getting away.

"Stay here," Jake said. "I'll be back."

"Are you out of your mind?" Zasha yelled over the gunfire. "I'm not staying anywhere alone."

"This isn't a game, Zasha! You could get killed."

"The last time I checked, the people shooting at you were also shooting at me. There's no way I'm staying alone."

She had a point. Jake didn't want to take a chance with her life, but she was safer by his side than alone and scared.

"Dammit! Run straight for the exit as soon as I start shooting, all right? Don't look back." Zasha nodded. "Go, go, go!" Jake rocked from behind the bar and emptied his clip as Zasha ran for the exit, weaving through the crowd.

Outside, Chinelo raced through the parking lot with the rest of the guests. He spotted an unattended Sprinter van with the keys inside and entered.

"Hey, you think I can bum a ride?"

He looked up to see Zasha hanging by his window. Before he could react, he was cuffed to the steering wheel and Jake had a gun lodged in his neck. He knew he was trapped

"Zasha, get in," Jake said. She ran around and closed the sliding door behind her. Jake ordered Chinelo to drive, and they swerved from the parking lot and onto the main street. "Keep straight and don't try anything funny. And you," he turned to Zasha, "what the hell were you thinking? You could have gotten yourself killed."

"I'm sorry, but in case you didn't know, I have a job to

do as well. How was I supposed to know you were going to go Rooster Cogburn back there?" As much as she tried to defend herself, a part of her knew Jake was right. She should have never gone there unprepared.

"There were clear indications—"

"There were no clear indications. Next time why not just say, 'Hey, I'm going to shoot up the place here in a few minutes, you might want leave.'"

"It doesn't matter now. We're going to find a train station to drop you off at. Then you're going straight to your hotel. Don't say anything to anyone on your way back. I'm serious."

"And what about him?"

"That's up to the NSA to decide."

"The NSA?"

Jake knew he had said too much. The silence was relaxing, but he could see the wheels turning behind Zasha's eyes. She fixed her lips to sound off her first question, but a bullet through the rear window interrupted that thought. The remaining three Asian men were trailing them in their own car. Their headlights blinded Jake as he tried to get a bead on them.

"Step on it!" Jake commanded.

Chinelo pressed his foot to the floor as he weaved through the light traffic. Jake motioned for Zasha to get low as bullets ricocheted off the Sprinter. Chinelo veered off to the left, almost tipping the van over. "You can do something if you want," he said.

Jake leaned out the passenger window and let off a few rounds. A bullet flew through the pursuing car's windshield and sniped the passenger. Chinelo pulled the Sprinter closer to the curb. The top of Jake's head missed a light pole by inches. "Watch where you're going!" Jake yelled.

Chinelo steamed through a busy intersection with a red light facing him. Cars blasted their horns right in Jake's ear as Chinelo barely dodged a pileup.

Jake ducked back inside just before a car T-boned them and they spun out of control into the intersection. A whirl of thick white smoke from the screeching tires surrounded the Sprinter. The sound of metal crashing and the smell of burning rubber took Jake to a dark place in his mind. His vision narrowed as he wondered where he was for a second. When the smoke cleared, both the Sprinter and the other car were facing each other. The other vehicle sat and revved its engine, but Chinelo stood his ground. Jake commanded Chinelo to go, but he blocked his voice out, hands on the steering wheel. His old wound reopened above his right eyebrow, and was bleeding down the ridges of his face.

"Drive this fucking car right now or I will shoot you!" Jake yelled.

"It does not make a difference," Chinelo replied. "Either you uncuff me or we all die together." He turned to face Jake. "It is your decision to make."

Jake saw the fearlessness in his eyes. The thought of Zasha being in the van with them turned his stomach. "Zasha, get out of."

"No, I'm not leaving without you."

The chasing car screeched its tires as it charged full speed toward the Sprinter. Jake's ears drowned out any sound. Death was a mute predator. He could feel Zasha tugging at his arm, but his stance was rooted. His heart stopped beating. His body went numb. To his surprise, a feeling of relief came over him. Then the thought of his family came to mind. Their smiling faces lit up his vision, and his eyes grew wide. Their smiles soon turned into the blinding headlights in the distance. Before the chasing car could make it through the intersection , an eighteen-wheeler smacked directly into its left side at full speed, hurling it down the road.

All sound was restored for Jake. His first breath felt like someone releasing a chokehold. He took a moment to put his thoughts together and looked at Chinelo, who never broke a sweat.

"Zasha, get out," Jake said again.

"Right," she said, jumping out of the Sprinter. Jake didn't even look to see where she was going. He knew she'd do the right thing.

"Drive." There was a certain level of respect gained from Chinelo. He turned the key, and the engine sputtered for a few clicks. Once it turned over, he put the Sprinter in drive and squeaked away.

19.

Undisclosed Location

Jake stared at Chinelo through a one-way mirror while Parker and two other NSA agents talked amongst themselves on the side. He'd brought Chinelo to Parker, who'd returned the favor by blindfolding him all the way to a safe house in the middle of nowhere. He didn't care where they were, but the car ride wasn't long, so it couldn't have been too far from the city.

Jake thought about his conversation with Chinelo back at the hotel. He rubbed his thumb under his ring finger, trying to convince himself that he was making the right decision, but there was doubt lingering in his subconscious. He couldn't trust Chinelo, but he was working with a liar. He even accepted that he, himself, was a liar. But there was something genuine about Chinelo that he couldn't be ignored .

"I guess congratulations are in order," Parker said, walking up to Jake.

"Not at all. I was just doing my job."

"No, you weren't." Parker stared hard at Jake. His eyes did a quick rundown to find anything out of place with the man's demeanor. When he couldn't find anything, he extended his hand. "This was above and beyond anything that you were called upon to do. We are grateful."

Humility looked weird coming from Parker. Jake didn't know what to expect in dropping off a Venom at his doorstep, but he was confident there was an ulterior motive behind this sudden humbleness. Jake nodded and gave him a firm handshake. His phone buzzed in his pocket. It was Lieutenant Simons calling for the fourth time. He wasn't prepared to take that call just yet, so he ignored it.

Parker turned toward the mirror and chuckled under his breath. "So, how'd you do it?"

"Do what?"

He faced Jake, biting his bottom lip as he smiled. "Catch a Venom. You guys go to the same juice bar? Or did you just run into each other on the way home?"

"Good old-fashioned police work, that's all."

"Then maybe you should be doing my job. I mean, the top government agencies in the world can't find these people, yet you did it in less than twenty-four hours. That's some kind of police work indeed. Certainly isn't old-fashioned."

"Are you trying to ask me something specific?"

"No, it's just that…finding this type of person, let alone catching him, would take some very extreme measures, maybe even illegal. And I know a Boy Scout like you would never do such a thing, which is why I'm having a hard time wrapping my head around us being here right now."

Jake stepped into Parker's space with a proud smile. "How I did it is none of your concern. Your main concern should be playing your role to the best of your abilities, because right now I seem to be the only one picking up the slack." Jake's smug moment put a cigarette burn in Parker's ego, but he was able to cringe through a laugh.

"It seems like you found yourself on the right end of this after all. Let's hope you stay there."

Jake's phone buzzed with a text from Zasha: *We need to talk*.

He ignored the text. "I have to go handle some things back at home. Do you still need me?"

"No, I think we're done here…for now. But the fun is just about to begin for our friend. You sure you want to leave so soon?"

Jake left without any reaction. Parker signaled for one of the men to follow him. Maybe help him get home without him knowing where he came from. Jake couldn't help but question whether Chinelo would be alive to see tomorrow. Or if he'd dimmed the only light that might have guided him through the darkness.

"I'll call you tomorrow then," Parker shouted right before the door closed behind Jake.

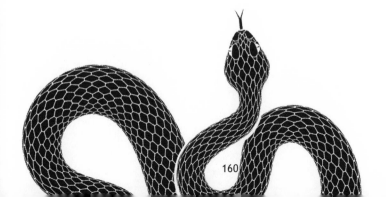

20.

Jake stood in an empty hallway, gripping a fifth of vodka under his coat. He looked both ways before sneaking the bottle out and taking another sip. A hearty belch rumbled from his mouth, followed by a hiccup. He looked at his watch. He was late. He guzzled the rest of the vodka without taking a breath. His body was full and empty at the same time. He pulled out a travel-size bottle of mouthwash, gargled and spat in the corner. Two splashes of eye drops fell into his crusted eyes. He paced for a few seconds and bounced on his toes before wondering if he even wanted to go through with this. He took a deep breath and entered the room.

When he stepped in, someone was already speaking. Sally's gaze shadowed Jake all the way to his seat. She noticed that something was off. Her years as a recovered mediator had taught her how to pick up on the signs early. Her evaluation was cut short by the applause of the group. The speaker stepped down and took his seat, receiving some supportive pats on the back.

"Thank you for sharing, Jimmy," Sally said. She turned her attention back to Jake. "It's nice of you to join us, Ray. But you know the rules. Latecomers automatically speak. To *The Hot Seat*."

Jake scrambled to his feet and found his balance before

he took a step. Each stride was concentrated. The faces of recovering alcoholics idolizing their hero stuck with him as he walked to *The Hot Seat*. He sat down with a white light beaming on his face. It seemed a little hotter than usual. A little brighter. More revealing. His stomach rose to his chest every time he opened his mouth for air.

"These past couple of days have been nothing short of a test for me, Jake said. "A test for my dignity. My integrity. My sanity. It's made me question the difference between what's real and what I tell myself is real. Then again, I've been living a lie almost my whole adult life."

Jake looked out to the crowd as they hung on his every word. He cleared his throat so his voice wouldn't crack. "If I'm going to start living my truth, I might as well start here, in front of complete strangers who know nothing about me. You're the closest thing I have to stability." He wiped the sweat from his face and took a deep sigh. The words were on the tip of his tongue, but the courage to speak them was taking a while to catch up.

Finally, he said, "My name isn't Ray. It's Jake. Jake Penny and…I'm a detective. I work for the Brooklyn division of the NYPD." Everyone mumbled their concerns amongst themselves. "Don't worry , I'm not here to bust anyone. I work in homicide. I hid my identity from you, but I was hiding who I am long before I showed up here. I was ashamed…ashamed of who I was and what I've done in the past."

Sally watched in shock. "It's quite understandable why you would want to hide your identity Ra, I mean, Jake. No one here is going to judge you. We're glad you made this breakthrough with us." Everyone agreed with various sounds of approval. "Please continue."

Jake could feel the weight lifting off his shoulders. "My sobriety has been snapped. I drink every day. All day. I'm drunk now." The audience gasped. "I was drinking right before I came in here. I'm a functioning alcoholic. I'm addicted to painkillers, and sometimes I question whether I want to live or not. My actions are a direct cause of my losing everything. I lost my pride. I lost my purpose. I lost my family." His voice cracked. "My wife Lea and my daughter Andrea were both taken away from me because of my selfishness."

"What happened to them, Jake?" Sally asked.

Jake looked down at his burned hand. He ran his fingers across the scars as faint screams echoed in his head. He looked back up at Sally with his bloodshot eyes fighting back the tears.

"It's all my fault."

"Jake, just take a second to—"

"I have to go." Jake knocked over *The Hot Seat*, dashing out of the room.

Outside, he stumbled into the street. A car blared its horn. He gathered his balance and walked toward the nearest train station. In the opposite direction, parked behind a few cars, was a black Mustang Bullitt , waiting and watching.

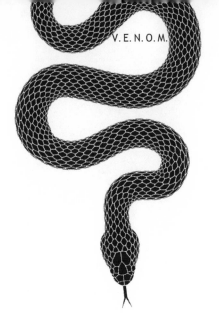

V.E.N.O.M.

21.

Zasha took in the energy of the city as she made her way back to her hotel after a long day of shopping. Manhattan was beautiful at night, but she was beginning to feel homesick, mostly missing the beach. She stopped at a boutique to get her last-minute shopping out of her system. Her sights landed on a decorative mirror. In it she noticed two jaundice-like eyes staring at her from a short distance. She continued to walk, but now her body was rigid. The man let a few people walk in his path, then followed behind them .

The hairs on the back of Zasha's neck became static with each passing step. Vendors on the block advertised their products in her face; some passing out flying for the upcoming parade, but she continued with tunnel vision toward the hotel. She looked back and saw the same man weaving through the crowd, getting closer. His face resembled a punch-drunk fighter's. She picked up her pace to a brisk trot; her heels clicking in a rapid cadence. She slid her fingers across her lips and pulled out a razor. No doubt something she'd learned growing up in her rough neighborhood .

The hotel entrance was just around the corner. *Home free,* she thought. She took one more glance behind to see how close the man was, but ended up crashing into Jake and knocking herself over.

"I'm sorry. Are you okay?" Jake asked.

"Yeah. No worries." She looked back as Jake helped her to her feet. The man following her was no longer there. She quickly dropped the razor into one of her bags.

"Are you busy?"

"No. Not at all. I was actually calling it a day." Zasha's tangled look turned into a smile when she realized she was safe. "What are you doing here?"

"I wanted to see if you were okay. After the other night, I wouldn't be surprised if you skipped town."

"Oh, right," she said, as if she'd forgotten all about it. "I'm fine. In my line of work, you know you're doing something right if you're getting shot at."

"You said we needed to talk. I thought we could do that over the best pizza in town. I know a place just twenty minutes from here if you'd like to join me."

Zasha took another look around to make sure no one was following her. "Right now?"

"Yeah. That's why I asked if you were busy."

"I have an idea. Why don't we order in, huh? My treat."

"Are you sure? The whole point of this place is the atmosphere. It's truly New York."

"I know, but I've been walking around all day, and if I'm being honest, I was looking forward to coming back to my room. Plus, I like to have my settings more intimate."

"Intimate?"

"For interview purposes. No distractions."

"Oh, right."

Jake couldn't count how many times his life had been in danger during the past forty-eight hours, but he felt the most nervous when talking to Zasha.

"I have a great view," she added.

He wasn't expecting her to move so quickly, but he was more concerned about the interview. He hadn't sorted through his lies well enough to give her any details.

"I don't know, it's getting late, and I have to wake up early for—"

"Don't worry, I'll have you in by curfew. Besides, what type of gentleman would you be if you left me alone when I'm asking for company?"

"The damsel in distress. Nice touch, but too soft for you."

Zasha had a smile that could melt the sun. The curves of her lips sank into two dimples, and her rosy cheeks meshed well with her freckles. Her eyes held him hostage. He could feel himself giving in to her wishes. A weaker man would have already done it.

Then suddenly, an excited voice yelled out, "Zasha!"

Her sights traveled over Jake's shoulder to see Brian standing a few feet away with a dozen roses. He was a skinny fellow with sleek glasses that accented his pointy nose. Zasha's smile turned into a confused stare. "Brian? What are doing here?"

"I called your office to see if you did some more digging on the case, and your assistant told me you were already in New York. You didn't tell me you were coming."

Zasha bounced her focus back and forth between Jake and Brian. "I know. It was a last-minute decision. I'll have to talk to my assistant on how to properly relay a message."

"Don't give your assistant a hard time. She has a lot going on with her boyfriend, her parents are pressuring her about marriage, but she's thinking about going back to school to get her masters and…" Brain caught himself rambling and decided to stare Jake up and down. On the outside, he seemed to be observing the competition, but on the inside, he was a little intimidated. "Who's he?"

"This is Detective Penny. He's the lead detective on the case, and he's giving me an exclusive. Detective Penny, this is Brian…a colleague of mine."

The two had an empty handshake. "Nice to meet you," Brian said. He turned his attention towards Zasha. "These are for you by the way." He handed her the roses.

"Thank you."

"So, do you want to grab something to eat? Maybe catch up? I made a reservation at this great Thai spot downtown. I know how much you love Thai."

"I can't, Brian."

"Why not?"

"That exclusive I was talking about is being given now."

"That's not a problem. We can all go out."

"I'm not doing an interview with anyone else," Jake said.

"Why not?" Brian asked, a little defensive. "I broke the story. She's just here to help. If anything, you should be giving me this exclusive."

"*Brian*, we're going to have to take a rain check on that get-together. I'm handling business right now."

"You mean stealing my story."

"I mean doing my job. Detective Penny is very selective about who he speaks with. You can't imagine what I had to go through to get this opportunity."

"Well, I hope it wasn't too backbreaking."

"What's that supposed to mean?"

"Nothing."

Zasha massaged her forehead before her headache could grow any worse. "He doesn't like speaking on the record to strangers, okay?"

"But I'm not a stranger. You know me."

"You are to him."

"I can do this another time," Jake said. "It's not a problem."

"No. Now is the time. Brian, please."

Brian let out a nervous laugh. He was the odd man out but didn't understand why. "I took three trains and two buses to come and see you."

Zasha sighed. "Technically you took three trains and two buses to come and see me unannounced. I already had plans with Detective Penny and I can't, no, I won't be unprofessional and drop everything just because you want to catch up on old times. That may be how you do things at your job, but at my level, it's inexcusable." Zasha took a hard gulp after that last word. It pained her to be so direct, but it needed to be done.

The lump in Brian's throat grew with each passing second. He looked over to Jake, who diverted his attention elsewhere. "Wow. I guess that pretty much sums up our relationship."

"Brian, don't make this about us."

"No, you know what, I wouldn't want you to be unprofessional. Lord knows that's all you ever cared about."

Zasha tried to hand him back the roses. "You can keep them. I'll see you around."

Brian turned and walked away without waiting for a response. Zasha walked toward the hotel entrance but stopped as she realized that Jake hadn't moved . She said over her shoulder, "You coming?"

* * *

Zasha stayed in the deluxe suite on the Astoria Level of the hotel. The suite came with two bedrooms, a personal housekeeping staff, original Art Deco motifs, and as promised, one of the most illuminated views of the city.

"Maybe I should have become a reporter," Jake said as he marveled at the room.

"It's investigative journalist, and it has its perks. You only live this life once, right? Why not enjoy it?" Jake answered with a subtle grunt as he continued to look around. "You want something to drink? The mini bar hasn't been raided yet."

Jake's mouth watered as soon as she made the offer, but he wanted to keep it professional. "No, I'm fine."

"Okay. Make yourself comfortable. I'll order the pizza. What's the name of the place?"

"Rocko's on Forty-Ninth Street. Do you need the number?"

"Nope. I'll look it up. Just relax."

Jake sat on the couch while Zasha went into the other room to make the call. He ran his rough hands across the silk pillows. His scar was a reminder that he didn't belong here.

Zasha came back in a white short-sleeved t-shirt, black jeggings, her hair down to her mid-back, and no shoes. Her aubergine fingernail polish matched her toes, and her skin looked soft enough to leave fingerprints. Her make-up was wiped off, but that didn't take an inch away from how stunning she looked. Even now, in her most comfortable form, she still looked like she was ready to slay a fashion show. Jake felt guilty for staring, but not enough to stop.

"Okay, the pizza is ordered, my bags are down, and I can finally take a breath." She jumped into the couch and sat Indian style facing Jake.

"You ordered for me?"

"Yep."

"But I didn't tell you what I wanted."

"I'm sure you'll like what I picked out for you. You want to start while we wait?

"Start what?" Jake knew exactly what she was talking about, but he thought maybe that slight delay might interrupt the whole process and they would have to do it another day.

Zasha smiled as she pulled out her phone and started the voice memo app. "January 9th. 7:45 pm. Interview with Detective Jake Penny." She put the phone down and looked Jake straight in the eye. "Where are you from, Detective?"

Jake was taken aback by the question. Any reasonable person wouldn't have had a problem answering, but her forwardness made him suspicious. "I thought we were going to talk about the Wei Pei case."

Jake had pieced together something on the way up to the room, and he wanted to get it all out before he forgot anything.

"We are, but I find that the interview process is a bit more fluid if we lay down the personal groundwork first." Jake adjusted his sitting position as he rubbed his ring finger.

Zasha picked up on the nervousness, but she'd come prepared. "Okay, how about this…we'll trade off questions. I ask you something, and then you can ask me something. We'll do this until we lead our way into the case. Sounds good?"

Jake took a deep breath and nodded.

"Okay, you're up first. Where are you from?" Zasha asked.

"You probably never heard of the place, but it's a small town called Harper. Harper, Kansas."

Zasha tilted her head, waiting for more, but nothing came. "Anything else? Did you like it there? What were your parents like? Any siblings?"

"The town was just like any other place, nothing special. I grew up with just my mom. No siblings."

"What was it like growing up there?"

"What a minute, that's already five questions, and I haven't asked you one yet."

Zasha smiled because she'd been caught trying to pull a fast one. "You're right. It's your turn."

Jake pretended to think of something, but he already knew what he wanted to ask. "Who was that guy downstairs?"

"Wow, straight for the jugular, huh? Okay, like I said, Brian is a colleague of mine."

"Yeah, okay, but who is he really?"

"What do you mean?"

"I've gotten really close to people I worked with, but none of them would bring me roses in the middle of the night."

Zasha sighed. "Fine. We dated briefly in college."

"Why'd you break up?"

"I was protecting him."

"From what?"

"From me." Jake's ears perked up. "I wasn't fit to be in a relationship at the time. He was so sweet, still is. He brought normalcy into my life. But I quickly found out that I and normal don't really get along. So, I called it quits. He wanted to continue to be friends afterward and that's what we did."

"I came unannounced too, you know?"

"What?"

"You blew him off because you said he came unannounced. I did the same thing."

"This is more important. He'll understand."

"And why is this so important to you?"

She paused to collect her thoughts. Her eyes grew soft, but her concern was quickly masked by a smile. "I would answer, but it seems that you used up all of your questions," she finally said. "My turn. Why did you come to New York?"

"I needed a change. New York was the start of a new beginning."

"You mean for you and your family."

Jake waited a second before he answered. "Yes. For my family and me. My wife, Lea, was a teacher. She had gotten a job at P.S. 375. And I was a stay-at-home dad until I got picked up by the Academy. Is it my turn now?"

Zasha nodded.

"What happened between you and your sisters?"

"What makes you think anything happened?"

"You mentioned something at the diner about losing them. I just get the feeling that you blame yourself for whatever happened."

Zasha stared at him without blinking. She'd underestimated his savvy. It was almost as if he'd tricked her into doing the interview.

"If you don't want to talk about it, that's fine," he continued.

She cleared her throat and ran her fingers through her hair. "There were three of us. I'm the middle child. My mother died giving birth to my younger sister when I was seven. So, my sisters, our dad and I moved to the Serbian province of Vojvodina. Not the best years of our lives. I lashed out as a child, a lot, and got put into a special school for little girls with behavior problems. My older sister, she…committed suicide a few years later. She just couldn't take my father anymore. My younger sister tried to run away but was later caught and put into a foster home. When I turned seventeen, I had an opportunity to make a change in my life, and I did it. Next thing I knew, I was on a plane to the States, heading to college. I never heard from my father again, and my sister got into some trouble while I was gone, so she's trapped in the system right now. I'm doing everything in my power to bring her here. Give her a fresh start."

"I'm sorry to hear that."

"Don't be. There are times where I feel sorry. Like my actions were a direct result of where she is now. That's why I'm doing what I'm doing."

Jake admired her strength but felt she was hiding something. She looked down at his scarred hand. Jake's body tensed up as he anticipated her next question.

"So, what happened here?" She gently touched his hand, but he pulled away. There was a painful silence between them. She reached again, this time with caution, and reassured Jake with her soft eyes. He was lost in them—to the point where he didn't even notice her reaching for his hand again. She gripped his palm, then stroked the disfigured side with her fingertips. She placed his palm on her face and shuddered under his calloused hand. It was like his pain was transferred to her body. "It's okay," she whispered. "You can tell me."

Jake's hand shook under her control. He had never felt

anything so soft and warm. Not since his wife. "I got into a car accident. I don't remember much leading up to it. I just remember waking up on my face. Glass everywhere. The car was upside-down in the road. It seemed like we were the only people left on Earth."

"We?"

Jake took a moment to catch his breath. "My family was still in the car. Somehow my body was tossed out the car as they continue to flip down the road" A single tear fell down his face, but Zasha wiped it away with her thumb. "I was cut really bad on my hand, but I couldn't feel a thing. I just wanted to get to the car. I kept telling myself *get to the car*. When I got there, it reeked of iron, gas and smoke. I remember the combination of them hitting my eyes and almost blinding me. My daughter was unconscious, but my wife was pinned down by her seatbelt, her eyes screaming for help. The car was totaled. No easy angle to get in. Finally, another car was coming down the road. I ran out to flag him down, but…an explosion planted me on my face. I got up and ran to that car as fast as I could. I stuck my hand in the window and burned myself trying to save my family. The driver must have come, because someone was pulling me away from the flames and I blacked out after that. I woke up to nothing."

Zasha came within inches of Jake's face, their eyes locked onto each other. "I don't know about you, but I could really use a drink right now."

"Yeah, me too," he agreed, eagerly.

Zasha gave him one last look of sympathy before making her way to the mini bar. "What are you having?"

"Nothing that's below forty percent," he said as he cleared the lump in his throat.

The doorbell rang. Zasha stopped to look at Jake, who

was already on alert. "That must be the pizza," she said. "I told the front desk to let him up. Take whatever you want from the bar, and I'll be right back."

As she walked down the hallway, Jake took an extended exhale to deflate. That was the first time he had ever told that story to anyone. A part of him felt relieved, but another part thought that he'd said too much.

He went over to the mini bar and checked out the assortment of hard liquor in the refrigerator. He picked up a mini bottle of vodka and thought about how wasteful it was to make something so good so small. Even if he drank everything in the fridge, it would only be enough to get him buzzed. He had to remind himself that he shouldn't get too comfortable. He stuffed a couple of bottles in his coat pocket and made his way back to the living room.

"You know what, maybe I'll just take a rain check on the drink. I should probably take my pizza to-go, and we finish this interview another time if that's not too—" Jake walked straight into a hostage situation.

Three Chinese men, dressed in matching trench coats, walked inside. One of them held a six-inch blade to Zasha's neck. The other two had handguns with silencers, pointed at Jake. Zasha stared straight at Jake with her neck stiff. She let out short breaths every time she felt the tip of the knife prick her in the neck.

Jake held his hands up to his chest, trying to calm the captors. "Don't hurt her," he said.

"Take your weapon and throw it to her feet," the captor said.

"Okay, but don't do anything crazy."

"I will if you don't toss your weapon."

Jake pulled his gun out slowly and threw it to the floor.

"Now, you need to come with us. Someone would like to speak with you."

"I'm not going anywhere until you let her go."

The Captor chuckled, and the others followed suit. "I'm sorry if I misled you into thinking that you had a choice in the matter. You *are* coming with us. And I will do with her as I please." He tightened his grip on her neck, and Zasha let out a yip. Jake flinched but fought the urge to steamroll the captor. He didn't have a good angle anyway. If he moved now they would shoot him, kill Zasha, or both. It was time to reassess his options.

"Everything is going to be okay, Zasha," Jake said. "I'm going to get you out of this."

Zasha's jaw tightened as she closed her eyes. When she opened them, she saw a genuine look on Jake's face. It wasn't fear. It wasn't guilt. He was actually concerned for her, and believed that everything would be okay if he took action.

"I'm so sorry, Jake," Zasha said. "I honestly didn't want it to be this way."

Those words came off her lips so softly, but pierced Jake in the heart like a hunter's knife. *Why is she apologizing?* he asked himself. *What has she done?*

Zasha took a deep breath. She could taste the stale cigarettes on the captor's clothes. His hands were freezing cold. They had been waiting to strike for a while. The tip of the knife pinched her delicate skin, but her focus was on the position of her feet compared to the captor's. His right foot was in between both her feet, which meant he stood at an angle. *Perfect.*

She plunged her head back as hard as she could. She could feel a small bone being crushed on her skull.

A small gash nicked her neck, giving her a jolt of energy.

She grabbed the captor's wrist and used her momentum to stab him in the neck with his own knife while using her right hand to pull out the super-shorty shotgun from his trench coat. She turned to the henchman on the right and shot him through his chest.

The henchman on the left opened fire, but Zasha used the captor as a shield and backtracked with full force into the remaining henchman, crashing them both into the wall. She kicked the gun out of the third henchman's hand and ripped his face with swift punches until he fell to the ground. She stood over him, glared into his dazed stare, then snapped his neck with no effort. She walked toward the captor, shotgun in hand, and watched him gargle on his own blood as he tried to put pressure on his wound. Zasha snatched the knife out of his neck causing him to bleed out in seconds.

She took a second to catch her breath, but the hairs on the back of her neck never let her down. She whipped around with the super-shorty shotgun tucked under her chin and pointed at Jake, but he already had his weapon drawn. Her strawberry blonde hair fell over her left eye, but her sights were as good as any marksman.

Jake stood there lost for words. His mind was still trying to process what he'd just seen. "Your neck," he finally said.

"I'll live," she replied in a cold tone.

"Who the hell are you?"

"Like I said, I'm sorry. It wasn't my intent for you to find out this way. Or at all for that matter."

"You're a Venom."

"*Was* a Venom. That was a long time ago. I'm not that person anymore."

"You know what they're trying to track down, don't

you? You knew what was going on this whole time."

"Look, I would love to continue with our question trade-off, but the way I see it, we have about six minutes to leave this room undetected. If we're lucky, they'll find this mess tomorrow."

"I can't leave a crime scene. And I can't let you leave either."

"Then that only leaves me with an option that I'd rather not exercise." Zasha racked the shotgun.

Jake placed his finger on the trigger. "Don't make me do this, Zasha. Don't make me choose."

"The choice should be simple. I'm not here to hurt you, Jake, but I will if it means protecting myself."

"Why should I trust you?"

"You don't have to. Trust your gut. I know something inside you is telling you to listen to me. I can protect you."

She took a step closer, but Jake cemented his stance.

"People saw us come in together," he said. "There's surveillance everywhere. I just can't walk out of here like nothing happened. I could be implicated if I—"

"I will take care of everything. No one will know you were ever here. We both want answers, Jake. We can get them together. But the longer we stand here, the more likely you won't get those answers."

Jake's didn't move a muscle.

Zasha sighed. "Look, there are only two ways this can end, Jake. You let me go, and we continue to help each other or…we both shoot and leave it up to chance. Either way, I'm walking out of this room. So, what's it gonna be, cowboy."

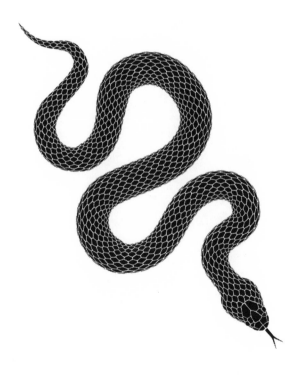

22.

Parker looked over the body of the henchman with the broken neck. He observed the corpses from a squatting position. Death never bothered Parker, but seeing these guys like this troubled him. Things were starting to escalate, and time was running out. He could only hope to accomplish his mission before it was too late.

Jake came to the door of the suite, but two plainclothes agents who could pass for cyborgs stopped him before he could enter. Parker whistled his approval and the two men stepped aside. Usually, a crime scene was flooded with essential personnel: forensics, detectives, coroners, photographers. But for the moment there were only four people on the scene, including Jake.

He surveyed the room, and a reenactment ensued in his head. On the outside he was calm, but on the inside, his heart was fluttering more than a caged bird. Every step he took was soft. Every breath short. Parker stood up. He didn't greet Jake with his usual smile. Instead, he gave a face that was hard to read. Jake was prepared for anything at this point.

"What do you think?" Parker asked as he walked by the mini bar.

"I don't know," Jake said. "I haven't had time to dig into the scene yet.

"Looks like our perp had no problem paying for overpriced booze. I need this whole area dusted for prints."

Jake cursed himself in his head. He pressed his hand against the empty bottles in his left breast pocket as regret fueled his anxiety. This wouldn't be the first time alcohol had put him in an unfortunate predicament. With his luck, it might be the last.

"These guys are with Jun Li," Parker said. "Which means they're either getting closer to what they're looking for, or less patient. Either way, there'll be more bodies to come, I'm sure of that. Say, where were you for the past three hours?" he quickly added.

Jake's heart stopped. "What?"

"Where were you for the past three hours?" he asked again. "I tried calling you, but you didn't answer, and you weren't at your apartment. I needed to talk to you about something."

"I was out having a drink. A Coke actually. I usually turn my phone on silent after duty hours."

Parker narrowed in on Jake and monitored him from head to toe. "There are no after duty hours. At the very least you should return my phone calls." He smiled to put Jake at ease, but his apprehension stayed in the back of his mind. "Just so I know you're still alive."

Jake mustered up a smile in return, but his emotions weighed on his conscience. "It won't happen again."

A small commotion ensued at the door.

"Excuse me, this is a crime scene within my jurisdiction and I demand to be let through," Lieutenant Simons barked at the agents guarding the door, but they didn't budge.

"Don't worry, I'll handle this," Parker said as he walked towards the door. "Lieutenant Simons! How can we help you?"

"Well, you can start by calling off your mutts and letting me through."

Parker did a subtle nod, and the agents stepped aside. "Anything else?"

"You mind telling me what the hell is going on here? I have a team of guys downstairs saying they can't come up to do their jobs because they don't have *clearance*?"

"That is correct. This is a classified crime scene until we can collect enough data for our investigation. I can't allow too many hands to be in the pot. You understand, right?"

"Then what is he doing here?" he asked, pointing at Jake.

"Detective Penny has upgraded himself to a valuable asset to the case. He's assisting me with the particulars of his findings."

"All this for a dead Chinese guy in the sticks?"

"That's a need-to-know, Lieutenant. Only people with the proper clearance can get those answers."

"Well, Detective Penny has been suspended from duty and his being here is a violation of my direct orders."

Parker took a step toward Lieutenant Simons, blocking his view of Jake. "Your orders might mean something to you, but they don't mean shit to me. If you have a problem with how I run my investigation, then you can take it up the chain, but you'll soon find out that chain ends with an answer you won't like."

Parker melted Lieutenant Simons on the spot with his stare. Simons turned his attention to Jake to redeem himself. "Can I speak to you for a second, outside?"

Before Jake could follow Lieutenant Simons out the door, Parker placed a hand on his chest to stop him. Jake's boss rolled his eyes as he held a clinched fist to his lip.

Parker turned to Jake and said, "I still have something I want to talk to you about, so make it fast." He withdrew his hand.

The hallway was empty for Jake and his boss. Jake knew Parker had crossed the line, but unfortunately for Lieutenant Simons, he had no clue how far that line went into the darkness. "Listen, I don't know what top secret bullshit you have going on with your boyfriend back there, but you seem to have forgotten who you work for."

"It's not like that, Trent."

"Then what is it like, huh? What the hell are you doing with this guy?"

Jake tried to find the best answer without sounding like a complete idiot. "I can't really explain what's going on right now."

"Why not?"

"Because…I don't fully know what's going on."

"You can't be serious. After everything I've done for you, you're going to ice me out for this prick?"

"That's not what I'm doing. I don't know the full details of the case. I'm just the front man while they do their real investigation."

"What do you mean real investigation?"

"I can't get into that. But you have to trust me."

"So, let me get this straight. You're the front man for the NSA, which is doing an investigation on something and you have no idea what it is?"

"Yeah."

Lieutenant Simons rubbed his chin as he thought about his next sentence. "That's bullshit. That's bullshit, and I'm going to tell you something else… You're just riding the coattail of this Parker character until he tosses you under the bus. And make no mistake, that moment is coming."

A part of Jake came to terms with the fact that his boss might be right. There was no guarantee that Parker was going to protect him if things went left. Jake looked back at what Zasha had left behind. He needed answers now more than ever.

"I don't trust this guy," Lieutenant Simons continued. "And neither should you."

"Just give me two days. Two more days and I'm done with this whole mess."

Lieutenant Simons let out a sigh. "Fine, but let it be known that from here on out everything you do is under his command and not the precinct's. So, when you're in a jam because of his actions, don't expect me to get you out of it."

Lieutenant Simons shoulder checked Jake on the way to the elevator.

Jake walked back into the room, straight to Parker. "What do you think you're doing? Unlike you, I still have a life after this."

"I'm glad you brought that up. It's precisely what I wanted to talk to you about earlier." Parker put his arm out to create a path away from the bodies. "With everything going on, from you catching a Venom, to your superior up your ass every ten seconds, and now this hotel incident... it's just going to get worse from here. Your safety might not be yours to keep if you continue with us."

"What are you saying?"

"I'm saying that you've done more than anyone has asked of you, but...I think it's best if we end your tenure while we're ahead."

"What?! You just made this big deal about me upgrading to a *valuable asset*, and now you're cutting me loose?"

"As much as I hate to admit it, your lieutenant is right. You don't belong here. If something happens to you, then that's your blood on my hands. So, from this moment forward you are relieved of duty, Detective Penny."

"That's bullshit!"

"That's me saving your ass. Someone from my staff will debrief you and tell you how you should carry on until this investigation is over."

"Just for once will you be straight with me? It's not like you're going to hurt your chances of solving the case faster if you do. You owe that much. Tell me why you're doing this?"

Parker sighed. Through all the bureaucracy and ego-throwing, Jake had reached him on a human level. "We got some intel about a high-profile Venom being here in New York as we speak. We don't know if he's a lone wolf or if he's teamed up with Jun Li. The bottom line is, more people like him are coming, and they specialize in making people like you suffer."

"You think this Venom was the one who did this?"

"This?" Parker asked through a chuckle. "No, no, no, no, this was a rushed job. If this were a top shelf Venom, we wouldn't have known about this until it was too late."

One of the agents walked up to Parker and whispered something into his ear. Jake could only make out the words *security feed* before he left. Jake's nerves were shot, but his face was as still as an untouched puddle.

"Okay, I have to go," Parker said.

"Let me see the footage," Jake said.

"You don't need to—"

"Just let me see the footage. I got you this far. You do this, and then I'll go home."

"Fine, but after this you're finished."

* * *

Jake and Parker were escorted by the hotel manager, a heavyset man with a pencil mustache. He trotted to the monitor with them both close behind. "I can't believe something like this could happen at my hotel," he whined. "This could ruin us! Eighty-seven years of history down the drain. For what?! A senseless act of violence? I hope you find the people who did this."

"We're hoping to," Parker said. "Just play the surveillance so we can see what we're working with." The video played and no one was more focused on the screen than Jake.

"Okay, we're going to start six hours before the gunshot was heard and fast forward from there," the hotel manager explained. He fast forwarded the video, and Zasha stepped out of the room with her face covered.

"Stop!" Parker said. "Who is that?"

The hotel manager got a closer look then thumbed through the documents he was holding. "That should be the guest. Her name is…Martina Alverez. She had a couple of more days left in the room.

Parker grabbed an agent. "Run that name. I want to know everything about her."

"Yes, sir." The agent scurried off.

"Keep going," Parker said.

The hotel manager continued. "Now, some of the workers said she came back around 7:15 pm."

"Alone?"

"Most accounts said alone, but some people said she could have been with someone."

The hotel manager skipped to minutes before her

arrival and let it play at regular speed. Jake held his breath leading up to the moment. Zasha appeared in the frame with a figure behind her. Even Parker's heart skipped a beat. Before the person behind her was revealed, the video jumped to the three henchmen standing outside the door waiting to come in.

"What the hell just happened?" Parker asked.

"I-I-I don't know," the hotel manager said. "There must be a glitch." He rewound to the original spot and played it once more, but nothing changed. Jake couldn't help but let out a sigh of relief through his nose.

Parker cursed as he knocked someone's belongings all over the floor. "Get every inch of footage throughout this whole building and outside for the past forty-eight hours and get it to me now!"

The hotel manager twiddled his fingers as he watched Parker pace through his fumes. "But that could take all night. Even days."

"You have two hours to get it done." Parker whipped toward the second agent. "I want every guest and employee screened before we shut this place down. And I mean *everyone*."

The hotel manager's eyes grew wide. "Um, excuse me, did you say, *shut down*?"

Parker sighed as he rolled his eyes. "That is correct. Cease operations until further notice."

"But you can't do that," the manager said through a nervous laugh. "We're the Waldorf Astoria. We're booked to this time next year. People are still staying here. This is just unacceptable."

Parker gestured for another agent to come over, completely ignoring the hotel manager. "Get Wu Xiaohui on the horn and tell him we need to get the ball rolling on shutting this place down. If he asks why, tell him it's for new renovations and restoration."

"Yes, sir." The young agent ran to complete his task.

Parker turned toward the hotel manager with a gracious smile. It was a gift, how he could go from ballistic to charming on a moment's notice. "Congratulations, you just got yourself a paid vacation."

The hotel manager stood there speechless. Parker left most people like that when he flexed his power. He turned to Jake with a much more serious look. "Speaking of vacations, go home, Jake. After the debriefing tomorrow, you can take some time off. Pick any place in the world and you're there for however long you want, on the government's dime. We'll take it from here ."

Parker extended his hand to officially part ways. It was the first time Jake felt like he was his equal. He hesitated for a moment then returned the favor with a firm grip. "Despite the rough beginnings, it was a pleasure working with you," Parker said. "I'll be seeing you around."

"Hopefully not," Jake replied.

23.

Jun Li sat in a room lit by candlelight, looking over the shoulder of Koa as he wrote Chinese symbols in a straight line. The frustration of learning a new language showed in Koa's handwriting as he became more careless. Jun Li sensed the negativity and slowly guided the young boy's hand to make the correct symbol.

"It is okay to make mistakes," Jun Li said. "The most important thing is that you keep practicing. Eight lessons a day should have you competent in no time."

"But what if I don't want to learn this stuff," Koa said.

"This *stuff* is a part of what makes you special. I will not allow you to walk this earth depending on someone else's language and culture."

Koa sighed as he massaged his forehead. It was at this moment that Jun Li was struck by a memory of his own, and he was able to relate. He took the pencil from Koa and sat next to him.

"I wasn't an excellent student growing up either. I had no one to help me."

"Where were your parents?" Koa asked.

"I never met my father, and my mother died when I was young . I grew up in an orphanage with hundreds of brothers and sisters just like you. I had no interest in studying, but the head mother made us. She had the teeth of a donkey, and there was a rumor that she bit off the toes of bad students in one snap."

"Was it true?"

"I don't know. After I heard that, I went straight to the top of the class, so I never had to find out."

They both enjoyed a laugh.

"Listen," Jun Li started. "If you promise to try with the lessons, then I promise I'll take you to that parade you're always talking about."

A smile sparkled on Koa's face. "Really?!"

"Of course. Just me and you."

Koa looked down at his lessons and his smile began to fade. "Did we do something wrong?"

Jun Li's face became serious as he moved in closer. "No. Why would you ask that?"

"I read a book that said bad things happen to bad people. We didn't have parents. So what does that make us?"

"You listen to me, we did nothing wrong. In fact, I'm fighting the bad people as we speak."

"You are?"

Jun Li nodded. "They took everything from us, and I'm going to take it back with interest . You don't have to worry about anything. I'll take care of you because that's what we do for each other."

"Would that make you my dad then?"

Before Jun Li could answer, a man who worked for him entered the room. "Sir, we have a problem. The men we sent died trying to apprehend our—"

Jun Li cleared his throat aggressively, then signaled his eyes to Koa. The man was in such a rush that he hadn't noticed Koa sitting right there. He understood what Jun Li was saying, and they both continued the conversation in Mandarin.

"The men are dead."

"How is this possible?" Jun Li asked.

"The detective had help. A woman. She is of the nation."

Jun Li's interest snapped to attention. "Is that confirmed?" The man nodded. "Do we know who she is?"

"Not yet. What would you like us to do?"

Jun Li looked to Koa, who went back to his lesson and pretended he wasn't listening. Jun Li knew he couldn't understand, but he still wasn't comfortable having this conversation in the boy's presence . He smiled and caressed Koa on the head. "Do you know where this detective lives?" Jun Li asked in English to the man.

"Yes, sir."

"Pay our friend a visit. And send him my regards."

V.E.N.O.M.

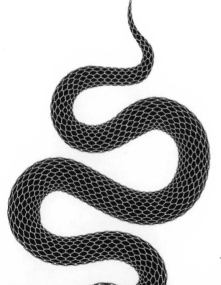

194

24.

Jake stumbled up the subway steps and onto the sidewalk. A pit stop by Arty's was necessary after tonight. In some ways, this was his private celebration for being done with the case. For a moment it felt like everything had gone away. Zasha, Parker, Chinelo and even Lieutenant Simons were all short memories that he didn't want to bother with.

Jake was only a block away from his house, but his lack of balance made it seem like a mile. He walked by a group of people, including Jay, and they laughed at him tripping over his own feet.

"Looks like someone had a good day at work," Jay said over the laughter. "What job do you know pays you to get drunk all day?"

Jake ignored the banter and continued down the block.

"Wait a second, Detective Jake." Jay ran back and put his arm around him. The initial aroma caught him off guard, but he was able to get some fresh air between breaths. "You know I'm just messing with you, right? I think you're pretty cool, even though you ain't never help a brother out—"

Jake pushed Jay as far as he could and almost fell in the process. "I don't have time for your shit," he said through a rumbling burp. "I don't have time for anyone's shit. Don't touch me again."

The laughs of Jay's entourage were now focused on him, and it poked at his ego like a needle. "You talking all that big stuff. You The Man now? You ain't nothing but a lonely drunk."

Jake turned toward his building and climbed the steps on an angle. He stumbled back a few steps. Then stomped up the steps, determined to get to the entrance.

"Yo, deadass, you're pathetic, man," Jay continued. "You can't even get up the steps."

"Leave me alone," Jake slurred. "I just want to get upstairs to my bed."

Jay's friends tried to get him to stop, but he was just getting started. "Yo, watch this," he whispered to his entourage. "You want to get to your bed? Catch up on re-runs of The Hardy Boys? Well, I wouldn't go upstairs if I were you, cowboy. There might be something waiting for you."

Jake stopped in his tracks. All his senses flared up. The sick feeling in his stomach evaporated. This couldn't have been a coincidence. He turned around with his head heavy. His beady eyes shortened Jay's smug smile, and Jay knew he'd said something wrong.

"What did you say to me?" Jake clumped down one heavy step at a time, then let his body weight build momentum toward Jay. Jake grabbed the man by the neck and threw him to the ground. "What did you just say?!"

"I ain't say nothing, man," Jay yelled, his voice raspy.

"Repeat what you just said!"

"I said don't go upstairs." The surrounding people looked on, shocked, while some recorded with their phones.

"No! Say it like you did before. Say it!"

"I wouldn't go upstairs if I were you, *cowboy*."

Jake loosened his grip to think, but reattached when the right question came to mind. "Who told you to say that?"

"I don't know."

Jake pressed his knee into Jay's neck. Jay let out a choking scream. Some of his friends couldn't bear to watch. "Johan, I swear to god, I will turn you into a fucking a hashtag all over the internet if you don't tell me who told you to say that!"

"I don't know," he said with more conviction. "I don't know who she was, all right?"

"She?"

"Yes! All I know is she was a badass white girl that I thought was in the wrong neighborhood until she started asking if anyone knew you. I told her I did. She gave me a hundred dollars and told me to give you that message as soon as I saw you. That's all I know, Jake. I swear!"

Jake uprooted his knee from Jay's neck. The man's frightened eyes brought Jake back to his senses. He had never acted that way with someone who didn't deserve it. With his adrenaline decreasing, his regret did the complete opposite. He tried to save face by helping Jay to his feet. The bright light of everyone's phone made Jake a little disorientated.

Throughout the crowd, he saw the boy he'd given money to for good grades. "Hey, I—"

The boy shied away behind someone's leg, and the whole community built a human fence around him. Jay coughed up a lung trying to catch his breath, and massaged his neck.

"I'm sorry," Jake said. "Please, think… Was there any reason why she didn't want me to go upstairs?"

Jay took a hard swallow. "She didn't say, man. I think you broke my neck."

Jake looked to the top floor where his apartment was. The whole level was without light, but that was nothing out of the ordinary. Jay watched as well to see what was going on. There was complete silence on the street.

"Maybe she was just tweaking," Jay said. "I know a lot of peop—"

An explosion erupted, bringing Jake's whole floor down. Everyone ran in a frenzy, trying to find cover. Everyone except for Jake who watched in disbelief. The white light blinded him for a few seconds, but he didn't let that stop him from taking it all in.

"No, no, no, no! God no!" Jake screamed while dropping to his knees and fighting tears. The heat boiled on his face as his whole body started to warm up. Ashes began to fall on his face, and the smell of smoke clouded his lungs.

The flames danced in his glassy eyes as every piece of his family's memory was incinerated. Clothes. Pictures. Toys. All gone in a blink of an eye. People tried to help him up, but he refused their aid. He couldn't stand even if he wanted to because his heart anchored him to the ground. Throughout the cluster of sirens and people watching and recording, Jake's eyes landed on a sketchy individual in the crowd. He was of Asian descent, but that wasn't what caught his attention. The man was unusually calm, standing in the middle of chaos. He showed no emotion. He didn't pay attention to the flames or the falling debris. He just stared at Jake with his lifeless eyes. A subtle smirk etched on his face as he turned to walk away.

Jake could feel the fire spreading through his chest as he rose to his feet. His subtle steps turned into a brisk walk. His eyes locked in on the back of the suspect's head. He didn't want to risk losing him. The crowd grew thick, but

Jake was able to bulldoze through them. The suspect was now at a full sprint toward the entrance of an underground train station, and Jake was right behind him.

Jake dashed down the stairs and onto the platform. A quick survey of the area showed no signs of the suspect. People waiting for the train watched Jake in his frantic motion and observed with caution. Finally, he spotted the suspect walking in the opposite direction on a platform two tracks over. A train was approaching on the same track, but before it arrived, Jake ran across the tracks, causing everyone to wonder what he was doing. He climbed up to the platform but lost the suspect again. The train arrived, and passengers exited so fast that it clogged up the platform in a matter of seconds. People blended together trying to make it to their next destination. Jake's head was on a swivel trying to find the suspect. He looked to the train, but the cars were too full to tell if the man he was looking for was inside. The train left, and Jake's pursuit slowed down. All that was left were the people waiting for the next train. Jake cursed himself in his head for coming up short. He pulled himself together in one spot, then made his way toward the exit. As he passed a cement pillar, the suspect jumped out and threw Jake to the floor near the edge of the platform. Everyone made space and watched the brawl in shock. Some people pulled out their phones to record.

The suspect pinned Jake to the floor, crushing his windpipe with a forearm. Jake grabbed the suspect's nose and squeezed as hard as he could. The suspect released his grip but managed to keep Jake on his back.

Jake landed a punch to the suspect's face but received a knee to the gut in return. He vomited but didn't let that bother him.

The suspect pulled out a small knife and used all his strength to press the blade into Jake's eye. Jake was barely able to hold the attack off. The two men used brute force to hold the knife suspended in the air. It was a matter of who got tired first. The horn for the next train howled down the tunnel. Jake inched closer to the edge of the platform, until the top of his head lined up. The headlights of the speeding train came closing in on them. Jake released his hold and let the blade come down, slicing into his cheek and stabbing the ground. A war cry from Jake gave him enough strength to lift the suspect forward and the train ripped his head off. The suspect's body flew down the platform leaving a bloody trail . Jake's unofficial celebration had turned into something more. The people he'd been chasing now wanted him dead.

* * *

The whole block was shut down, with police barricading civilians away from the train entrance. Jake gave his statement to an officer as his face was being patched up. Lieutenant Simons pulled up to the scene, and before the car could come to a complete stop, the door was open with him tracking directly to Jake.

"Please tell me this is not what I'm hearing it is," Lieutenant Simons said. "It cannot be fucking possible for you to be standing here as the nucleus to all of this." He realized he might have come on too strong, so he took a deep breath. Afterall, this was his friend he was talking to. "I'm sorry. That's not how I should have started. Are you okay?"

"Yeah," Jake said.

"What happened?"

"I already gave my statement."

"I'm not officially asking… What happened?"

Jake waved away the medic helping him. "I was attacked. I had a gut feeling about this guy, so I approached him, and he pulled a knife on me."

"And your apartment? What happened there?"

"I don't know. I came home and—" Jake's throat clogged up just thinking about it.

"All right, all right. Is there anything else that I should know?" Jake shook his head. Lieutenant Simons sighed. He took a quick look to see if anyone was listening, then sat next to him. "Jake, things are starting to unravel. I don't know what's going on, but people are starting to suspect there were outside influences."

"Are you talking about Parker? Because he has—"

"No, no, no, nothing like that, but… I got to ask, buddy… Were you drinking tonight?"

Jake's face tightened up. After all he'd been through tonight, he couldn't believe his friend was giving him the procedural questioning.

"You know it's going to come up later," Lieutenant Simons continued. "It's better if it comes through me first."

Jake cleared his throat. "What exactly are we doing here, Trent? We should be out there looking for whoever set this up."

Lieutenant Simons rolled his eyes as he planted his face into his hand. "Cut the crap, Jake, and tell me you're willing to take a blood test."

"You're supposed to have my back."

"And I do! I'm just trying to get ahead of this thing before it gets any worse."

"How could this possibly get any worse?"

Lieutenant Simons paused. "There's a video… Well, multiple videos of you using excessive force on a minority before all of this happened. It's spreading like crazy all over the internet and the news picked up on it. You put that, with your recent suspension, and this pending blood test, and I don't know what comes out of the other end. So, I need to you be cooperative with me."

"Trent, you know me.

This is all just a big misunderstanding."

Lieutenant Simons looked away from Jake's deteriorating eyes. He wanted to believe him, but they had to go through the process first. "Commissioner Diaz wants to meet with you first thing tomorrow morning. I imagine he's pissed beyond belief and wants answers. I can probably pull some strings, get him to agree to get you extensive help under *my* strict supervision, but I can't make any promises. You have a real problem, Jake. I'm just trying to help…"

Lieutenant Simons' voice was drowned out by a roaring V-8 engine. Parker pulled up on the scene without any resistance. He never looked in Jake's direction. He just sat there waiting, engine rumbling. Jake could smell the exhaust from where he was sitting. Without acknowledging Lieutenant Simons, he walked toward the car.

"Hey, hey, hey!" Lieutenant Simons yelled. "Where do you think you're going?" Jake ignored him and kept walking. "Don't do this, Jake. Detective Penny, I'm talking to you! If you leave this crime scene, we're through!" Jake stopped and turned around. "You get in that car, and I can't protect you anymore. He's only going to make things worse."

"How much worse can it get? They took everything from me."

"Who are they?"

Jake paused for a moment to think about his answer. He concluded that he didn't know who *they* were. No one did. Jake realized this wasn't going to be fixed by sticking around here.

Lieutenant Simons walked up to him to make one last plea. Jake considered it, but Parker beeping his horn only made this more of a reality. From that moment, he did the only thing he could do.

25.

Lieutenant Simons' office was dead silent as he and Jake sat waiting for Commissioner Diaz. What was once a place where two friends could speak comfortably, was now a tomb where their fates were hanging by a thread. Jake could still sniff out remnants of Parker's cologne. The fragrance made him look over his shoulder in hopes of him walking through the door. Parker had told Jake in the car that he'd be here to explain things to Commissioner Diaz, but the more time passed, the more Jake knew that wasn't going to happen. Lieutenant Simons stared at Jake while tapping his fingers on his desk at a rapid cadence. It was the wait that was giving him a migraine. Not just for Jake, but for his future as well.

Finally, a young female officer stuck her head in the office. "He's here." She quickly closed the door.

"I wish I could say the same about your friend," Lieutenant Simons said as he stood to attention. A feeling of embarrassment slithered down Jake's spine as he followed suit. All he could do was take the hit and prepare for the worst.

Commissioner Diaz walked in without a sound. He was a Hispanic man of medium height who wore a discount suit. Even though he was the highest-ranking officer on the force, his thirty years as a cop wouldn't allow him to collapse into the political pitfalls that came with being commissioner. He took pride in being for the people while also being a part of the establishment. His gaze stabbed into Lieutenant Simons, then over to Jake .

"Commissioner Diaz. Thank you for meeting with us on such short notice," Lieutenant Simons said.

"Spare me the customs and courtesies, Lieutenant. I've had my fair share since I walked in the door." Commissioner Diaz unbuttoned his jacket and rejected the seat offered to him with a simple hand swipe. "Sit. Both of you. Now, I don't care who says what, but one of you needs to tell me what the hell is going on ."

Lieutenant Simons jumped at the opportunity. "Sir, we've already taken corrective measures to—"

"Let's start with him."

Jake adjusted himself in his seat. He noticed the commissioner had no problems with looking him in the eye while he prepared himself. Jake saw in the commissioner's face that no matter what he said, the his mind made up about what happened. "There has been a chain of events that hit us in a way that we weren't prepared for. I can't explain these events or why they're happening, but we're doing everything we can to rectify the situation."

The commissioner thought before he spoke. Stroking his left brow seemed to calm him, but when he stopped to look at Jake, his eyes grew dark. "Chain of events. Situations. Rectify. It sounds like someone was front-row during media training," Commissioner Diaz chuckled, but everyone knew this was far from funny. "This *chain of events…* You wouldn't happen to be talking about the murder of eight innocent Asian people over the past three days, would you? Not to mention at least one of them has a direct connection to you. Is that what you mean by a chain of events?" The more Commissioner Diaz raised his voice, the more bothered Jake became.

"Yes, sir. That's part of it."

"No, no, no, see, that's the part that you see at your level. What I see, up here, is a community banding together and protesting at the mayor's office to have your ass on a platter. You should be thanking your god that your identity hasn't been released to the public yet. Which I can almost guarantee won't be for long. I have Chinese diplomats, ambassadors and everyone who thinks they're important in my ear trying to figure out what's going on in my city. So, I need a better explanation than this just being a chain reaction."

"What about my apartment, sir? That has to show you that something is going on. That I'm being targeted."

"Oh, yes, your apartment. Let's talk about that one, shall we? You said that someone told you there was a bomb in your apartment right before the explosion, correct?"

"Yes, sir."

"Then why would you assault the very person who, according to you, saved your life?"

"I… I didn't mean to. Things got a little carried away, but I know him from the neighborhood."

The commissioner gave Jake a pretentious smile. "So that gives you the right to violate his, because you're neighbors?"

The sarcasm was pissing Jake off. "No, I…" Jake calmed down before he raised his voice any louder. "No, sir, it doesn't," he said calmly. "But he was warned by someone else that a bomb was placed in my apartment."

"By whom?"

Jake paused to think of what name he should give. "He'll tell you."

Commissioner Diaz clicked his teeth. "That's where you're wrong. He won't be telling us anything. He's lawyered up and suing the goddam city over your misconduct."

"But my apartment—"

"The fire marshal said there was a gas leak. Possibly someone left the oven on after cooking."

"Oh, that's a bunch of bull…crap, sir."

Lieutenant Simons watched on the edge of his seat. One more outburst could be the end of Jake.

"Sir, do I look like the type of person who cooks?"

"No, you don't. You look more like a person who would enjoy a drink or two after a long day. Possibly during one too. Why did you refuse the blood test, Detective?" Jake said nothing. Instead, he looked over to Lieutenant Simons, who was purposely looking down. "In fact, why did you leave the scene in the first place?"

"Someone picked me up."

"They picked you up so you wouldn't have to take the blood test?"

"No. Trent, help me out here, will ya? You were there."

Commissioner Diaz looked to Lieutenant Simons, both eyebrows raised in shock. "Trent? Lieutenant, do your subordinates always call you by your first name?"

Lieutenant Simons juggled his thoughts when the spotlight was put on him. "Let's try and keep it professional, Detective Penny. He asking you the questions, so you answer them."

Commissioner Diaz focused back on Jake. "I was told that you've recently taken part in an AA program. How's that going?"

"The program's good. I feel like I'm making progress."

"Really? Because your moderator said the last time you were there you reeked of alcohol and ran out like a madman."

"That's not one hundred percent true."

"Which part?"

Jake struggled to think of what to say.

"Do you still drink, Detective Penny?" Commissioner Diaz continued.

"Every now and then, yes. They say it's best to wean yourself off in the beginning stages."

"Was last night one of those *now and thens*?"

Jake scoffed. "With all due respect, sir, what does this have to do with my apartment blowing up in my face? Or the fact that I was attacked in a train station. Are we forgetting about that?"

"The officer who took your statement reported that you were slurring your words and you wobbled when you walked."

"Well excuse me for having a stutter and shaky legs after stopping a guy from stabbing me in my fucking eyeball, right after I watched everything I owned blown to dust!"

"Jake!" Lieutenant Simons interjected.

The room took a moment to decompress. Jake gathered his composure and tried again. "I think it would best if we waited for Parker. He should be able to clear things up."

"Ah, yes, this infamous NSA agent who no one has ever seen or heard about."

"Lieutenant Simons is the one who introduced me to him. He knows him. He's real."

Commissioner Diaz looked to Lieutenant Simons, who said nothing. Then he said, "His existence is not in question here, Detective. However, whether he was here or not, is."

Jake rubbed his ring finger. "What?"

"I checked with Special Agent Ethan Parker's office, and they confirmed to me that he was on vacation. Fiji. Been there since last week."

"That's impossible."

"It's possible, and I think I've had enough. So, here's what's going to happen: you, Detective, are on administrative leave indefinitely for violating the terms of your return to duty with the AA program. This was the least destructive thing we could pull out of our asses for the media, but don't think that you are off the hook so easily. You will be investigated thoroughly by the Internal Affairs office."

Commissioner Diaz turned his attention toward Lieutenant Simons. "I have a press conference in twenty minutes in front of City Hall, to address the mess caused by your officer. Afterward, I want you in my office so we can discuss your decision-making and ultimately your future at this precinct." Lieutenant Simons took a hard swallow as he nodded.

Commission Diaz turned back to Jake. "I pray that you get better, Detective." He turned and left the two to think over what had just happened, and what would happen in the future.

Jake paced with his hand running through his hair as Lieutenant Simons masked his anger with a bitter smile. "I hope you're happy," Lieutenant Simons uttered.

"Actually," Jake started. "I was thinking more confused. What the hell was that? You left me hanging out to dry."

"I told you that would happen if you got in the car last night, and you did. That was your decision, now you live with it."

"My decision? I haven't been making my own decisions since this all started."

"You want to know what you've done up to now? You just pissed away any chance of piecing your life back together, and you managed to bring me down with you."

His words hit Jake right in the chest. "That's not fair, Trent. You know I would never do that intentionally."

"It's not about being fair, Jake. It's about taking accountability for your own actions. I'm paying for mine just like you're paying for yours. I get it, losing your family is tough, but I was there for you from the beginning. Not Parker, me. You're becoming self-destructive, and it's affecting the people around you."

"We can fix this. All we have to do is talk to Parker."

"How?! We can't talk to someone who doesn't want to be found. I saw him last night. Hell, you left with him. But somehow, our commissioner walked in here and told us he's been in Fiji this whole fucking time. You know what that tells me? Either we're fucking delusional or this rabbit hole is dark and cold and whoever has their hand in it isn't getting it back.

"Trent, I—"

"Get the fuck out of my office. Please, I just need a minute."

Jake decided not to push the issue and left on a bad note. More and more questions began to cloud his mind.

26.

The afternoon personified justice. Flags flapped in the brisk wind and the sun shined through passing clouds. As Commissioner Diaz addressed the media from the top step of City Hall, Jake watched from a distance, listening to the echoes of what was being preached to the public. He took his vodka-filled water bottle and washed down a few painkillers. No point in doing it in complete solitude anymore. His career was over, and he had no more friends. The least he could do was try to forget about his immediate problems. Lieutenant Simons caught his gaze as he stood in front of the pack. No doubt trying to ease the blow that was set to come later. A part of Jake felt terrible for dragging him down. All he'd wanted was the best for Jake, and in return he'd gotten a big middle finger from the government. *Maybe I could talk to Parker to get things straightened out,* Jake thought. But then again, Parker hasn't been Mr. Reliable lately.

At the podium, Commissioner Diaz was coming to the end of his speech. It was a bit long-winded, and Jake could tell it took a lot out of him mentally. But the commissioner had the remarkable ability to speak from the heart, so he did. "…and I want to assure the residents of New York City that every measure is being put into place to close these investigations swiftly and accurately. We will work diligently to build on our already solid relationship between law enforcement and the community, and to make sure we put measures in place to prevent these sort of incidents from occurring in the future. I want everyone to know that this my number one priority."

Three Kawasaki Ninja H2R bikes turned off Centre Street. Each bike had a rider and passenger. All were dressed in black-and-red-leather biker suits. Their helmets were matte black with tinted visors. The bikes came to a stop and revved their engines nonstop during the speech. Jake locked in on them. He knew something was about to go down. Commissioner Diaz rolled his eyes and signaled for security to handle the distraction. The revving grew louder as the guards closed in.

Everything went silent for Jake. The timing. The bikes. The open road to the bridge. It was all too convenient. A muffled, distant *pop* slapped his eardrum and interrupted his train of thought. The pop seemed to have come out nowhere, leaving Jake to circle around looking for its source. His gaze landed on the commissioner, whose features were distorted. A hand was clutched to his chest, and blood ran through his fingers. A woman took notice and shrieked.

Three more muffled *pops* came from nowhere, and the commissioner fell onto his back. The crowd scattered in different directions, screaming at the top of their lungs. Lieutenant Simons dashed towards the commissioner to give aid. Jake sprinted in that direction as well, but was thrown off when the motorcycle passengers hopped off the bikes and fired rounds into the crowd.

Jake took cover behind a wall. He saw Lieutenant Simons get sniped by a stray bullet. The passengers emptied their clips then hopped back on the bikes. The riders fled the scene, going toward the Brooklyn Bridge.

Jake chased after them, but was cut off by Parker's car. "Get in!" Parker said. Jake got in, and they swerved off after the shooters.

Parker ripped through traffic as he closed in on the motorcyclists.

"You finally show up." Jake asked.

"Get ready to shoot," Parker said, completely ignoring his question.

Jake pulled out his gun. The passengers on the bikes turned with their reloaded guns, raining bullets on all the vehicles behind them. Cars veered out of the way and crashed into each other, trying to avoid the gunfire. Parker's hands burned into the steering wheel as he slid through the skidding vehicles. He went full-throttle even with bullets drumming on the hood and windshield. Jake took cover, but quickly realized there was no damage to the vehicle. The car was bullet-proof.

"We have to catch them before they get off the bridge or we'll lose them in traffic," Jake said. Parker rammed the back wheel of one of the motorcycles, and the passenger came flying onto the hood. The bike collapsed sideways, and Parker ran right over the rider. The front tires lifted off the ground and catapulted the passenger off the hood, smearing him all over the asphalt.

"You can start shooting when you feel comfortable, sunshine," Parker said. Jake hung out the window and adjusted his sights against the wind. He missed the target with the first few rounds. "Dammit, Jake, have you ever been to a range?"

Jake relaxed his body as much as he could. He held

his breath as he aimed. The target was in sight. Before he could let off a round, a crash from the back of the car knocked him off balance. He turned around to see a cop car trying to run them off the road, followed by a whole fleet of cop cars .

"This is the wrong time for your people to get involved," Parker said. He spotted a semi-truck coming up on the road. "When I'm about ten feet away from this truck, I want you to shoot out the back tires." Jake looked at him confused. "Just do it, all right?!" He pulled up right behind the semi-truck and Jake shot out every back tire.

The truck skidded slowly to the left, almost tipping over. The bumper of the semi-truck nicked the tail end of the second motorcycle and flipped it over. Parker slingshotted around the truck before it blocked the road.

"The bridge is ending," Parker said.

Jake slipped outside the window and set his sights again. The wind didn't allow for his eyes to be open all the way. His ears were blown out, and his hand shook from every bump in the road. He let off a shot. The bullet went through the passenger's shoulder. The momentum caused the bike to shift off balance and wipe out . Both the rider and passenger slid down the road—coming to a smoky stop. Jake and Parker stopped forty feet out. They stepped from the car and ran toward the fallen suspects.

The smell of burning rubber and gas put a common sickness in Jake's stomach, but he blocked out the memory for now. The bike was completely totaled. The rider and passenger didn't look any better.

A sharp sting went through Jake's chest. *I'm going to kill them both,* he thought. For the first time since this thing had started, Jake didn't know which side of the law he was on.

He just wanted to do something terrible to the criminals for once.

The passenger took off his helmet and cleared his mouth of any blood as Jake and Parker approached him. "I will not tell you anything," the passenger said, his voice trembling. "My loyalty is with Jun Li."

"That's good to know." Parker let off a round right in between his eyes, and continued to walk without a hitch. A wave of relief rushed through Jake's body, but he would have been more satisfied if he'd been the one pulling the trigger.

The rider was no more than ten feet away. He tried to crawl, but his right leg was broken. Parker stepped in front of him and kneeled. He flipped the rider on his back and removed his helmet. To his surprise, the rider couldn't have been older than twenty-five.

"I got some good news and some bad news for you, chief," Parker said. "The good news is, from the time it took me to walk here from my car, I decided that I was only going to kill one of you. The bad news is…your selfish comrade over there took that option away from you. So why don't we just skip the *I don't speaky any English* part and get right to it. Where's Jun Li?"

"I don't know anything, I swear," the rider said in a cracked voice.

"Of course you don't. How 'bout I phrase it another way. Tell me where Jun Li is before I break every bone in your body?"

"I told you, I don't know anything. I'm just driver."

Parker stood up and walked to the rider's broken leg. "You know, we're all just role-players in the grand scheme of things. But like any role-player, I know there's something you want. Maybe even something you need." The rider moaned through his teeth as Parker stepped on his broken leg. "You might want to hurry. If the police get here before we make a deal, you're going to a place far worse than jail, and I might not be generous and help you out then. You picking up what I'm putting down?"

"You're honestly not thinking about helping this piece of shit, are you?" Jake asked.

Parker raised his hand to cut him off. "Clock is ticking. What do you want to do?"

The rider fumbled his words before he spoke. "I need protection. And full immunity. You promise me that, and I tell you what you need to know."

Parker ground his teeth, then sighed. "Okay. You give me the right information, and I'll see if I can arrange something."

"*Bullshit*," the rider said in Mandarin. "You make arrangement, and I tell you information."

"You're not in a position to negotiate, son." Parker pressed down on the broken leg, and the rider winced in pain.

"You need information as much as I need protection."

Parker pressed down harder, and the rider began to talk faster. "If they take me, I'm dead regardless. If you don't get information, this will all be for nothing." Parker released his foot. He looked toward Jake and could sense his disapproval. For the first time in their encounter, Parker second-guessed a decision based on Jake's reaction.

"Okay, I can have you extracted from America back to China with no criminal charges. That includes the act of terrorism you just pulled back at the City Hall."

"No good."

"That's the only option you have, son. Take it or leave it."

"Jun Li will find me and have me killed. I'd have a better chance staying in America."

"Where I'm from it's better to fight for your life than wish you were dead. Make no mistake, whoever takes custody of you will make it their top priority to keep you alive as long as your body can hold up. Last chance to make a deal with the devil."

The rider's troubled face curled into a delighted smile. A chuckle rumbled under his breath. Then full laughter sprouted out. Parker raised an eyebrow. None of this mattered to Jake. He just wanted the absolute worst for this degenerate. "You were right," the rider said. "There is something I want. I wanted to see where your loyalty was. And the answer is…you have none to be found."

The rider laughed more through a choking cough. "Even when death is certain, I would never help you. I can die honorably knowing I had a hand in your country's demise, but most importantly, you will die a soulless coward who was willing to aid his enemy for his own benefit."

Parker clenched his fist until his fingers went numb. He booted the rider's head, making him go unconscious. The laughter was replaced by the propeller of a helicopter whirling in the air above them. Parker walked back to the car without saying a word.

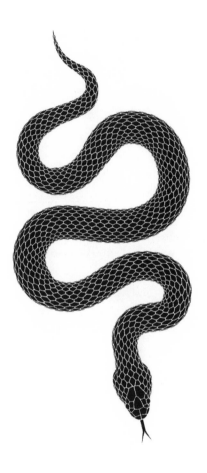

27.

Undisclosed Location

Later that night

"I just got word from the hospital," Parker said, walking up to Jake. "Is Simons in stable condition and expected to pull through . Only one bullet caught him in the shoulder."

"And the commissioner?" Jake asked.

Parker shook his head.

Jake stared through the Plexiglas at Chinelo, who was chained to a chair and more banged-up than he remembered . Jake caught a glimpse of his own reflection. The bloodshot eyes anchored by sandbags. The wrinkles forming in his face. The few gray hairs sprinkled in his stubble. The past two days have done more to him mentally than an ordinary man could withstand.

"This isn't your fault, Jake. I told you things were going to get dangerous, and if I'm one hundred percent being honest with you, the worst is yet to come. We can still set you up somewhere nice until things blow over. There's no shame in that."

Jake looked away from his reflection and into Parker's eyes. There was a different kind of motivation burning inside him. "We both know we're far past that."

Parker nodded, then signaled for someone to open the

door to the interrogation room. "We don't have much time, and we're out of options. From this point forward, we do whatever needs to be done to bring these fuckers down. They brought themselves to the light, which means they're getting desperate. More people will be hurt. You sure you're ready for that?" Jake walked right into the interrogation room. Parker took that as a yes and followed right behind him.

Jake stood off to one side while Parker sat in front of Chinelo. Chinelo's head nodded off, and his eyes rolled to the back of his head as he tried to hold onto consciousness. Someone had done a real number on his face. Parker observed him for a moment with a smirk on his face, then adjusted his tie and cleared his throat.

"I'm not going to waste my breath with silly questions for silly answers, because time is of the essence and we're stuck. We've exhausted all our leads, but my gut is telling me there's a piece of this puzzle that you're hiding from us. Whenever you're ready to tell us, that would be greatly appreciated."

Chinelo's lips never separated. Instead, he narrowed his eyes to Parker's, trying to figure out his angle.

"I looked through your resumé," Parker continued, "and saw that your Venom name is Red Shadow. I'm always curious when I come across you people, how did you get that name if you don't mind me asking?"

Chinelo eased in as far close as his chains would allow. "Because everywhere I go, my enemy's blood follows me." He smiled, showing off his blood tainted teeth.

Parker did an impressed scoff. "I'm not going to lie… that's pretty badass. You think that's trademarked?"

"Enough of this shit!" Jake shouted. He marched

from the dark walls and pointed a pistol point-blank at Chinelo's forehead.

"Jake, what are you doing?" Parker asked.

Jake didn't answer. He didn't even hear the question. All he saw was the barrel leading straight in between Chinelo's red eyes. The pistol shook in his hand, but his trigger finger was steady.

"Jake, I know you're anxious right now, but maybe you can hold off killing this bastard until we get what we actually need."

Jake's hand stopped shaking. "Tell us where Jun Li is."

Chinelo stayed silent. His eyes dared Jake to pull the trigger and Jake cocked his gun to show him he was willing to take him up on it. "Tell us where he is, or you're going to die here. It's that simple."

"Do it," Chinelo said. "You'll be helping everyone in this room if you do."

"Don't push me. Right now, I could care less if you tell us anything. Your life means nothing to me."

"Well, it kind of means something until we get that information," Parker said. "Don't let him get in your head, Jake. Me personally, I don't give a shit if you kill him or not. I just want the intel before you do it."

Chinelo mustered out a bruised smirk on his face. "I say you should, but I know you won't," he said to Jake. "You can tell a lot about a man when he is in the face of death. For you, I can see a lot of rage in that deteriorating heart of yours. There's only one way to find out if you are strong enough to control it…and that is to let it consume you."

Chinelo closed his eyes and pressed his head against the barrel of the gun. After a few seconds, Jake snatched the gun away and pounded a dent into the steel table with his fist.

"Take a walk," Parker said.

As Jake stormed out of the room, Parker signaled one of the agents to follow him. He then turned back to Chinelo with a thrilled smile. "And he's the calm one. Imagine how I am if I don't get what I want. Do we really have to play this game?"

"There is nothing you can do to me."

Parker chuckled. "I think that's something we both can agree on. You're a tough son of a bitch, Chinelo. You actually have top-level agents complaining about torturing you. Can you believe that? You've probably prepared extensively for moments like this. V.E.N.O.M. has taught you well, no doubt about that."

Chinelo spat his blood-infused saliva on the steel table. "I have no ties to V.E.N.O.M. anymore. If you want information about them, then I'm sorry, but you have tortured the wrong person."

"So, you're exonerated from any wrongdoing because you don't go by Red Shadow anymore?"

"No. We all have a debt to pay for what we've done. Even you."

Parker scoffed as he took his seat. "Tell me, what exactly was your role in V.E.N.O.M.?"

Chinelo locked up once again.

Parker's smile never left his face. "Touchy subject? I get it. I wouldn't want anyone digging up my old skeletons either. I'll tell you what we do know." An agent from outside brought Parker a thick file. He opened it and started from the top. "Oladimeji Chinelo Adebayo. Wanted in thirty-six countries for a long list of things, but I want to focus on what you specialized in: arms dealing. You were supplying seventy-five percent of the V.E.N.O.M. organization and its associates with weapons. In fact, your most infamous deal was through V.E.N.O.M. to military-aligned rebel groups who looked to combat the ECOMOG." Parker slammed the file on the table.

Chinelo closed his eyes as he looked away.

"You sold heavy artillery to people that overthrew your government and military. People lost their lives. Their homes. Children bled on the same streets they used to walk to school on. You killed your own for profit. If you ask me, it takes a special kind of icebox to be able to do something like that. I'm sure there's someone out there dying to bring you out of hiding."

"Then do it! It is what I deserve." Chinelo's voice cracked.

"Not until you tell me what I need to know."

"What do you want from me?"

"Jun Li."

"I do not know where he is."

The room went silent. Parker loosened his tie and sighed as he leaned back in his chair. "Okay. What about Ester Sinclair? Can you tell me where she is? Hmm? Maybe you know her by her birth name…Dimilola Tinah Adebayo."

Chinelo's face tightened up. His bloodshot eyes bulged past their sockets.

"Is that a yes or no? Maybe a picture would help." Parker pulled out a school photo of an eleven-year-old girl dress in her school uniform. Her hair was long and natural. Her skin was rich with melanin. Her smile was missing a tooth, but couldn't be any more beautiful. "I'll ask you again… do you know where this girl is? Because I do. She lives in South Africa. She goes to Alexandria Christian Academy. She's an April Fool's baby. Her favorite color is orange, and she despises beets. Not much of a fan myself. The intel says it's just her and her *mother,* who works a regular clerk job, nothing fancy. But once a month, the mother receives a deposit to her account. Nothing ridiculous enough to warrant a red flag, but just enough to question where it's coming from. Turns out, it's coming from thin air. It's being used to support that beautiful little girl." Parker placed the picture of her on the table, to let Chinelo gaze at it. "Would you like to see a video of your daughter on a playground?"

Chinelo jumped at Parker, but the chains kept him grounded. "If you touch her I swear that I will kill you and anyone who stands next to you." His breathing grew heavy. Parker put the picture away in his pocket.

"I work for the U.S. government, sir. I would never partake in criminal activity, no matter who the receiving party is. However, you pissed off a lot of people in this world who do partake in and, in some cases, enjoy criminal activity. So I'm sure it would be nothing for those people to filet little Ester's skin off her bones and show you a video of them doing so."

Chinelo's hard exterior was cracked. He eased back in his chair and calmed his demeanor. "Please, do not do this. I will give you my life for hers."

"Right now we are the only two people on Earth who know this information about your sister and daughter. Tell me where Jun Li is, and I will keep it that way."

"I do not know where he is," Chinelo said through his teeth.

Parker stood from his chair. "Then we have nothing more to talk about." He walked toward the exit.

"Wait! I can tell you where Xi Yuen and Jun Li met every

month." Parker stopped in his tracks. Finally, something he was interested in. A smirk ran across his face, but he made sure to erase it when he turned around and retook his seat.

"The old man in West Virginia would meet with Jun Li every month?" Parker asked.

"For almost a year straight. I would drive Xi Yuen to New York to meet with people in a restaurant in downtown Manhattan. Hakkasan."

"And why were you trusted with such a task?"

"One hand washes the other and both wash the face. Xi Yuen was second in command in V.E.N.O.M., and Do Shen loved him like a brother. I dealt with both directly. When the nation crumbled, and Xi Yuen and his wife fell ill, they could barely take care of themselves. They needed help from someone they could trust. My sister and daughter needed protection. It was an even exchange and Do Shen bridged the arrangement."

"What was this meeting all about?"

"I do not know. I never went inside."

"Then this means nothing. They could have been talking about their orgy the night before over brunch."

"You believe what you want. But after the house of Xi Yuen was raided, I came to New York out of desperation. I did not know what to expect, but I still went to the Hakkasan restaurant. I told them everything that had happened."

"Was Jun Li there?"

"No. To express their gratitude, they gave me ten thousand American dollars in cash and produced a passport for me right there on the spot. They told me never to return. If you want to find Jun Li, that is the place to start."

"When was the last meeting?"

"The day before Do Shen was killed."

"Okay, we can work with that. I knew you had it in you. Good work."

"What about my family?"

"This just buys them time. We have to see if what you say checks out."

"It does."

"I trust you. In the meantime, someone's going to clean you up and give you a nice pair of trousers. You're coming with us."

"Why?"

"Because if we go into that restaurant and it turns out to be nothing, I want you to see me make the call for the vultures to pick your family apart. If it does, in fact, turn into something, and the end result is me getting my head blown off, I want them to know who to blame for their front being exposed. Then *they* can order the vultures on your family."

28.

It was just before eleven o'clock at night, but people were still walking into Hakkasan. Jake, Parker, and Chinelo sat quietly in a parking lot across the street. Chinelo sat in the driver's seat with Parker keeping things secure in the back seat and Jake in the passenger seat.

Chinelo's bruises were patched up, and he wore a casual suit. "What exactly is your plan?" he asked.

"Plans are restricting," Parker said. "In situations like these, I find it more productive to improvise."

Chinelo looked in the rearview mirror. "Are you insane? That is the most idiotic thing you could do."

"Hey, easy there, Negative Nancy. You're the idiot who's going to lead us in there."

"He has a point, Parker," Jake interjected. "We need a plan."

"Being led by fear rather than faith is the primary cause of failure, guys."

Jake rolled his eyes. "So now you have faith?"

"I like to think of it as infinite intelligence. No negativity necessary."

"There is nothing intelligent about doing this," Chinelo said. "You are a lunatic, and this one is the only man who can say he put a gun to my head, twice, and lived to talk about it."

"If it makes you feel better, I wasn't going to shoot you," Jake said.

"Maybe you should have. Because what the fool in the back is talking about doing is suicide."

The car fell silent. Chinelo was right, but Jake didn't know how he was going to convince Parker. A snicker from the back seat caught Jake and Chinelo off-guard. The snicker turned into chuckles, and the chuckles into full-on laughter.

Chinelo looked in the rearview mirror again to see Parker laughing hysterically. "You are mad," he said.

"What's so funny?" Jake asked.

Parker spoke between laughs, wiping tears from his eyes. "I… I did the same thing to you when we first met with the whole gun-in-the-face bit. The look on your face…" Parker laughed harder. "You almost shat a brick."

Jake scoffed. "Why is that so funny now?"

"Because you took a page out of my book and it totally backfired."

Parker continued to laugh. A smile crept on Jake's face. Even he could see the humor in it. After a brief thought, he chuckled under his breath, then fixed his face to be more serious. He looked to Chinelo, who was always grave in his appearance.

"Aw come on, Red Shadow," Parker panted. "Laugh a little. You'll live longer."

"Excuse me if I do not see the hilarity in this foolish scenario," Chinelo said.

Parker got his last laugh out as he caught his breath. "On a serious note, we have to go inside. There's no other option."

"And do what?" Chinelo asked. "We do not know if the

person we want to talk to is even there."

"We won't know until we find out." Parker's voice dropped to a serious tone. "This is nonnegotiable. We're going in together whether you like it or not."

"Why do you do it?" Jake asked Parker. "Why do you ask for the Venoms' names?"

Parker smiled. "I'm, uh…somewhat of a collector. I've been tracking Venoms for the past six years now. The odds of a person knowingly coming across one are a billion-to-one. I've tracked down three, including this handsome young fellow."

"Is it worth it?" Jake asked. "From what you're telling me, these people barely exist. It seems like you're chasing an idea more than an actual person."

"I used to ask myself that very question. Is there a purpose to all of this? Then I always go back to the very first Venom I ever brought down. It was by mistake actually. Pure luck. He was a tough son of a bitch, too. Almost killed me when we threw blows. But I walked out of there by the skin of my teeth. My life was never the same after that day."

Parker went into deep thought.

"What was his Venom name?" Jake asked.

Parker snapped back to reality. "Sole Survivor. That is, of course, until he met me." Parker's eyes turned cold as the event played back in his head. "He was a colleague of mine, you know? He wasn't some random mercenary making his bones, no, no no, no. This was a person I'd seen every day. He was an American who worked for the NSA while working for V.E.N.O.M. right under our noses. V.E.N.O.M. poisoned the root of our government, and a small part of me thinks that no matter how long the shot is, I can still make a difference. Restore the innocence in our country. That's a good enough reason, right?"

* * *

Inside, the restaurant was filled with patrons enjoying their meals over mixed conversations. The layout was a modern Chinese style, with dim lights to set the mood. The diners wore casual suits and martini dresses. And then there were Jake, Parker and Chinelo, standing behind a velvet rope waiting to be seated.

A hostess finally came to them with a bright smile. She had a petite frame and long silky black hair, which seemed like the dress code there. "Good evening gentlemen and welcome to Hakkasan. Whose name will the reservation be under?"

Parker stepped forward and said in a hushed voice, "No reservation, ma'am. My friends and I are just tourists, and we were looking for a fancy restaurant to try in the city. Trip Advisor brought us here."

The hostess' face fell to disappointment. "Oh, I am so sorry, sir, but we only take reservations throughout the year. It gets hectic here."

"That's too bad. This one here loves Chinese food." Parker pointed at Chinelo's solid face. The hostess cringed a smile but could barely look at his swollen face. "He ate it all of his life, and now he's a bamboo stick. I promised him we would have the best Chinese cuisine in New York. There must be something you can do."

"I really am sorry, sir, but there's nothing I can do without a reservation."

Parker looked the hostess up and down. His gaze made

her straighten her back. He waited a moment before he asked, "Is there someone else I can talk to? Maybe someone with authority?"

"Of course, but they're going to tell you the same thing. If you make a reservation for next time, you can avoid this confusion."

"Let me be more specific. Is there someone I can talk to about making fake passports?"

The hostess' face turned milk-white. She looked back at Chinelo, and familiarity suddenly crossed her face. "I-I don't know what you're talking about, sir."

"Listen here, sweetheart, I don't have time for petty games. Now I came a long way for some very important people who are in need of a service. That service is getting official passports made in a short amount of time. Do I need to make a phone call and tell them I'm getting pushback from a fucking waitress?"

"No, no, no, no… Please, wait right here." The hostess scurried off to a man who looked to be security. She whispered in his ear, and the man glared in Parker's direction.

"What the hell are you doing?" Jake asked, still eyeing the hostess and security.

"Getting results," Parker said.

The security man gave the hostess a nod and walked in the opposite direction. She greeted Parker again with a forced smile. "Right this way, sir."

They were seated at a table close to the bar. The hostess handed them menus and shuffled away without saying anything.

"Okay, now what?" Jake asked.

"We wait," Parker said. "They know we're here, so they'll have to come to us."

"I still think we should leave while there's still a chance," Chinelo quickly added.

"No one's going anywhere."

"Chinelo's right," said Jake. "We don't have a plan. This place isn't going anywhere. I say we come back later with backup."

"And risk losing the person responsible for coordinating one of the deadliest terrorist attacks on American soil since 9/11? He had your commissioner killed, your lieutenant is hanging on by a thread and, worst of all, he put the lives of Americans in jeopardy. For once, we can use the element of surprise to our advantage. It's now or never, and I for one am not going to—"

Parker was interrupted by three Chinese men stopping right by their table. They were a young-looking trio with slender builds and tattoos covering their arms.

Parker waited a moment to see if they had a reason for being there, but when the staring became stifling, he finally asked, "Can we help you gentlemen with something?"

The front man smirked while looking over the table. His stance suggested that he was the unofficial leader. Jake confirmed that when the front man's smirk slid away and the other two followed. "You're sitting at our table."

Parker looked at the table, then back to the front man. "The beautiful young lady at the front desk sat us here. So, unless you literally own this table, I'm going to have to say…tough luck."

The front man's nostrils flared as he held his chin high. "None of you are welcome here," he said through his teeth, not to attract attention. "You should be thanking your god that we are allowing you to leave quietly."

Parker chuckled. "Actually, it should be the other way

around. You should be thanking me for not bringing hell down on this restaurant. So why don't you do us both a favor and fetch me the person I originally called for."

The front man grabbed Parker by the shoulder, but Parker used his momentum to smash his face into the table and pin him down with the barrel of his gun lodged into his cheek. Gunmen from every angle of the restaurant popped up like a flash mob from their respective tables. The music turned off, and all eyes were on Parker.

"Well, this just got interesting," Parker said.

A middle-aged Chinese man made his way through the gunmen and stopped at their table. He was short with a round face and a braided ponytail. He looked over the crowd, now a mixture of gunmen and frightened patrons. "If you are not with these people, I suggest you leave now," he said. About sixteen patrons scurried out the front exit. The sight of Chinelo made the middle-aged Chinese man drop his head and close his eyes. When he opened them again, it was as if he realized that he was just now seeing reality.

"Who are you?" Parker asked.

"I am Yang Chui, the owner of this restaurant. What are you people doing here?"

"We came here to visit someone," Parker said.

Yang took a beat then said, "There is no one here who wishes to see you."

"I think there is." Parker pointed his gun right at Yang and everyone held their breath.

Yang's demeanor stayed tranquil. He even let his top row of teeth show in a bitter smile. "My grandfather used to tell me this proverb when I was a child. He said, 'a courageous foe is better than a cowardly friend.' You, sir, are neither courageous nor cowardly. You are just a fool absorbed in your own prideful bliss."

Before Parker could reply, a sliding door opened from the lounge upstairs. Jun Li walked out in a black linen suit and a white button up shirt. As he closed the door behind him, Jake caught a glimpse of Koa's face watching with hatred in his eyes.

Jun Li walked along the support rail, tapping his Chinese Cobra ring with the cadence of his footsteps. It was a slow tap that hooked everyone's attention. He took his time as he walked down the stairs and locked eyes with Jake, finally coming face-to-face with him.

Jake's stomach felt empty. His hands shook. He'd imagined the infamous Jun Li to be taller, but when he saw the sea of shooters spread apart to make way for him, he could feel his power.

Jun Li stood next to the Yang and placed a reassuring hand on his shoulder. "Go back upstairs with Koa," he said in Mandarin. "I'll take care of things here."

Yang had a concerned look in his eyes. "This is a public restaurant. We are known on a global scale. I can't have my place on the news."

Jun Li nodded and directed Yang man up the stairs. Once he was in the lounge with Koa, Jun Li signaled for one of the gunmen to block the door. With a snap of his fingers, all the gunmen lowered their weapons and removed all the tables and chairs from the floor, including the one Jake and Chinelo were sitting at—forcing them to stand.

"We have respectfully put away our weapons," Jun Li said to Parker. "I ask that you do the same." Parker threw the front man to Jun Li's feet, and his gun was snatched from him by a henchman.

"What is it that you want, Ethan?"

Jake looked to Parker, wondering how Jun Li knew his first name, but Parker didn't miss a beat.

"I just want to talk," Parker said.

"The floor is yours."

"I was thinking in a less…jammed environment. Somewhere we can both be comfortable."

"I'm very comfortable here. Whatever you have to say to me can be said in front of everyone."

"Okay. I can play that game too. Everyone here is going away for a very long time, to a place that no one knows about. In fact, if everyone could file into a single line, we can get you all piled up in the van out front."

Jun Li chuckled as he turned his sights on Jake. "What about you, Detective Penny? Are you here to read me my rights? To do what's best for your country? Or does Ethan have another speech he's spewing these days?"

Jake's rage rattled his face.

"How's your apartment by the way?"

"You son of a bitch!" Jake rushed towards Jun Li, but Chinelo was able to stop him.

Jun Li's smile turned into a grimacing stare. It was almost as if he were surprised that Jake would try something like that in front of his men. "I'll go with you, Ethan, but you have to do one thing."

"Which is?"

"You have to come get me first. Show me how much I'm really worth." A wall of henchmen barricaded themselves in front of Jun Li. "Destroy them without guns," he commanded in Mandarin.

A group of henchmen formed a large circle around Jake, Parker, and Chinelo, who stood with their backs against each other, waiting for the first attack. The henchmen stalked them, waiting for a chance to strike.

One henchman ran full speed at Chinelo, but Chinelo whipped out a high kick to the face before he could get within arm's reach.

The guys separated from each other's back and now were faced with four henchmen a piece to take on.

Jake started off by setting his feet. Two henchmen in the front and two in the back. One henchman lunged at him, but Jake caught him midair and broke the floor with his back. The second henchman grabbed Jake by the arm and punched him in the face. Jake absorbed that energy and let his anger fuel his momentum. He hit the second henchman in combination to the ground, then immediately raced for the third henchman. A tiger roar from the pit of his stomach gave him the strength to lift the third henchman over his head and slam him to the floor. More henchmen followed, but Jake powered through them one by one. He could hear bone crunching and separating under the skin of the thugs from his knuckles. He turned around to find a knife inches from his face. Parker had stopped a henchman from stabbing him in the skull, and held him in a headlock.

"Watch your six," Parker grunted out as he snapped the man's neck.

Jake was shocked to see Parker had saved his life, but didn't have time to process the moment as a cluster of henchmen rushed towards Parker.

Parker fended them off with kicks and punches. The more henchmen came, the more he demolished. Every kick he threw was bone-crushing. Every punch was muscle-bruising .

One henchman charged at Parker with a kitchen

knife. Parker dodged each stab by inches. He grabbed the henchman by the arm, dislocated his shoulder, tossed him and picked up the knife.

"Come on," he snarled at the remaining henchmen. "I got a real treat for you."

Chinelo was stuck with the most henchmen surrounding him. They circled him, trying to figure out how to overcome his reach advantage. Chinelo backed his way into a corner with a broom. He detached the head of the broom and swung with grace. One by one he picked the henchmen apart, hitting knees, ankles, necks and the crowns of their heads. He sprang from the corner and took out more henchmen in the open space. His strikes were deadly, and his counterattacks were just as lethal. A surge of energy pulsed at the back of his neck. It was like a sixth sense he had for defense. He turned around swinging the stick with brute strength, and splintered it through Koa's head. His body fell beside the knife he'd been wielding.

The room froze. Silence. Koa broke into a seizure, foaming at the mouth, and his eyes reeled into the back of his head. Jun Li rushed to his aid, holding him tight, but Koa convulsed until his body came to a complete stop.

Chinelo dropped what was left of the broom and stared with his hand over his mouth. Even Parker took a hard swallow after seeing everything transpire. All the henchmen spoke sporadically among themselves in Mandarin. Jun Li stood, took a deep breath with his eyes closed, then opened them to face Chinelo. There was a certain calmness that came with Jun Li's anger. One that his enemies would be unwise to take for granted. His knuckles cracked as he tightened his fists and went into his fighting stance.

Jun Li made the first dash. His speed was so impressive that both his feet looked to be off the ground at once.

Chinelo threw a kick, but Jun Li dodged it and attacked his ribs with lightning punches. Everyone could hear his ribs cracking after each punch. Chinelo took a swing to create space and recover his position. His breathing got raspier, and stance became fixed to ease the pain. Jun Li taunted him with a couple of jab steps and Chinelo flinched, never underestimating his agility again. Jun Li charged once more, but this time, he kicked Chinelo's legs. Chinelo dodged as much as he could, but he was moving in quicksand. Jun Li jumped in the air and spin-kicked the sweat off his head.

Chinelo stumbled back as the room spun, but managed to stay on his feet. Jun Li stalked him, and soon Chinelo saw two of him. Chinelo swung wildly, trying to create space.

Jun Li was more amused than defensive. He decided to stop playing with his food and immobilized Chinelo with a blade shoved into his lung. Jun Li forced the blade as deep as he could, all the while staring at Jake .

Chinelo dropped to his knees, gasping for air. He grabbed Jun Li by the arm but didn't have the strength to secure a firm grip. His breaths became heavy. Shorter. A weight on his shoulders bogged him down until he fell to his side.

Jun Li ripped the dagger out and handed it off to a henchman to be wiped clean. He walked toward Jake and Parker. Once he was within arm's reach, he gave them both a glance over. "I don't think I'll be going anywhere with you tonight," he said in a somber voice. "However, a question still remains… What are we to do with you two?"

All the henchmen prepared for Jun Li's next command. Jake surveyed the room. They were outnumbered. Outgunned. No way out. He contemplated making the first move, until one henchman rose from the bunch.

"Sir," the henchman started in Mandarin. "The authorities have been notified. They are eight minutes out."

Jun Li pondered to himself. His smile suggested that he enjoyed having their fate in his hands. "No. Let them stay," he said to the henchman. "Why wait on them?" "We have two men of the law ready to get a head start on the crime scene." He winked at Parker before turning his back on them. With a snap of his fingers, everyone filed out of the restaurant. "I'll be seeing you guys around."

A couple of henchmen went to pick up Koa. "Leave him. I want everyone to see what they did to my boy ."

Jun Li's eyes became glassy as he left with his henchmen close behind.

Jake walked towards Chinelo's lifeless body, but Parker stopped him. "We have to go."

Jake snatched his arm away. "We just can't leave them here."

"And where are we going to take them?"

"You're telling me with all your power you can't do anything about this?"

"I can make people move. That's not the problem. What I can't do is make them not see a double murder. So, if you want to sit here and explain to the police why you have two dead people in the middle of the floor, be my guest." Parker walked to the front entrance.

Jake looked over Chinelo and Koa. More bodies added to his conscience. He turned to leave, but Chinelo's cough stopped him. His chest rose slightly, but the rest of his body wasn't moving. In the Army, Jake lived by the warrior's ethos of never leaving a man behind, but there was nothing he could do. His values had deserted him a long time ago. Jake watched as Chinelo took his last breath.

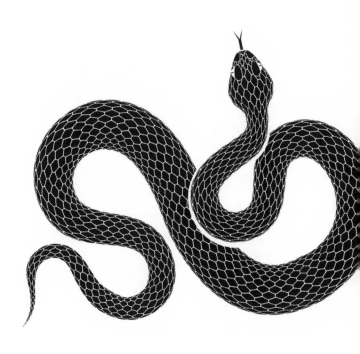

29.

Jake and Parker entered what was left of Do Shen's house. The musty debris irritated Jake's nose. He coughed to clear his scratchy throat, but the itchiness just clawed its way back up.

"No one will look for you here," Parker said. "At least not tonight. Don't worry, you won't be here for long, but it's the best I can do for you right now."

Jake turned with a perplexed face. "The best for me? You're not staying?"

"No, I have to check in. Do a status report."

"Then I'll come with you."

"Absolutely not. Staying completely off the radar is the best thing for both of us right now. We are so near to closing this, and I don't want to jeopardize it by risking our safety."

"How are we any closer than before? It seems like we're in the same place, if not worse."

"We boxed Jun Li into a corner. Tonight wasn't about bringing him in. It was about letting him know that the end is near. Guys like him, you just don't slap handcuffs on them. It has to be handled behind the scenes. He's going bring everything he has, and when he does, he'll make a mistake. That's when we'll take him down."

"So, am I just supposed to stay here with my thumb up my ass?"

"Until I get a feel for what's going on out there…yes." Jake stormed away. "Where are you going?" Parker called out.

"I need a minute."

In the bathroom, Jake questioned his integrity in the cracked mirror. His whole world was crumbling around him, and there was nothing he could do. He washed his face with cold water, then pulled out his prescription bottle with an assortment drugs inside. The bottle rattled in his hand, as he forced himself to pour the pills down the drain.

He placed his forehead on the mirror and felt a solid presence behind it. He pressed the mirror with the tip of his fingers and watched the outside of the mirror retract as he let go. Jake opened the mirror, which doubled as a medicine cabinet. The inside was rusted out, and a revolver was strapped to the back of the mirror. Do Shen's paranoia became Jake's tool to search for the truth.

Parker walked around the living room until he stepped on a green notebook hidden under the debris. The cover had a gold Chinese symbol, and there was a ribbon bookmarked midway through. Parker opened the book to see everything written in Chinese. His better judgment told him to toss it, but not before he went to the bookmarked page. There were sketches of a custom casket with meticulous detail. The next page had more designs, along with a business card: Greenwich Funeral Home / Adam Greenwich, Jr. / Director

Before Parker could connect the dots, a sharp blow to the back of his head knocked him face-first to the ground. He rolled over, holding his throbbing head and trying to focus his blurry vision on the shadowy figure descending upon him. When his vision centered, he saw the barrel of the revolver under his right eye, and Jake on the other end. "Jake, what the hell are you doing?" he asked calmly.

Jake cocked back the hammer and pressed the cold steel against Parker's flesh. "What are you looking for? And what is your connection with Jun Li?"

"Let's take a second to breathe, okay? You're not thinking logically."

"Don't try to get into my head. Just answer the questions."

"I don't have any connection with Jun Li."

"Don't lie! He called you by your first name."

"What does that mean? I'm a part of one of the many covert operations in the *world* trying to bring him down. You think he's not doing his homework too? I'm surprised he didn't call me by my childhood nickname."

"That still doesn't answer the question of what you're looking for."

"I feel like if we take a moment to collect our thoughts, maybe we can—"

Jake let off a round inches away from Parker's ear.

Parker's ear rang with stabbing pain.

Jake pressed the sizzling barrel on Parker's cheek. Parker winced as the mixture of gunpowder and flesh cooked under his nose.

"The next one will be the last one. Now, tell me what you're looking for."

"You think by knowing more than you already do, it's going to change anything? Nothing changes!"

"Last chance."

"And then what, Jake? You go back to living your shit life in a burnt apartment? You should know better than anyone by now that's not how it works. You're scared and confused, and I get that. Killing me isn't going to solve that issue. If you put the gun down, I promise to forget this happened."

"You sound very confident speaking to someone who doesn't have much to lose." Jake held the trigger tight making the hammer creep back. Parker's eyes widened. The barrel ticked like a minute hand, getting closer to releasing a round.

"All right, all right, I'll tell you what I'm looking for."

Jake loosened his trigger finger. "Start talking."

Parker took a moment to catch his breath. Until now, he'd always known that Jake wasn't capable of pulling the trigger without a good reason. But this time, he wasn't so sure. "We're looking for…critical information."

"Could you be a little more specific?"

"Information that could rupture our national security. Destroy the Geneva Convention and turn us back into a world where death by the thousands was a Tuesday. For the sake of the United States of America, we need to retrieve this information before Jun Li or…prepare for another global war."

"What the hell is this information?"

"Do Shen's collateral ."

"I thought you said it didn't exist."

"Now I'm telling you it does, and no one is taking any chances that it's not real. There are records of covert operations conducted by V.E.N.O.M. Everything from when, where and who ordered the jobs that literally dictated how we wrote history. That's not even the best part. There's one thing that everyone wants that's included in this data… The Catalogue."

The way Parker said it sent chills up Jake's spine. "The Catalogue?"

"The real identities of every person enlisted as a merc for V.E.N.O.M. All two-hundred and fifty-six of them. That list alone is worth at least one hundred million dollars and can cause ten times as much damage. Whoever's in possession of it will become the closest thing to God on earth ."

"Or a target," Jake said. He let the revolver slide from his hand. His mind went blank as he walked toward the broken window. He didn't fear much, but this came with a terror he'd never felt before. He turned around to see Parker already on his feet. He prepared for any repercussion Parker was willing to throw at him, but Parker simply dusted his suit off and stood his ground.

"Are you sure this is a real thing?" Jake asked.

"I'm sure. Every country that was involved with V.E.N.O.M. is taking extreme measures to prevent their own exposure and use The Catalogue to their advantage against others. Including us."

Jake thought about Zasha being on The Catalogue. It was all coming together now.

"I told you we weren't always diplomatic."

"What happens if no one finds it?"

"Then the myth gets buried with the legend tomorrow. Sure, there will be some people still looking for it, but if they haven't found it after all this time, then humanity will live to see the sun another day."

As Jake turned his attention away for a second, Parker picked up the green book with the casket plans and stuffed it in his left breast pocket. "Listen, I'm going back to the city to check in. You sit tight. We're going to end this thing together. Do Shen will be buried, Jun Li will move on empty-handed, and you will be on a beach somewhere sipping pina coladas on the government's dime."

"Somewhere like Fiji?"

Parker paused. A smile followed soon after. "Sure. Whatever you want."

"Hey," Jake said as Parker tried to leave. "I'm sorry… about just now."

Parker's smile was bright even on a bruised face. "Don't mention it. We're all a little tense, but this'll be over soon enough. I'll see you in the morning."

"And thank you… For what you did at the restaurant."

Parker nodded and left.

* * *

Jake slept on a couch with his legs hanging off the end. It was ironic that the tensest part of his life was also the moment when he could sleep on his own. Maybe the past few days had taken so much energy from him that it was impossible for him not to sleep.

A noise coming from the back of the house jolted him awake. He rose from the dusty couch and surveyed the area carefully. Everything seemed to be in order, but he knew better than that. With the revolver in his hand, he crept to the back door. He could see no farther than his nose, so his steps were cautiously planted.

At the back door, he aligned himself with the trim. His breathing slowed to a gasp. He mentally counted down, then emerged from the swinging back door with the revolver aimed to kill. Nothing but trees and an old swing set swaying in the wind. Jake retreated into the house, closing and locking the door.

"That's some type of security you got there, cowboy," a familiar voice said from the shadows. Jake popped into action with his gun pointed at Zasha.

"Please, let's skip the formalities," she said, walking toward him. "We have a lot to discuss."

She dressed in a black skin-tight one piece and a black skull cap. Her perfume was faint but still enough for Jake to pick up. He lowered his gun. "What are you doing here?" he asked.

"Nice to see you too. By the way, you're welcome. I know with all the chaos you've been involved in over the past couple of days it might have slipped your mind that I saved your life."

"For all I know you could have planted that bomb yourself."

Zasha crept closer, her hips swaying in her natural catwalk. Her piercing green eyes caught every ray of light that found its way into the house. "That's not my style. I'm more up close and personal." She stood on her toes, hovering right below his chin.

Jake grabbed her by the arms, breaking her trance, and she shivered from his cold grip. They stared into each other's eyes, and Jake was brought back to the last time they'd seen each other. Deep in his heart, he could never hurt her. The thought of someone so sensual possibly being the end of him made his mental battle with her that much more arduous. "Parker told me about The Catalogue," he finally said.

Her face turned white as she shook loose from his grip. She turned her back and crossed her arms.

"You're on there, aren't you? That's why you wanted to be so close to the case. So when the opportunity presented itself, you could swipe it right from under our noses."

"There's no proof that it exists," she said over her shoulder.

"Parker says he's sure it exists. Surely you agree with him if you blew your cover for it."

"I did what I did to save your life."

"You don't care about me."

Zasha turned back around, her eyes glassy. "You don't know anything about me. Especially the things that I care about, so don't address me with that judgmental tone."

"I'll tell you what I do know. I know that you're a liar. No matter how you try to spin it, your objective was to find The Catalogue. It was never about helping me. You used me. You used my vulnerability and tried to manipulate me into helping you. You're a criminal."

Zasha scoffed. "Look at the pot calling the kettle black."

"What are you talking about?"

"You don't know? It's the biggest headline in the news right now. New York homicide detective wanted for questioning in connection with a string of civil rights violations and the murder of a Chinese diplomat's son."

"You're lying."

"Why would I?"

She had a point. It had been proven before that the people he was up against had the means and the motive to let this narrative leak. "None of it is true. Parker can vouch for me. Ethan Parker. He's with the NSA. He was there when the boy was murdered."

"That's funny because the reports didn't mention an Ethan Parker. They don't mention anyone except you."

"That's impossible. There were several witnesses on the scene. They saw me with two other guys. One of them was murdered as well."

"Only one murder was reported... The one they pinned on you."

"I have to find Parker." Jake rushed to the front door.

"If you leave now, you'll risk being taken in. Once they have you in their clutches, there's no way of getting out. They will make this story airtight, with no loose ends."

Jake stopped in place, still facing the door.

"This Parker fellow, have you ever seen his credentials?"

"What?" he asked over his shoulder.

"Obviously he has some type of clout to keep your head above water for so long, but with your own eyes, have you ever visually seen his credentials? His ID? A badge? A piece of paper stating that he even has the authority to be here?"

Jake thought back to all the times Parker had thrown his weight around. Not once did he even glance at Parker's credentials, let alone question him. Then there was the one time he was handed Parker's badge, but Parker had quickly snatched it away. When he really thought about it, he didn't know Parker at all .

"I'm going to take that as a no," Zasha continued. "So, in reality, you don't know who you're working for, what he has you doing or the reason for it. Is this some kind of fantasy for you? Wasn't good enough to get recruited into the FBI or the CIA , so you happily joined the ride just so you could say you were a part of something."

"No."

"Then what is it? My theory is you're just a lost puppy looking for any excuse to forget about your dead family."

"Stop it!" Jake turned in a fury and stomped right up to her. "Stop it right now. Don't you *ever* bring up my family again! You understand me?"

Jake's voice heightened all her senses. "Are the pieces starting to fall in place for you, Jake? Or are you too blind to see what's already in front of you?"

"Why did you come here? You don't need me. You're out for The Catalogue just like everyone else, so why come here?!"

"Because I can help you."

"That's a lie. All you people do is lie. Just like you probably lied to me about your sisters."

Zasha threw a fierce slap across Jake's face that echoed through the house. The room fell silent. Jake noticed her hand twitching from the blow. She hurt herself more than she'd hurt him, but she did leave a blistering hand mark on his face. He went into the kitchen and put some water and ice in a bowl. He took a towel and soaked it in the ice water, then took her hand and gently wrapped it in the towel.

Zasha's breathing calmed down as she fell into Jake's stare.

Jake pulled her close and kissed her.

"Wait," she said. She slid a razor blade from under her tongue. "Last line of defense."

She grabbed the back of Jake's neck and climbed him until she was attached to his waist. Jake took her to the couch that could barely fit him, but they both made it work as they tore each other's clothes off.

30.

Jack woke to birdsong and sunlight. It was the most extended sleep he'd experienced in nearly two years. It almost felt like he was waking up to a regular morning—almost. He opened his eyes to see Parker's blurry smile. "Rise and shine, sweetheart."

Jake fully woke up and searched around the room. "Where's—"

"The girl? She's hanging out for a bit." Parker nodded slightly to the left. Jake looked over his shoulder to see Zasha keeping her balance on a wooden table that wobbled at any sudden movement. The only cover she had was her bra and panties. Her tippy-toes were rushed with blood. Her hands were bound together, and her mouth gagged. The only thing that held her up was the noose tied around her neck, hung from a wood beam on the ceiling. Jake rushed to her aid, but stopped when Parker pulled out a gun.

"Ah-ah-ah, not so fast. Sit."

Jake sat with his focus on Zasha.

"I have to say, Jake…I'm beyond disappointed. I mean, here I am slaving away to build my trust with you and you're literally in bed with the enemy. How do you think that makes me feel?"

"It's not what you think."

Parker laughed. "It's not what I think, he says. Do you hear yourself? Can you even fathom how severely you've damaged your credibility? Did you think I wouldn't find out? How long have you two been working together?"

"We weren't working together."

"Okay, how long has she had you brainwashed?"

"Parker, listen, she was helping me a little bit, but this was before I knew she was a Venom. You were keeping me in the dark ; she was guiding me through it. What did you expect?"

"For one, to keep your pants on. But as a man, I can't fully blame you. Her body is nothing short of amazing." Parker caressed her thigh with two fingers. He inhaled her natural scent and couldn't help shimmying his shoulders. "I must confess, I undressed her with my eyes when I first saw her at the hotel."

Jake didn't say a word. His focus was on Zasha balancing on the table.

"Don't worry, nothing happened," Parker continued. "Not in real life anyway."

"She doesn't care about The Catalogue."

Parker rolled his eyes. "You don't say. So the very person we're trying to put away, the one you're working with, mind you, doesn't care about the one thing on earth that exposes who she really is? The one thing that could make her rich beyond her wildest dreams and make her country the number-one powerhouse of the world. You're telling me she doesn't care about that?" Parker thought to himself for a moment. "Tell me, why should either one of you leave this house alive?"

Jake had no answer. He knew how all of this looked, and after last night, Parker was repaying him with the favor of distrust.

Parker grew impatient with Jake's silence and kicked the table over. The noose constricted on Zasha's neck as she dangled in the air. Her face lit up instantly.

"Why should either of you live?!"

Zasha's eyes turned beet red as each passing second decreased her air flow. The veins in her neck grew so thick they began to pulsate.

Jake's heart pounded out of his chest as he watched Zasha dance with life and death.

"You're running out of time," Parker said.

"Kill me!" Jake yelled. "Kill me and let her live. I deserve to die!"

"It doesn't work like that, Jake. You can't just go parading around with a Venom and expect the repercussions to be that easy."

Suddenly the dots connected in Jake's head. It was all about bringing one man down. "The parade. The parade!" Jake stood up to Parker's gun in his chest. "Jun Li will be at the parade. That's where his next attack is. We go there and stop it before anything can happen."

Parker stared coldly at Jake, but the wheels were turning behind those soulless eyes. "I guess that is a possibility. What about her?"

"We use her to tie everything together," Jake said quickly. "Catalogue or no Catalogue, there's still a lot of questions that need to be answered. Those loose ends can be tied tight if we have a Venom in our possession *alive*. She takes the fall, everything else gets buried with Do Shen."

Parker stepped back to create space. "And what about you? Where do you fit in all of this?"

"I'll fit wherever you put me."

Parker pondered the idea for each precious second

passing. Zasha's body was cemented in Jake's pupils as she swung in the air. A subtle twitch from her foot was the only sign of life from her numb body. Parker finally shot the rope , and she came crashing down to the floor, her body making a hard thud.

Jake ran to her aid as she slowly regained consciousness. Her neck was branded with rope burns, and every breath was a wheezing struggle for her.

"You better hope you're right, Jake."

* * *

Parker made Jake zip-tie Zasha to a chair by her wrists and ankles. His eyes were filled with guilt, but she wasn't upset with Jake. She knew he was only doing what was necessary.

"Hurry it up," Parker said. "We only have a few hours before the parade begins. I wouldn't want Jun Li to miss our surprise visit."

Jake looked at Zasha with his pupils wide, trying to signal something to her. "I'm coming back for you," he whispered. He kissed her deeply. When their lips parted, Jake made sure to look into her eyes one last time and give her a subtle nod. Zasha locked her lips as he walked toward the door.

Parker came behind him and checked the zip ties' security. "We can make this a little tighter." He squeezed out a couple more clicks in each zip tie, cutting off some circulation. "There. That's much better. Now, don't worry about a thing, sweet pea. This'll all be over sooner than you expect."

Zasha mustered up whatever moisture she had left in

her mouth and spat in Parker's face. "Go to hell," she said, her voice hoarse.

Parker took a linen cloth from his pocket, wiped the spit away and gave her a charming smile. "You're very beautiful. I can see why anyone would fall for you." Parker leaned in closer and whispered, "Maybe later, when it's all said and done, we can sit in a room and you could give me your Venom name. Hopefully by then you'll still have your lips." Parker tied a gag around her mouth, winked and exited the house behind Jake.

* * *

The Bullit shot down I-87 south in restricting silence. Jake's demeanor was straight-edge, but his mind was racing a mile a minute. Parker talked on the phone as he drove, but would glance over at Jake every now and then. When he hung up the phone, Jake's face was boiling over.

"There's a fine line between wanting to do what's right and actually doing it," Parker said. "The greatest thing V.E.N.O.M. ever did was exist right in front of our eyes and still be able to do the things they did. Like it or not, everything I do is for my country, no matter how deep my hands are in the shit. You need to figure out which side you're really on, Jake."

A muted response from Jake threw more fuel on Parker's fire.

"You can be mad at me for roping up your little girlfriend and everything else I've done up until this point, but I will *not* let you take for granted how critical this mission is, or let you make hasty decisions like the one you made back there. She could have slit your throat in the middle of the night, you know that right?"

"But she didn't," Jake finally said.

"So that makes her a good person? You think if you had The Catalogue in your hand, she wouldn't chop it off to get to it?"

"She doesn't care about The Catalogue, Parker. Neither did Chinelo. The only person that seems to give damn about it is you."

"Oh, well that's just great. That makes perfect sense. Open and shut case. We're done. What else did she say to you, Jake? Did she tell about her role in V.E.N.O.M.? How she's ruined thousands of lives? No?" Parker scoffed. "I bet she told you the sob story about her family though. Her struggles as a child, maybe? I know for sure she questioned you about who I am and what I'm doing here. Am I getting warm?"

He was on fire, but Jake wasn't going to tell him that.

"Wake up, Jake. It's all a ploy to manipulate and confuse you. She's a sleeper agent with connections to Russia, sent here for one objective and one objective only: to find and bring back The Catalogue for her country. She will complete that mission by any means necessary. If you can't see that, then you're more of a danger to us than Jun Li."

The car fell silent again.

* * *

Parker stopped at a neighborhood between East Sixty-Sixth and Lexington Ave. The streets were filled with people walking in one direction, all in colorful costumes.

"The parade route is along 5th Avenue, three blocks south of here. It goes from 64th street all the way to 86th, which is too much ground to cover by one person. So, I have some of my guys posted at some hot spots. They're there to scope out the land, but also for your protection."

"You mean to keep an eye on me," Jake said.

"Well, you are a wanted fugitive who's been connected to a Venom, so you'll have to excuse me if I want to hedge all of my bets."

"And what will you be doing during all of this?"

"I have an important lead to follow up with at the funeral home before they release Do Shen for the parade. Some last-minute checks that couldn't be done and have the parade covered at the same time. Just keep a low profile, and you'll be fine. I'll be back as soon as possible."

Jake opened the car door, but Parker grabbed him by the arm before he could leave. "And Jake… don't do anything stupid. The guys on-site are authorized to take out *anyone* they feel is a threat to the mission. Not to mention your little girlfriend's quality of life depends on how you conduct yourself out there, so watch yourself."

31.

Zasha's hands were going numb, and so were her toes. Her restraints had been so tight they had broken through her skin and left streaks of blood. She adjusted her jaw back and forth, making her wince in pain. She slowly used her shoulder to remove the gag, careful not to strain her neck more than it already was. One milestone at a time. Her lips parted, and out slid the razor Jake had passed to her. She bent forward, each degree introducing a new level of pain, and skimmed the razor over the zip-tie with precision. Her lower back locked up, but she knew she couldn't stop. Her will to live wouldn't allow her. Plus, she already had it in her mind that she was going to kill Parker when she got out of this. It was only about one step at a time. She cut the zip tie on her left wrist, and carefully lifted her arm. Flexing her hand subdued the numbness, but she wasn't out of the woods yet. Before she could cut the right side, the sound of tires on gravel and screeching brakes snatched her attention. Two car doors opened and closed, followed by two different sets of footsteps approaching the house. Zasha quickly placed the blade under her tongue followed by putting the gag back in her mouth. She turned the broken zip-tie over her wrist and sat stiffly in the chair.

The front door creaked open, and two men entered the house. The first man, named Gus, was tall and skinny with a patchy beard. He was middle-aged and had four gold caps on the fangs of his teeth. His accomplice, Roger, was a heavyset man, well over three-hundred pounds, with a sausage nose and severe acne. He carried a black leather bag that was as big as his belly.

"Well, well, well, what do we have here?" Gus said. He walked around Zasha to get a better look. His knee-high rubber boots squeaked over the rusty wood floors. "They didn't say the subject was gonna be this gorgeous. What's your name, sweetheart?"

Zasha kept her lips sealed and her body stiff. The broken zip tie lay next to her foot, but they didn't seem to notice. Gus tried to caress her face, but she avoided his dirty finger, revealing the burns on her neck. "Now why did they gone and do that?" he asked, loosening the gag to observe closer. "What's the matter? You don't wanna get to know me? I'm actually a pretty good guy depending on how you act."

"Why do you always do that?" Roger interrupted.

Gus rolled his eyes. "What now?"

"You always get too personal with the subjects."

"Well excuse me for not being a fucking robot on the job all the time."

"The instructions were crystal clear. They want the job quick and without a trace. We need to be focused." Roger pulled out an extra duty tarp and laid it under and around Zasha. He then pulled out a leather apron. The strap settled in the rolls of his neck. He carefully pulled out a collection of knives and placed them on a folded towel laid out on the coffee table. Each blade shimmered brighter than the last. He seemed to have been thorough with his ritual. The sight put a pause in Zasha's heart.

While Roger prepared his station, Gus studied Zasha's body more. His lustful eyes traveled from her face down to her breasts. He pulled out his machete and caressed her flesh with the tip, from her chest all the way down to her belly button. "I know we're supposed to be professionals and all, but...I think she deserves the best five minutes of her life. What do you think?"

Roger stopped setting up his cutting station, and his chin wobbled as he shook his head. "No. Absolutely not! We're on a strict schedule as it is. The job is supposed to be clean, which means you would have to be completely sterile. To be completely sterile, you would have to use a condom. To get a condom would mean you would have to go into a store. And to go into a store creates—"

"Witnesses. I know."

"So you should also know that it's just not possible."

Gus stabbed his machete into the floor next to Zasha's leg. She took a mental note of it. "Aw come on, five minutes isn't gonna change anything. When was the last time we got a subject like this? Eight months ago? Look at her. This isn't someone you just let go by. Plus, I got some condoms in the truck. I'll be done before you set up." Gus walked to the door.

"Gus," Roger started. "Bring one for me too," he said, not making eye contact.

"Attaboy!" Gus said as he clapped. He turned to Zasha and said, "Looks like today is your lucky, cutie pie. You're fixing to get the best eight and a half minutes of your life." Gus hummed his way outside to the truck.

Roger removed his leather apron and wiped the beads of sweat from his forehead. "He's right you know? You're probably the most beautiful subject we've ever had." Roger wheezed after every sentence as he took in Zasha's beauty. "It kinda makes me wonder what you did to deserve this." He crept closer without making eye contact.

Zasha wanted to move, but couldn't give up her position just yet.

"Gus and I have been doing this for a long time, and as crude as Gus wants to seem, we're not complete savages. It's just a job. We actually try to be as humane as possible by giving our subjects morphine even if their terrible people. But you really pissed someone off. In fact, they paid extra to omit that part of the process. It's a shame, because besides the fact that I'm excruciatingly keen to routine…I really hate the screams of a woman. High frequencies bother my ears." Roger ran his swollen fingers across Zasha's face. Her skin was the softest thing he'd ever felt in his life. And then his guilt began to soften his eyes. He pulled out a syringe from his bag and flashed it in her face. "I have some morphine in this syringe. I know I'm not supposed to give you this, but I'd be willing to overlook that if you'll do something for me. The client mentioned something about a secret name. Are you familiar with that?"

Zasha nodded.

"If you give me the name, I can make sure we do this the humane way. What do you say?" His breath smelled of rotten meat and made her lips curl into her mouth.

Her breathing stuttered as she worked her lips to whisper, "Eclipse. My secret name is Eclipse."

Roger scoffed into a nervous laugh. He didn't think it was going to be that easy, but he was relieved, to say the least. "God, you're so pretty. It's a shame, because by the time Gus is done with you, you're goin g to be all cut up and bashed to a pulp. Then I get his leftovers. I've never gone first before."

"That seems to be the real pity here," Zasha said.

Roger took a beat, then finally asked, "What do you mean?"

"Obviously you're the one carrying this dynamic duo. Without you, bean stalk over there would have been caught after his first job. As far as I can tell, you're the real leader."

"Why are you saying this?"

"My time is up, and I've accepted that. Like you said, I pissed someone off that I really shouldn't have. If I could do one last thing on this earth, it'll be to give someone like you exactly what they deserve."

Roger took a hard swallow as he eyed the front door. Still no sign of Gus. He put away the syringe, planted his face under her chin and took a deep breath. The smell of flowers from her breasts put a fire under his hormones. His tongue lathered up her neck and chest.

Zasha's skin crawled under the surface from the combination of his slimy tongue and chapped lips pressing against her delicate skin, but she kept her heartbeat steady. She reached for the machete, grabbing the handle one finger at a time. While Roger was living his fantasy, Zasha slid the blade out of her mouth and clamped down hard. She found a clear spot on his sweaty neck and tore into his flesh over and over again. Roger screamed and backed away, holding his open wound.

Zasha's mouth looked like it belonged to a crazed vampire after a delightful meal.

"Are you crazy?!" Roger stuttered. He took a staggering step forward while reaching for one of his knives. Zasha pulled the machete from the floorboard and thrust it through his sternum.

Roger stood before her, wheezing for air. He rapidly blinked while trying to make sense of what just happened.

Zasha took the blade from her mouth and sawed off the other zip tie. Once she got her right wrist free, she went to work on her ankles, but Roger was no longer in control of his body. All three-hundred pounds tilted over and collapsed on her, flattening the chair. The machete lodged itself deeper into his chest and sliced its way through his spinal cord.

Zasha clamped her mouth shut so she wouldn't scream. The bulging veins in her neck settled once she let out small gasps of air. Suddenly, the front door creaked open, followed by the sound of rubber boots squeaking toward her.

"Sorry it took so long," Gus said. "I couldn't find but one condom. So, unless you're willing to share, I don't—" Gus looked down to see Roger's lifeless body hunched over Zasha. A smile cracked on his dirt-tainted face. "You dirty little hound. You done got started without me. That's all right, every dog has his day. So much for sterile, huh?" Gus noticed Roger wasn't moving much. "Well, don't let my presence stop you. Go 'head and finish." The silence raised Gus' suspicion. "Rog? Don't tell me you have stage fright now."

Gus tried to get his attention by placing his hand on Roger's back, but he quickly retracted when he found his fingertips covered in blood. "What the hell? Roger?!" Gus pushed Roger's body on its side, and leaned in to grab Zasha, but she split Gus' right eye open with the razor . Gus fell back, holding his eye and screaming his lungs out. Zasha cut the last two zip ties at her ankles and hobbled for the front door , but Gus cut her off, wielding a ten-inch knife. "You think you're so cute, don't you? Did it feel good to kill Roger? Killing a man that was just doing his job?! You gone pay for that," he said with a cracked voice.

Zasha pulled her hair over her shoulder and used the razor to cut it. There was no need to give Gus any advantage. She threw her hair on the floor along with the razor. Her almost naked body was bloody from head to toe. Her ankles were throbbing, and she could barely feel her fingers, but she was never willing to back down from a challenge for her life. The way she saw it, this was just one more obstacle in the way of getting to the person she really wanted. She spotted the station of knives on the table, but they were too far. The door was closer, but where would she go if she was able to step foot outside? He was hurt, but she was worse. She couldn't outrun him, and he would slit her throat before she could call for help. Her best chance was to assess and then attack. His right side was vulnerable because of the missing eye, so that's where she would strike first. She readied herself in a fighting stance and waited. After all, patience was the most reliable weapon she could use.

Gus smiled. "You're just a feisty little cunt, aren't you? It kinda turns me on." He went into a defensive orthodox stance with the knife ready to swing. "Come on, bitch! I'm gone have fun with you."

Zasha didn't move. She had the patience of a lioness waiting for its prey to make a mistake. "Do you know how many women get sexually abused in the course of their lifetime? Of course you don't. You never had to live with that type of information. But I expect you to die with it."

Gus charged at her, swinging the knife at full power. She could feel the wind cutting along her body as she avoided each lethal blow. Gus stabbed the knife into the wall so hard trying to hit her that it got stuck. Zasha landed two punches to the ribs, and one kick to the jaw. Gus stumbled back without the knife, and Zasha gave him no room to recover. She foot-swept him to the ground, but he quickly rolled to safety. Gus squared back into his fighting stance. His breathing turned into a heavy wheeze.

"I've had fighters before," he said. "Nothing quite like you. I think you'll make a fine mantel piece."

Zasha went on the attack first, with a fierce roar behind her swings. Gus couldn't keep her sharp knuckles from piercing his body as she picked him apart. His fist grazed her chin, but she countered with a crushing uppercut that almost lifted Gus off his feet. Zasha sprinted and flew in the air to land one more blow, but Gus caught her and tossed her into the wall. Zasha tried to stand, but the ground tilted right under her feet, and she fell back down. Gus grabbed her by the neck and lobbed her across the room once more. He stumbled over to her body, squatted over her stomach and began to strangle her.

Zasha's arms flailed around looking for something to grab, but nothing was in reach. She felt as if she was falling from the sky and lightheadedness came with a plunge. Everything started to turn black expect Gus' face. His features seemed to be more prevalent than ever. The drool dripping from his jagged-toothed smile. The vein popping from his forehead. The blood dripping from the gash she had cursed him with. As a last resort, she grabbed the right side of his face and lodged her thumb knuckle deep into his eye socket.

Gus tried to hide his pain as he screamed through his teeth.

Zasha went deeper into the wound until Gus couldn't hold back anymore. He released her neck and shouted on the floor.

"You fucking bitch!" he yelled. "I'm gonna kill you!"

Zasha rolled over to her hands and knees, trying to catch her breath. She rose to her feet and planted herself on Gus' back, locking in a chokehold. "You like that?" she whispered in his ear. "Everything I do turns you on, right? Tell me you like it."

Gus staggered to his feet as he gasped for air. He tried to shake Zasha off, but her vice grip wouldn't let go. He ran, back first, into a cabinet and fell to the floor. Zasha screamed in pain but held on tight. Gus stumbled to his feet again and backtracked as hard as he could into the wall, putting a hole through it. Zasha's back seized up, but letting go was not an option. Gus fell to the floor and wasn't getting up for a third time. The room started to spin for him. His sights zeroed in on his only hope: the knife station left by his dead partner. He bear-crawled on his knees towards the station. Zasha tried to anchor him down, but she wasn't heavy enough. Gus slithered one leg at a time, inching toward his salvation. His shaking hand came within inches of the cloth to pull the knives down. One more push and he could have a weapon in his possession. Zasha locked her legs around his waist and rolled onto her back, becoming a boa constrictor squeezing the life from her prey. Her eyes bulged with rage as she kept any air from coming in or out of Gus' body.

"321,000 per year," she whispers. "321,000 are violated every year by people like you." Gus' body tremored violently, trying to make a desperate attempt to break the hold, until his body stiffened to a halt.

Zasha locked her hold so tight she couldn't feel her arm. She couldn't feel anything. She was completely numb. She pushed Gus off her and lay still, staring at the ceiling. Her eyes were too dry to cry. For a second she thought about her childhood with her sisters. That was the last time she'd had a feeling like this. A part of her died on the rusty floor with Gus and Roger. A part she would never see again.

32.

Jake searched through the crowded sidewalk, looking for anything that could be deemed out of the ordinary. The street was filled with colorful dragons and dancers performing next to monumental floats. The majority of the crowd was of Asian descent, and all seemed to be focused on Jake. The sparkling firecrackers triggered a panic in the pit of Jake's stomach, but he poised himself as best as he could. It had been thirty-two hours since a drop of alcohol had touched his lips, and about the same since he'd swallowed a painkiller. He realized that his sobriety was the spark for his paranoia to reach uncharted levels. He noticed every bump from each passing person. Every conversation seemed to be aimed at him, even if the person wasn't speaking English. The fact that everyone was a suspect to him, and that anyone could be conspiring to take his life, left him standing in place.

A thunderous boom from a cannon shot out red, yellow and white confetti. Everyone cheered. Jake could feel his chest tightening and his breath getting shorter. He closed his eyes and let the confetti fall on his face. He took three deep breaths then imagined his daughter's face in front of him. Her smile brought his heart to a resting a beat. It was so real that he could hear traces of her giggle. He opened his eyes and, like a magnet, spotted Jun Li staring down the block, sitting in a roped-off area next to a food vendor. A table and chair was prepared for a guest. The allure of Jun Li's nonchalant demeanor pulled Jake in closer. For a moment, he felt safe walking toward him with all these people as witnesses. But that feeling faded with every approaching step. Jake walked into the lion's den surrounded by four of Jun Li's men. Jun Li gestured for him to sit, and he did. A woman came over and poured them both tea. Jake was too busy staring at Jun Li to notice his tea steaming next to his hand. Jun Li took a sip and savored the taste as he watched the festivities. "What do you think?" he asked.

"A bit too loud for my liking," Jake replied.

Jun Li turned toward him with an intrigued look. "But that's the best part. I had a lot of brothers and sisters growing up in an orphanage. As children, we would chase behind every firecracker we would hear. Beijing always had the best ones. There were so many little explosions that the smoke would cloud our lungs until we choked and couldn't run anymore. I've noticed that the firecrackers in America are significantly weaker."

Jake slowly stroked his ring finger with his thumb. "What do you want from me?"

"I wanted to meet you, Detective."

"We've already met."

"I meant officially. It would seem that our binding commitments have prevented us from actually encountering one another like civilized human beings. Ironically, our cat-and-mouse game has been the gravitational pull that has forced us to meet face-to-face right now. So, here we are."

"Here we are."

They both stared at each other for a moment. There

was a certain peculiarity about Jake that interested Jun Li. "You should try your tea before it gets cold. It's the best my people have to offer." Jake guzzled the tea in one sitting. There was a nice burn in the back of his throat, but it went down smooth.

"Good?" Jun Li asked.

Jake approved with a single grunt.

"Now, back to business. As much as I've enjoyed our little exchange, I think I speak for both of us when I say it's been going on for far too long to benefit either one of us. My people have died. Your people have died. My plans have been spoiled, and your attempt to capture me has slipped from your fingertips time and time again. My question for you is: why can't we meet in the middle?"

"Why would I want to do that?"

"Well, for one, you're a fugitive with some severe allegations. From what I'm hearing, it won't take a trial to find you guilty. I can easily have that go away from my level, and you can have your life back. No, you can have a better life than before."

"My life will never be the same. Not you or anyone for that matter can make a difference. You just want The Catalogue."

Jun Li chuckled. "What makes you think I don't already have it?"

"Because you're sitting here, pleading with me to take my foot off your neck."

Jun Li's grin turned into a menacing scowl. "You think that I'm *pleading* with you?"

"Why else would you invite me to this fancy tea party?"

Jun Li scoffed. He looked to his men, who showed no emotion, then back to Jake. "Are you familiar with the term 'blood is thicker than water'?"

"Yeah, I've heard it."

"What do you think that means, Detective?"

Jake sighed. He wondered where Parker's men were. His leg bounced under the table, but his face was calm. "It means family bonds are more important than temporary relationships."

Jun Li clicked his teeth as he shook his head. "Just like an American. You take something of great value, and you dilute it to something so…rudimentary. How is the bond with your family?"

Jake's ears tingled as he stopped rubbing his thumb under his ring finger. "Nonexistent," he hissed out.

"And yet, you've been caressing your ring finger for the past five minutes. Which means despite the current status of your family bond, you still have a connection to them. Is that safe to say?"

"Always."

"Which brings me back to my point. The origin of the saying comes from an old proverb that states 'the blood of the covenant is thicker than the water of the womb.' So, actually, you have it backward. The bond between comrades is stronger even than your own family allegiance. Nothing brings together a covenant more than bathing in the blood of the enemy. You literally become blood brothers. That, Detective, is V.E.N.O.M. We are more prominent than any force that you can imagine, and we will crush whoever stands before us with the tip of our toe. So, do not, for one insignificant second of your life, underestimate how small you are in this world."

"I heard V.E.N.O.M.'s not doing too well these days."

"That will be a short-lived fact. The resurgence is near."

"That is if you find The Catalogue."

"It's a matter of when at this point. Your efforts will have been a waste."

Jake cleared his throat. "There was a point in time where there was nothing more insignificant than my own life. I'm not far removed from that point, but there is something that I learned being in that space. That nothing can defeat me if I don't let it."

Jun Li smirked at Jake's newfound courage. "That's the spirit, Detective." The woman came to refill their teacups, but Jun Li declined for both of them. "I realize that you may not feel inclined to do me any favors, but I'm going to ask you anyway." He snapped his fingers, and one of his henchmen brought a red box with a gold bow to the table. "Open it."

Jake didn't budge at first, but he realized he didn't have much of choice "A present? For me?"

Jun Li nodded for him to open the box. Jake took the top off, and what was inside turned his face white. His eyes grew soft, but his building anger kept them dry. Inside was a dated Motorola phone. Attached to its top was the head of Andrea's bunny. Jake gently picked up the phone and stared into the bunny's button eyes.

"I would be careful with that if I were you," Jun Li said. "You're going to need it in the next five minutes."

Jake's breath stuttered as he asked, "What have you done?"

"Do Shen's body is coming through this parade in a hearse. We need a distraction to divert him out without anyone noticing. That's where you come in. What you have in your hand is a trigger to an IED strapped to a float that will be passing by this very spot. You will punch in the code two-three-six from a safe distance, if you choose, and initiate our distraction."

"You might as well kill me now," Jake said.

Jun Li chuckled. "I like you, Detective. You're stubborn, just like me. But I've broken men who were ten times more stubborn than you. It's all about finding a breaking point. We all have it inside of us. You just have to look."

"I won't do it."

"Fine. But you can be directly responsible for some people dying or indirectly responsible for thousands of people dying. This whole parade is laced with explosives from block to block. If you don't detonate that IED when it reaches its discharge point, which is here, then I will detonate mine, killing thousands." Jun Li's eyes traveled past Jake, and a smile crept onto his face. "I can already see our float on the horizon…it's the red one."

Jake looked back to see a vibrant red dragon with yellow trim and a snake-like body stationed on top of a hidden van. The dragon's gaping mouth was full of crystalized fangs. It had green eyes that spiraled into the center, and smoke blowing from its nose.

"The Chinese dragon is symbolic for being lucky, propitious, powerful and noble," Jun Li said. "Western culture has portrayed it as nothing more than a hideous monster. Something for children to fear and men to slay. I'm giving you a choice, Detective. Call it empathy. Either be a noble fugitive or become the monster that you've created. Whichever you choose, don't let the smoke cloud your lungs."

Jun Li and his men dispersed from the table and disappeared into the crowd—leaving Jake alone.

Jake glanced at all the smiling faces. The laughter of children distracted him from his decision for a moment. He walked down the sidewalk with the detonator still in his hand. The dragon float rolled closer as Jake's thumb hovered over the number two button. He looked up one more time, and saw something he didn't like at all. A man with his daughter on his shoulders had snuck past the barricade to get a closer look at the dragon float. The little girl carried a an animal doll, just as Jake's daughter had.

He sprinted over to the man and put on his cop voice. "Sir, I'm going to need for you to get back behind the barricade."

The man waved him off and said, "Okay, okay, I just want to get a picture of this one with my daughter. Everyone's doing it."

"It doesn't matter what everyone is doing…" Another person with their child ran by. "…you have to be behind the barricade for your safety." Another group of people came rushing to see the dragon float. Before Jake knew it, there were too many people to control. He turned in all directions looking for help, but there was no one in sight. Jake's eyes landed on the little girl's monkey doll. He marched up behind the father and snatched the monkey from the unexpecting little girl. She turned with her eyes wide and screamed at Jake's back. Some spectators saw what happened and tried to stop Jake, but he muscled right through them. A young man in his twenties stepped in front of Jake like a hero and requested he give the doll back. Before the young man could finish, Jake had leveled him with one punch and pressed forward. His walk turned into a light trot as the crowd around him grew bigger. He looked over his shoulder and saw the little girl crying on her father's shoulder through the crowd. They were at a safe distance—safe enough anyway.

The dragon float made it to the detonation point. Jake

looked down at the detonator and saw a flashing red light. Suddenly, a firm hand grabbed his shoulder and spun him around. It was the local police coming to defuse the scene he'd caused.

"Sir, I'm going to need for you to come with me," the police officer said. Jake saw the familiarity in the cop's eyes as he slowly reached for his pistol. Jake threw the monkey in the air, sucker punched the cop and sprinted in the opposite direction while typing in the code: two-three-six. He took cover behind a cement barricade. A deafening bang blasted louder than any fireworks at the parade. Fragments and debris traveled over Jake's head through a screen of smoke car alarms rang out of control.

The crowd scattered for their lives in different directions, screaming for help. There were some bodies outlined in the smoke. Jake couldn't tell if they were children or not. He just knew that he had to keep moving. He turned, only to be met by the barrel of a standard-issue pistol. On the other side of that pistol was Lieutenant Simons, his arm in a sling.

Jake looked down to his right hand, where he still held the detonator, then back to Lieutenant Simons. He dropped it to his feet and raised his hands mid-torso.

"Give it up, Jake," Lieutenant Simons said. "It's all over. Come with me, and you'll be safe."

Jake didn't move a muscle.

"I know this is all a little confusing right now," Lieutenant Simons continued, "but believe me, I don't want to be in this position any more than you do. At the same time, I can't help you if you don't come with me."

"You can't help me at all," Jake finally said. "It's too late to go back."

"That's crazy talk, Jake, and you know it. We can sort everything out from the shootouts, the guy at the train, the diplomat's son and this moment right here. Everything can be worked out if you just come with me."

Jake took a moment to put everything together. Something didn't sit right with him. "How do you know what happened here?"

"What?"

"What are you doing here, Trent? Who sent you?"

"What are you talking about? No one sent me. I'm here to help."

"How did you know to be here right now?" he yelled.

Lieutenant Simons sighed. He couldn't bear to look Jake in the eyes.

"It was you," Jake continued. "You set me up from the beginning. You sent me to Catskills. You introduced me to Parker. You had them blow up my apartment."

"That doesn't even make sense, Jake! Are you hearing yourself right now? You sound batshit crazy, and it's killing me as your friend to see you go through this."

Jake dropped his hands to his sides. Any ounce of care he had was drained from his body. "*In Venenum Potentia ,*" he said, the words leaving his lips effortlessly.

Lieutenant Simons stared Jake in the eyes. His jaw tightened up, and his legs wobbled right under him. "Why did you say that?"

Jake took a beat to analyze his reaction. "Do you know what that means?"

"No, I don't," Lieutenant Simons said.

"You sure?"

Lieutenant Simons locked in on Jake as he aimed. His index finger left the trigger guard and wrapped around the trigger. His sight lined up with Jake's head. He took one deep inhale through his nose. Ready to shoot to kill.

Then an old truck crashed through a barricade and sped toward Lieutenant Simons. Before he could react, the truck mowed him down and stopped on top of him after he let off an accidental round that hit Jake.

Jake grabbed the right side of his face as he fell on his back. Zasha hopped out of the truck fully dressed but still bloodied, and limped over to Jake. She touched his body, searching for the entry wound. She couldn't find one. "Jake!" she shouted. "Jake, are you hit? Say something to me. Jake?!" Jake could hear his name being called, but it was by a distant, melodic voice.

"Jake. Wake up for me," and you will be. "Wake up for Andrea. We forgive you. We've forgiven you long ago."

"I'm sorry," Jake said. "This is all my fault. I should have protected you."

"You did your best, but now you have to wake up."

"No…I want to come with you. I want to be with you and Andrea."

"And you will be. But not now," the voice said. "Now, you have to wake up. Wake up!"

Jake opened his dark brown eyes, gasping for air. The first thing he saw was a blur of Zasha's face with gray clouds as the background. He heard her yelling, but her voice was muffled. His vision began to focus. She had some cuts and bruises on her face, and her hair was shorter. Her left eye was almost swollen shut. He still thought she looked beautiful.

"Jake, are you okay?" her voice came to full volume.

Jake touched her face to make sure she was real. "Aren't you a sight for sore eyes."

Zasha smiled and rested her head on his chest. He lifted his head slowly as he touched the top of his ear where the bullet nicked him.

"Jun Li took Do Shen," he grunted. "We have to stop him."

"Stop him from doing what? Does he have The Catalogue?"

"I don't know. But something isn't adding up."

Zasha helped Jake to his feet and to the passenger's side of the truck.

"No, I'll drive," Jake said.

"Are you sure?"

"Yeah."

33.

Jake drove down Madison Avenue, making sure they were as cautious as possible. Police cars in the opposite lanes raced to the crime scene they had both left behind. Jake checked his rearview mirror to make sure they didn't double back Zasha stared out the window. Her arms and legs were crossed. She had barely said a word since they got in the truck.

Jake grabbed her trembling hand. Without words, he told her everything was going to be all right. Her hand stopped shaking, but her mind was still rattled. Jake was on edge too, but now wasn't the time to show it, so they both sat quietly.

Jake found a rundown payphone next to a Laundromat, and made a phone call. He kept one eye on Zasha and one eye on the surrounding area, just in case any cops showed up.

"Hello?" the voice on the other end said.

"Parker. It's me."

"Jake? Where the hell are you?"

"No, where the hell are you? Jun Li was waiting for me the whole time. He knew I was coming."

Parker sighed. "I'm sorry. We didn't have much time to plan. When I made it back, the roads were blocked. There was an explosion."

"I know. I was there."

"Was it Jun Li?"

Jake paused as the screams of the victims echoed in his subconscious. "We need to meet," he finally said.

"I don't know if that's a good idea."

"I spoke with Jun Li. He may be close to getting The Catalogue."

"I have The Catalogue."

The way he said it so nonchalantly made Jake think he hadn't heard him correctly. "You have what?"

"Are you alone?"

Jake looked over to Zasha. "Yeah."

"I'm going to give you an address. Meet me there in two hours. Don't be late."

* * *

Jake was able to get them an hourly room at a motel. It wasn't the Waldorf Astoria, but it was enough to hold them over for now. Zasha turned the squeaky handle to start the shower. She let the warm water stream from the top of her head down to her toes. A trail of diluted blood spiraled into the drain. Her skin didn't feel pure anymore. She sat down in an upward fetal position and broke down crying into her knees. A gentle touch on her shoulder made her gasp and jump into a hyper-defensive mode. It was Jake, there to console her. Her instinct told her to stop crying immediately, but the tears wouldn't stop flowing. He climbed in the tub fully clothed and wrapped his arms around her as tight as he could. Her head rested on his solid forearm, as if that had been her favorite position for years. She continued to cry. For Zasha, there was nothing like having someone to cuddle with after taking a life.

Later, Zasha sat on the edge of the firm bed with the cleanest clothes she could find from the hotel's lost-and-found. She stared at the blank TV, lost in her thoughts. A glimpse of her reflection caught her eye, and she began to run her fingers through what was left of her hair. Then she glided her fingers right under her swollen eye, which still hurt like hell. Jake walked in, and she snapped back to reality. "You can't go," she said.

"It's the only way to clear my name," he replied.

"He tried to have me killed! There's no way you can trust him."

"He's all I have, Zasha. Without him, I don't have a chance. They'll crucify me."

"Do you really think he's going to make everything go away?"

"He has to. I know too much ."

"So that's your plan? Fix everything, or I'll tell on you."

"Pretty much."

"What if he hears that and puts bullet in your head? That seems like the more efficient way to handle this. That's what I would do."

Jake came face-to-face with her. "I don't have a choice, Zasha."

Jake sidestepped her, but Zasha stepped right back in front of him. She was about the only thing that could do that without physically touching him. "What about me? When your buddy finds out I'm not dead, he's going to have eyes on you for the rest of your life. Is that what you want, living under someone's thumb?"

"Then what do you suggest?"

"Let's just go. We can leave right now and disappear. I can make us some new identities, and we can be whoever we want to be, wherever we want to be. But we have to leave now."

Jake pondered the suggestion. He saw that this was the most vulnerable Zasha had ever been, possibly in her life. The fact that she would want to spend the rest of her life in hiding, with him no less, was flattering, but there was no easy answer. "I can't do that."

"Yes, you can."

"It's more complicated than you think."

"What's more complicated than giving up your destroyed life to evade getting caught up in a global conspiracy? Give me one good reason why you shouldn't come with me."

"Because I'm tired of running. I run from the guilt. I run from who I am. I run from the lies. I run from the truth. For once, I want to stand tall and do what's right. If I go down, then it's supposed to happen."

"Then I'm coming with you."

"No! You can't."

"It's not a request."

"If Parker sees that I lied to him, there's no telling what he'll do. Stay here. I promise I'll be back."

"Don't promise me anything," she said, her voice cracked. She made sure to wipe her tears before they escaped. "You don't get to do that to me. It's not up for discussion. Either you come with me, or I go with you."

"Dammit, Zasha!" Jake grabbed her by the arms and pressed her back against the wall. Her arm lined up with a rusted pipe that ran up to the ceiling. "staying here is not for you, it's for me!. I can't have anything happen to you. I have too much on my heart to add you to the list."

Zasha pressed her forehead against his, their lips inches apart. She nodded, then kissed him. "You're right. I'll stay."

Jake pressed his lips to her ear and whispered, "I know

you will." A clicking sound closed around Zasha's wrist. She yanked her arm but could only pull a couple of feet. Jake backed away to see the handcuff secured on the pipe.

"Jake! What the hell are you doing?!"

She reached for his face, but only her fingertips came close. "I can't risk anything happening to you. You understand?"

"Don't do this, Jake. Please don't leave me."

"It's the only way." Jake turned his back to open the door.

"If you leave, you'll never see me again!" she shouted. Her voice was still a little hoarse, but Jake heard her loud and clear. Her words kept him from opening the door. "You know I will get out of this eventually," she continued. "And when I do, I'm leaving for good. So please, don't leave me."

Jake turned around, and the sight of tears running down her face stopped his heart. "Maybe my leaving is the best thing for both of us. It'll keep you safe."

Jake exited without looking back. He stood for a second with his back to the door, wondering if this was really what he wanted to do. In the end, he knew this was the best for her. She was safer without him.

34.

The night was moonless and mute. Perfect for anyone trying to go unnoticed. The location Parker gave Jake was the abandoned Glenwood Power Plant. He knew the area somewhat, because the bus he took to work passed through Yonkers and gave him an open view almost every day. The nickname for the power plant was *The Gates of Hell*, and it lived up to the reputation. The building had been abandoned since the sixties.

Jake slipped through a flimsy fence and walked to the boarded-up entrance. A few mattresses were scattered around the building, no doubt dragged there by the homeless. Distant sirens filled the air, still answering the terror left earlier. He kicked down the boarded entrance and walked through the gates of hell.

Inside, Jake couldn't see past his nose. The temperature dropped five degrees, and the stench of mold filled his lungs. He pulled out a flashlight and crossed it under his wrist, with his pistol aimed into the darkness. The walk through the cathedral-like turbine hall was more reason for Jake to have a hyper-attentive focus. Every echo, splash and ping snatched his attention in their direction. Jake tried to tame his imagination from getting the best of him, but the sound of shuffling footsteps was far too real to ignore. Jake decided to follow the racket with his flashlight, but he couldn't quite catch it. *Maybe it's a dog,* he thought. The important thing was to stay focused.

He pushed forward, not sure where to go. A generator roared from behind him, and bright lights beamed from a circle of standing floodlights, blinding him. Jun Li and three of his henchmen ascended from the shadows and into the light. Two of the henchmen approached Jake with drawn machine guns.

Jun Li gave Jake a slow clap. "I must say…I'm quite impressed. You have a little more tenacity than most people would give you credit for. It's admirable." One of the henchmen nudged Jake to hand over his weapon. He did so begrudgingly, but as soon as he let go of his gun, he smacked the hand of the henchman behind him and punched him to the ground. The second henchman whacked Jake in the back of the head with his gun.

Jun Li smirked. "You are not one to waste time, are you?" He turned toward his fallen henchman in disgust, and yelled something to him in Mandarin. The man stood to attention in a split second, and forced Jake to come face-to-face with Jun Li.

Jun Li took a second to study Jake before he spoke. "I can sense an energy from you like nothing I've felt before. There's something in you, hiding. I want to bring it out for the world to see what you truly are."

From the shadows, an apparatus that could only be described as a crude wooden beach chair angled at one hundred and fifty degrees was wheeled out into the light by two additional henchmen.

"Have a seat," Jun Li said, tapping the chair.

Jake stood his ground until three henchmen forced him down in the chair. They fastened brown leather straps around him, keeping his back straight and his legs fully extended.

"My grandfather used to tell me the old way is the best way," Jun Li continued. "I always credited him with instilling a tradition in me. Being a proud countryman is not the easiest life to carry out, but the honor in it is immense, and fills the soul with an indescribable sentiment."

As Jun Li spoke, one of the henchmen handed him a paddle found in the debris. "If anyone were to get in the way of your newfound glory, it was your duty, as a proud countryman, to go through them. Even if that meant their existence must be no more." Jun Li's henchmen brought out a stack of bricks, four five-gallon water bottles, and a bundle of towels. "Are you familiar with the contraption you're sitting in right now? It's not the best engineering, I must admit, but it yields effective results. In my country, it's called a Tiger Bench. It was introduced to China in the early nineties. Officials would use it for spiritual discipline. I guess this is my way of staying true to tradition."

"Your grandfather would be proud," Jake said.

One of the henchmen grabbed two bricks and placed them under the heels of his feet. Jake grunted through his teeth as the leather straps tightened on his static legs. Jun Li cocked the paddle back and struck Jake's legs, causing him to scream. "That's for fixing your foul mouth that spoke ill of my grandfather."

Jake's legs burned and tightened up under the leather straps. He focused on his breathing rather than the pain. "I didn't know you were going take it this easy on me."

Jun Li smiled at Jake, then nodded to one of his henchmen. The lone henchman grabbed a towel and stretched it over Jake's face. A second henchman grabbed a five-gallon water bottle and poured the water over his face. Jake convulsed as he tried to break free, but the restraints were sturdier than they looked. After fifteen seconds of water-pouring, Jun Li ordered the henchman to stop, and ripped the towel off. Jake choked and inhaled intensely, trying to clear the water out of his lungs.

Jun Li grabbed Jake's face to make his point clearer. "A part of me really does admire you. Earlier today, you would have rather died than do anything to bring dishonor to your people, your country. When dying wasn't an option, you made a difficult decision. One that devastated some but benefited the greater good. This is another thing we have in common. We want what's best for our respective motherlands.

"Unfortunately for you, for my country to flourish, yours must burn. It's the most basic concept of all living things. But there is a silver lining in this exclusively for you. If you confirm to me right now that the Americans have The Catalogue, I will make sure that your life will be better than you can imagine. All you have to do is move your head. Yes or no."

Jake's throat was almost entirely closed, but he managed to clear out most of the water. When his breathing came back to normal, he kept his mouth shut and his eyes dead center on Jun Li.

Jun Li was as impressed by his perseverance as he was annoyed. He took a deep breath and ordered for his henchman to put another brick under Jake's heel. Jake winced in pain as he ground his teeth and the leather straps constricted tighter. He felt like his legs were going to snap at any moment, but he kept his composure as much as he could.

"You're not making this easy for yourself, Detective," Jun Li said as a henchman stretched another fresh towel over his face. Jun Li positioned his face next to Jake's ear and whispered, "Dying would be the easiest thing for you right now. I plan on keeping you alive for a very long time." Jun Li's henchman poured the water again. Jake twitched and turned, gargling between short breaths. "Now tell me…where is The Catalogue?!" Jun Li continued to strike Jake's legs. The last blow snapped the paddle against Jake's abdomen. Jun Li took a moment to catch his breath, and waved his man away from pouring the water. He commanded one of the henchmen to grab something similar to the paddle. Jun Li snatched the towel off Jake's face, and used a dry one to pat him. " Sh-sh-sh-sh, don't worry. It's just a brief intermission."

When the henchman didn't return promptly, Jun Li turned to the remaining four. "Go see what's taking that idiot so long," he barked in Mandarin. Two henchmen ran off into the shadows to look for the first one. "Excuse the unprofessionalism," Jun Li said to Jake. "Normally my torture sessions are a bit more…fluid."

A piece of glass shattered in the darkness. This was followed by a man's painful grunt . Jun Li's stare became more attentive as he looked at his remaining two henchmen. One of the henchmen took the initiative and paced with uncertainty toward the darkness. Before he could make it past the first standing floodlight, a muffled pop dropped him to the ground. Jun Li watched nonchalantly as the remaining henchman ran to the trouble—only to be shot three times.

Immediately after, Zasha emerged from the darkness with a silencer aimed directly at Jun Li. "Unstrap him," she said.

Jun Li removed the bricks from under Jake's feet, and loosened each strap one by one. As the last strap was unbuckled, Jake fell face first to the floor. "Now what?" Jun Li asked. "You two live happily ever after?"

Zasha walked around the tiger bench to Jun Li. "That's more than I can say for you."

"There's no better partner to dance with than death. You kill me, and you can leave this building. But what about the rest of the world ? How will you survive?"

"I'll live."

"Oh, no, my dear, you will do quite the opposite. Running for the rest of your life. Living like every day is your last. Then with him anchoring you down… That's no way to spend the rest of your time here on earth. But it doesn't have to be that way. I can make it so everyone walks away happy."

"I'm sure you say that to all the girls." Zasha's index finger closed in on the trigger. She pressed the barrel right between Jun Li's eyes. His face was still. Not a worried wrinkle on the surface. Almost as if he relished the possibility of death. "No blood spilled within the nation."

Jun Li was impressed by her logic. "You are a remarkable piece of work. You still respect the doctrine, even though you're not a part of us anymore."

"I have no quarrels with you. If you want to chase something that you will never find, then that's your business. But I need your word that you will respect the decree that once governed us, so we can be on our way. Otherwise, I'll have to exercise an option that I have no problem executing."

"You have my word that *I* will bring no harm your way."

Zasha weighed the pros and cons, and knew the risk far outweighed the words. Her finger crept closer to the trigger until the slightest shift in Jun Li's eyes caught her attention. Zasha switched her aim, but a loud bang stopped her midturn. Her eyes welled up as her pistol shook in her hand. She looked down stammering to herself as she saw blood spreading like fire through her shirt from her stomach. She looked up to Jun Li, who had that pretentious grin on his face. Her vision blurred as she stumbled backward. She tried to pull the trigger, but her legs collapsed right under her.

Jake watched helplessly as she blinked rapidly and her eyes wandered around, looking for an answer. A tear slid across the bridge of Jake's nose as he reached out to her. They were so close and yet so far away at the same time. A shadow glided across Jake's face and over towards Zasha. Jake looked up and saw Parker looking over her, with his gun smoking. He kicked her weapon away from her.

"She's a resilient one, that's for sure," Parker said. He turned his attention to Jun Li, gun ready to fire. "Now, the question is, what to do with you?" He inched towards Jun Li until he was within arm's reach.

"That is totally up to you," Jun Li said.

The two stared each other down without a sign of apprehension. Parker's signature smile was covered by a deadly stare. The tension was broken when Parker finally let a smile sneak onto his face, and lowered his gun. Jun Li followed with a smile of his own.

"You're the only one who never falls for that," Parker said.

"I never let the opposition see me sweat," Jun Li replied.

Parker looked down to Jake with the same sneaky grin.

"I would pay a fortune to know what's running through your head right now."

Jake's jaw tightened as every muscle in his face shook, and his fists clenched. All he could see was red.

35.

"Do you have it?" Jun Li asked.

Parker was too focused on Jake to answer.

"I said, do you have it?!"

Parker diverted his attention to Jun Li then nodded subtly.

"Show me."

"What's the rush there, Li-Li? Why can't we just enjoy each other's company?"

"I don't have time for your stupid games, Ethan. Show me now, or I walk out."

Parker reached inside the breast pocket of his jacket and pulled out a USB. "I believe this what you're looking for." He rotated the USB between his fingers, as if teasing a rabbit with a carrot.

Jun Li's eyes glinted when Parker tossed it to him. His search was over, and this was the moment that left him speechless.

"It's beautiful, isn't it?" Parker asked. "World domination in the palm of your hand."

"Where did you—"

"Greenwich funeral home. The director was in on it the whole time. Do Shen was willing to die with this secret, rather than have it end up in the wrong hands."

A gust of relief left Jun Li's lips as he clinched the USB tight. His mind started to wander to the things he'd planned to do, but his imagination was interrupted by Jake struggling to rise to his feet. "What about them?" Jun Li asked, keeping the USB tight in his hand.

"You don't have to worry about that," Parker said. "I'll take care of them."

"Fucking traitor," Jake coughed out.

"What was that, Jake?" Parker asked. "I couldn't hear you."

"I believe he's trying to express his displeasure in your decision to work with the enemy."

Jake's heart pounded through his chest as Parker walked closer to him. He tried to meet him halfway, but he slipped and fell. Parker knelt to his level and looked him in his eyes. "Is that what is? You think I'm a traitor?" He moved in close and whispered, "You have no idea what you're dealing with. But you will soon enough."

"You're a Venom?" Jake asked, voice hoarse.

"Of course not," Parker said through a chuckle. "I would never stoop so low." Parker stood up and turned his back. "But the sad reality is that we're all connected to the V.E.N.O.M., one way or another. Somebody works for somebody who works for somebody who has their hand in the cookie jar. In this business, you either get dirty or get caught chasing your tail. I got tired of running in circles."

"That doesn't mean you get to betray your country. Everyone who's fought and died to protect us is being spat on the face by you right now."

"I was betrayed first, Jake!" Parker yelled. "I gave my life to defending our nation. Securing the future. And for what? A badge of honor? A pat on the back? No one in the intelligence world is 100% clean, and I had to learn that the hard way. Well, lesson learned. Now it's time to apply it."

"Parker, listen to me. Think of the lives that will be affected if he leaves with The Catalogue. Your life will be affected if he gets his way."

"Oh no, I told you once before, I'm in control of my own destiny. If anyone is affected by this negatively…they deserved it."

"I hate to interrupt this moment you two seem to be having, but I have to arrange transport for me back to China. I assume you have my itinerary ready."

"I won't have anything ready until we talk about my reimbursement."

Jun Li sighed into a bitter smile. "You will receive half of your payment once I authenticate everything on the drive while on the plane, including The Catalogue. Once that plane lands safely in China, you will receive the other half within forty-eight hours. 500 million. American."

"Fair enough."

"And just a reminder, no Catalogue, no payment." Jun Li placed the USB in his pocket and walked toward the exit. "I would hope that you wouldn't take too long to dispose of them. I can have a car pick us up in ten minutes."

"That sounds good, but there's one thing I don't get."

"Whatever it is I'm sure it can be sorted out on the way to the airport."

"I think I'll ask now." Parker cocked his gun. Jun Li stopped and turned with his chin high.

"Now, the question is…do you always turn your back on people you don't trust?"

Jun Li chuckled. "The next five seconds can be very crucial for you. I advise you to choose your words and actions carefully."

"I think we both know I already have," Parker said. "I

saw you signal to the girl of my presence. Venoms stick together, don't they? All over a stupid code. You might be allowed to not kill each other, but you sure can die together."

Jun Li's face tightened. He took a hard swallow and cleared his throat. "You will never be safe. My people will find you, and your victory will be short-lived, if you can even call it that. If not my people, then someone else will unearth you from whatever hole you decide to crawl into, and end you for The Catalogue. It won't stop just because you have a pretty smile. Your whole life will be defined by this very moment, so like I said before, it's all up to you."

Parker took a few strides and came up to point-blank range .

Pride wouldn't allow Jun Li to break eye contact. "I hope you find what you are looking for in this world," he said in Mandarim. "Because your soul will forever be lost. I honor—"

Parker stopped Jun Li's speech with a single round to the forehead.

Jun Li fell straight back, collapsing on his spine. Blood poured from the back of his head as his foot twitched.

"And the plot thickens," Parker said. He stood over Jun Li's lifeless body and retrieved the USB. "You couldn't have possibly thought that it was going to end well for you, my friend." He looked over to Jake, who was kneeled by Zasha's side, stroking her hair. His stare couldn't be more menacing when he looked at Parker. "Oh, don't give me that look," Parker said. "I didn't kill anyone who didn't deserve it. If I didn't end him, he would have ended me eventually. Your life depends on anonymity in this world. One of us had to go."

Jake picked himself up to a slouching stance. "Jun Li's

right. You're not going to get away with this. It will never end. They'll keep coming for you until there's nothing left."

Parker chuckled. "Oh, but it's quite the opposite, Jake. It all depends on your paradigm. You see this as my demise when I see it as a way out. To finally have control over my life. No more chasing my tail. No more bullshit bureaucracy. As of 4:28 pm today, I was no longer a slave to the V.E.N.O.M. or to our broken government. It wasn't the smoothest of plans, but it's all falling into place now."

"The money isn't going to change anything."

"It was never about the money, Jake. I mean, I am getting something out of the deal, but this is more of a righteous rebellion. At least I'm fair. The highest bidder gets The Catalogue. No strings attached ."

"What about the service to your country? Protecting its citizens? Going through with this will go against everything you stand for. You sell those secrets to anyone, you're just as bad Jun Li."

"No, no, no, no, see that's where our plans split. Jun Li was really gunning for world domination in favor of his country. He was going to try to reinvent V.E.N.O.M. Can you believe that? Once he found out the identities of everyone on The Catalogue, it was either work for him or die. Trust me, as a person who's worked with him, the latter doesn't seem so bad. I, on the other hand, just want to be happy. I already got my eyes set on this little island with coconut trees, plentiful sea life and the clearest water you've ever seen in your life. That couldn't happen, me knowing the things I know."

"You sell that story to Trent?"

Parker chuckled. "Lieutenant Simons was a pawn just like you. Although, his desires were a little more tangible than yours. Too bad he couldn't stay alive long enough to enjoy being commissioner."

Zasha coughed a breath. She was still alive but had lost a lot of blood. Parker turned his attention toward her. "But as always, a job is never done until you tie up all the loose ends."

As Parker walked over to her, Jake tried his best to limp toward him. "No!" Jake's scratchy voice yelled. "Parker! We had a deal. If nothing else, stick to your word like a man."

Parker stood over Zasha, with his gun pressed against her temple. "I am sticking to my word. Except, you're going be taking her place. I thought about it and giving the blame for everything that's transpired over the past few days to an ex-Venom would raise too many questions. But pinning everything on an ex-cop with a history of violence, alcohol abuse, PTSD, the terrorist act you pulled at the parade and suffering from deep depression over the loss of his family…that's a bit easier to digest. In fact, the media will eat that shit up."

"Parker! Don't!"

"Just do me a favor, beautiful," Parker said to Zasha. "And tell me your Venom name. You have three seconds to give it up, or I will pull the trigger. One…" Zasha lay there defiant. She was willing to die in silence rather than give him what he wanted. "Twooo…" Parker secured his finger on the trigger.

"*In Venenum Potentia!*" Jake yelled.

Parker's finger jumped off the trigger. He looked at Jake as if he'd seen a ghost. Even Zasha's eyes grew wide.

"What did you just say?" Parker asked.

Jake struggled to his feet. "You heard me. It sounds familiar, doesn't it?"

"No, that's not possible." Parker pointed his gun at Jake

as he stepped toward him. "Who told you to say that?"

Jake shook his head. "No one. It's something that I lived by a long time ago. I'm sure you know where it comes from. The creed that everyone who ever slipped through your fingers lived by. All this time you've been looking, and I've been right under your nose."

Parker leveled Jake with a right hook. "Lies! It can't be." He picked Jake up to his feet and lodged his gun under his chin. "What is it?"

Jake stayed silent.

Parker shot a round at Zasha without looking, and it missed her by inches. "I will kill her and make you watch. Now, tell me...what is it? What is your Venom name?" he asked through his teeth.

Jake looked straight into Parker's eyes and took a deep breath. "The Wraith," he whispered. "My Venom name is The Wraith."

Parker scoffed in disbelief. "You? The unkillable ghost?" He let out a nervous laugh, then cut his smile short to a grimace. "I don't know where you heard that name from or who told you to utter those words, but you can't possibly expect me to believe tha—"

Jake twisted the gun out of Parker's hands and threw him over his shoulder to the ground, then spin-kicked his abdomen. Parker gazed up, partially frightened but more astonished by Jake's quick reflexes. Even Zasha looked on, speechless. Jake had a different look in his eyes. His stance had more confidence, his demeanor was more militant. It was at this moment that Parker knew Jake was indeed... The Wraith.

Parker chuckled in amazement as Jake pinned him down with his own gun. His chuckles then turned into hysterical laughter. "You have got to be shitting me!" he yelled. "You? Of all people, you. Oh, I've seen it all now." Parker gave Jake a round of applause, but he wasn't biting. "This whole time you've been wasting away as a drunken detective when you're a Venom, one of the most infamous Venoms I might add. I don't even know where to start."

"You can start by handing over The Catalogue," Jake said. Even his voice had been smoothed over by calm confidence.

Parker's face dropped as he revealed his hands. "Wait a minute, wait a minute, Jake. Considering this new information, I think at the very least we have to communicate. You wouldn't want to pass on a grand opportunity, would you?"

"Don't listen to him, Jake," Zasha said. "Shoot him! Shoot him right now! He can't be trusted."

Parker rose to his feet slowly, with his hands exposed. "Don't you dare shoot me without hearing what I have to say first."

"He tried to have me killed at the house when you left. I am bleeding out right now because of him. Just shoot him already!"

"Okay, in hindsight, the house call was a dick move, but you would have done the same thing if you were me, Jake. And it's true, she has lost a lot of blood, but she's not going to die from that wound. Not unless we work together."

"Get to the point," Jake said.

"Chasing Venoms was my life. You know how rare it is to come in contact with one. We have two in attendance right now. Two and a half if you count Jun Li's corpse."

"You're running out of time, Parker."

"Let me go. I'll sell The Catalogue to the highest bidder. In exchange, I will transfer five million dollars to each of you within twenty-four hours, plus ten percent of what I make off the sale."

"What about the destruction in New York? The whole country is on alert because of what you colluded to."

"That will be taken care of. We both know that. In the meantime, you can get her stitched up, create new identities for the both of you, which I'm sure is nothing new to you, and disappear...together. The best part of it all, you have my word that your names will be removed from The Catalogue before the sale."

Parker had finally said something that caught Jake's attention.

"That is what you want, isn't it? No more running. No more hiding. No more killing. You can officially retire from V.E.N.O.M. today, without owing anybody anything. Tell me that's not something you think about every day ."

Jake pondered the enticing offer. It had been a long time since he'd shown his face as The Wraith, and it was already exhausting. Parker had a concerned look on his face. It was a look Jake had never seen from him before. But the idea of walking away—for good—put air under his feet.

"Jake," Zasha cracked. "As crazy as it sounds, I don't see any other way of getting out of this. Now, I don't trust this son of a bitch as much as you do, but...that doesn't mean he's not right, about people like us. We can start a new life, as long as we all trust each other."

With Zasha on board, Jake had to make the hardest decision of his life. The idea of having peace of mind wrapped around his subconscious and released   calmness in his body. The serenity helped him to lower the gun, and a smile crept onto Parker's face.

"These past few years have been extremely rough for me," Jake said. "We've all done terrible things, and now we're paying for the secrets we don't want to be brought to light. It's not about how long you can run from those secrets, but will you still be alive long enough to face them?" Jake soaked in the words of Chinelo. His mind had reached a level of clarity never touched before. He reaffirmed his shooting stance, and tightened his grip on the gun. "I'm facing mine right now."

Parker's face wrinkled in anger. "Jake, let's think about this a little longer. Even your girlfriend thinks it's a good idea."

Jake shook his head. "I can't let you leave with The Catalogue. This one thing isn't going to make up for all the years of terror, but it's a small start."

"Bullshit!" Parker yelled. "The only reason you care about this thing is because your name is on here. In what world is it okay for me to give you The Catalogue?"

"It doesn't exist. But it'll make you feel better."

Parker laughed as he repeated what Jake said. "Jake, I'm begging you, and I never beg, but please…don't be a hero. It's not your thing."

Jake thought back to his AA meetings, and how the guys there had looked up to a lie. He'd been lying his whole life, but now he made the decision to not lie anymore—especially to himself. "I know who I am. I'm nobody's hero. But I'm not the bad guy either, not anymore."

"Well, that's just great. You found the perfect time to grow a conscience."

"Throw me The Catalogue, Parker. It's over."

"Okay." Parker reached in his left breast pocket. "And here I was celebrating an early retirement. But you just had to bring me down, didn't you?" He launched a knife into Jake's forearm and charged at him. Parker grabbed the gun, and a few stray rounds went off in different directions before Parker disarmed the gun and knocked Jake on his back. "You're a little rusty there, Wraith. But then again, drugs and alcohol will do that to you. I thought you were a part of the common folk we both know so well." Jake slid on his back to safety as he took the blade out of his arm. Parker dropped the clip out of the gun, flipped the bullet out of the chamber and tossed the rest. "I can't just shoot The Wraith. There would be no honor in that."

Jake made it back to his feet and went into his fighting stance.

"I used to hear stories about you. Legend has it that you could never be killed," Parker continued. "You did every operation to perfection. When it was all said and done for Do Shen, you were next in line to take over everything. At least in Jun Li's mind, that was the case. He could never stop talking about it. I kind of wish you would have made your big reveal before I killed him." Parker laughed. "Boy, the look on his face would almost be worth The Catalogue, almost." The despair crept on Parker's face. It was eerily human of him. "This is your last chance to reconsider. Take the deal."

Jake locked in his fighting stance and tightened his fists. His decision was final.

Parker stretched his neck and loosened his arms. "Today wasn't a total waste. I get a big retirement, and I get to bag the biggest trophy in V.E.N.O.M.'s history."

Jake watched Parker's feet. The way his body swayed. The twitch in his eye. He was fighting Parker in his mind before a single blow was thrown. Parker was a skilled fighter, and if Jake wanted any chance to compete, he was going to have to outsmart him. Parker rushed at him with a flurry of punches. Jake blocked each blow and managed to land a few counter punches, but Parker didn't quit. Jake threw a punch and missed. Parker took advantage and propelled his elbow dead center into Jake's nose.

Jake took a moment to shake off the blinking colors and catch his balance. He threw a few more punches in combination, but Parker's defense was as smooth as a champion boxer's.

Parker grabbed both of Jake's arms and delivered a head-butt to his face. He then heaved some punches to Jake's gut and pounded a sharp elbow to his back.

Jake doubled over but scurried away as Parker followed him. When Parker least expected it, Jake rushed at him and picked him off his feet.

Parker caught his footing and pummeled Jake in the back until he let go. Parker sent a flying knee to Jake's mouth, knocking him down on his back. Jake spat out blood as he caught his breath. His whole body was sore, and he saw two of everything.

Parker walked over to some rubble and pulled out a laptop he'd placed there from a black satchel . He inserted the USB into the port and pressed OK. One percent of The Catalogue had been uploaded onto the hard drive. Parker placed the laptop on a box and let it work. He turned around to see Jake crawling on his hands and knees.

"The world is an irrational place, Jake. Everyone's worried about a war on foreign terrorism while peeking over their shoulders for domestic terrorism, treason, espionage and everything else they can fear. Then there's us. Two men from the shadows, fighting each other indirectly for years over the very fears these people hold to their hearts. Tell me, would freedom be any freer if it were granted by Kim

Jong-un? Or what about V.E.N.O.M.? You were a part of that. You think you're any better than the terrorists of the world because you did your crimes covertly? I'm going to let you in on a little secret. It doesn't matter. We don't get to decide anything. The world spins because someone tells it to spin. And if they want it to burn then, dammit, it'll be hell on earth. Me selling The Catalogue and then leaking it to every major intelligence agency around the world isn't going to change that. But it does give me leverage." Parker looked over at his laptop. Twenty-six percent of The Catalogue had been uploaded . "As much as you try to fight it, I know you understand. Let the savages eat each other and may the best country win."

Jake rose to his feet, slouched over. "I understand it. The problem is, you don't. No matter what you do…you're still somebody's bitch."

Parker snarled as he plodded toward Jake. He threw two hooks, connecting on both, then chucked Jake to the ground. He lifted his size 12 shoe up and tried to smash Jake's face, but Jake recovered the knife and stabbed his foot.

Parker's screams reached the ceiling and echoed throughout the empty hallways. Jake snatched the knife out of Parker's foot and rolled to safety. Parker limped away to find something to lean on, leaving a blood trail. Jake rose again, knife in hand. The dust in the air was making it hard for him breathe. His left eye was closing, but his will was unscathed. Jake saw with his one good eye that sixty-two percent of The Catalogue had uploaded.

Jake trotted toward the laptop, but Parker jumped in his way. Jake stabbed and sliced through the air, but Parker dodged each blow from a stationary position. Jake jabbed the knife at Parker's chest, but Parker caught the blow. Jake put all his weight behind the blade as it inched toward Parker's chest, but Parker was able to kick the back of Jake's leg causing, him to fall to on one knee.

Parker twisted the knife out of Jake's hand then wrestled him to the ground. He landed on Jake's back and wrapped his arm around his neck with a strong force behind it. "Look," Parker whispered in his ear. "We can watch together. The beginning of the end starts any minute now. This is what we've both been waiting for."

As the upload reached ninety-one percent, Jake stretched his arm as far as he could to reach for the knife, but his fingertips barely tapped the surface. Each tap inched the blade a little closer.

"Parker, don't do this," Jake said. "Don't fall to our level."

"I have no choice, Jake. This is the only way."

Jake spun the knife with his finger and was able to grab ahold of it. "Parker! Last chance!"

Parker showed no signs of slowing down.

Jake lodged the knife blindly into Parker's neck. He could feel warm liquid pouring down the back of his head, followed by Parker's grip getting loose. Parker rolled over, holding his wound and trying to retain as much blood as possible. He grabbed Jake by the shirt, but he could barely hold on. His blue eyes were wide with shock. The room spun and his vision blurred.

Jake caught his breath, sitting up while watching Parker struggle for understanding.

"Jake?" Parker gargled out. His blood-drenched hand reached for help. Jake firmly grasped his hand and pulled himself closer to Parker. They both looked into each other's eyes. "I just wanted my life back," Parker whimpered.

"I know," Jake said.

"It was never personal between you and me. It was survival. That's all I know…survival."

Jake fought back his tears, seeing Parker like this. He knew the one person who was the key to his redemption was compromised by the lies fed to him by his own country. He wondered if Parker could be pulled to the shadows, if there was any hope for him to change. Parker's hand began to slip, but Jake held on tight. "Would you like to pray?" he asked.

Parker laughed into a violent cough. He looked off into the distance, as if someone was calling him. His gaze floated to Jake and signaled for him to come closer. They both bowed their heads in silence. A single tear slid down Parker's cheek as he took in his last breath, his grip now lifeless.

Jake opened his eyes to see Parker's empty eyes staring at him. He closed them out of respect. "You have control now," he whispered.

Jake went to the laptop and yanked the USB out at ninety-nine percent. He limped over to Zasha, who was in and out of consciousness. Her face was pale and her lips purple. He dropped the USB on the floor next to her, and stomped it to pieces.

EPILOGUE.

Garibaldi, Oregon

Jake walked down the aisle of a local food market, shopping for groceries. He had a full beard, and his hair was almost to his shoulders. As he decided on what to buy, he saw a boy, no more than eight years old, misbehaving with his mother. Other shoppers looked on with judgmental stares as the mother dangled on her last nerve.

The cashier checked Jake out, and the mother with the disobedient boy pulled her shopping cart right behind him. The boy settled for the moment when the mother murmured a threatening pep talk in his ear. The little boy then turned his attention to Jake's burnt hand and held his disgust in his mouth.

Jake noticed the boy gawking at him and gave him a polite smile. The boy's mother grabbed him close and whispered something in his ear. They both had matching green eyes and pale skin. "I'm sorry," the boy's mother said. "He knows it's not nice to stare."

"That's quite all right," Jake said. "He's just a curious boy." Jake turned his attention toward the little boy. "You want to know how this happened?" The boy nodded, forgetting he was disgusted in the first place. The mother wasn't as excited. "When my daughter was about your age she told me there were monsters under her bed. I didn't believe her, so I told her to go back to sleep, but she was very adamant about this being a fact. For days she had been telling me about these monsters until one night I decided to prove her wrong. I stuck my hand under her bed, and do you know what happened?" The little boy shook his head without blinking. "I felt something bite down and yank me under the bed." Jake acted out the story in dramatic fashion.

The boy's eyes grew as his imagination took him to another place. His mother put her hand over her mouth trying to figure out where this was going.

"Were you scared?" the little boy asked.

"Of course I was scared. There was a monster that had me pulled into his world and was ready to eat me."

The little boy gasped. "How did you escape?"

"That was the easy part. It's a scientific fact that every monster has three weaknesses. Would you like to know what they are?" The little boy nodded frantically. "Okay, first thing's first, monsters hate the taste of vegetables. They can't even stand the smell of it. Luckily, I ate all my vegetables at dinner as a kid growing up. So, he spat my hand out immediately."

"I don't blame him," the little boy said.

Jake chuckled as he started winning the mother over. "So, if you don't want to get eaten by a monster, you have to start eating your vegetables at an early age. Number two, monsters hate smart people. It drives them crazy because they're so dumb. Good thing I made a lot of good grades when I was in school. I did all of my homework and read five books a month."

"Five books?"

The mother threw up two fingers behind his head. "You can start off with two," Jake said. "And the third and most important thing of all…you have to listen to your mother. No matter what she says, you must do it. She knows what's best and she won't let a monster get you no matter what."

The boy looked up to his mother who shot back an approving stare. "Are you sure you did all of this stuff?"

"Absolutely! How do you think I lived to talk about it?" Jake asked as he showed his burned hand.

The boy's eyes lit up with excitement. "Cool!"

Jake winked at the mother, and she mouthed a thank-you through a flirtatious smile.

"So, what happened next?" the boy asked.

"Actually," the mother said. "I think Mr. —"

"—Nick. Nick Wilkinson," Jake said.

"Yes, I think Mr. Wilkinson has told enough stories for today. Especially ones so graphic. But you can get the PG version later after Mr. Wilkinson tells me his story over a cup of coffee."

Jake smiled at her advances. "I'm sorry, I just stopped drinking coffee recently. A promise I made to Mrs. Wilkinson."

The mother's face turned ruby red. "Oh, I'm so sorry to hear that…for the coffee, I mean," she stammered. "I didn't see a ring, so—"

"I don't always wear it, because of work. I'm sorry if I made it seem like there was more to the story."

"No, it's my fault. I should have known better. The good storytellers are always taken."

Jake paid the cashier in cash and gathered his bags. "You guys have a great day. And remember what I said," he directed at the boy. The mother gawked at Jake's body as he walked away.

Jake opened the back of his Land Rover and placed the groceries inside.

"Nick!" a voice yelled from behind. Jake turned around to see a man of medium height trotting in his direction. He wore circular wire-frame glasses and had dry black hair that didn't move.

"Dr. De La Cruz," Jake said. "How are you?"

"Nick, please, we discussed this, call me David."

The two shook hands. "Okay…David. What can I do for you?"

"The wife and I are planning our next dinner party." David moved to the side so Jake could get a view of his wife putting the groceries away.

"Hey, Nick!" David's wife yelled.

Jake waved with a friendly smile.

"And where are you hiding your beauty, Diana?" David asked.

"She's at home. No doubt building a list of things for me to do."

"Don't they always. Hey, when are you guys going to get off that rock and come and see us again? You had fun at the last dinner party, right?"

"Of course. That was an amazing gesture when we first came here, and we met a lot of great people because of you."

"Then you should come to this next one we're throwing. It's going to be more of an intimate crowd, open bar. I know you don't drink, but it'll be all-around fun. Whaddaya say?"

Jake looked over at David's smiling wife, then back at him. He took a few breaths to appreciate how ordinary his life had become. "Let me run it by the wife and get back to you."

"Of course. Tell her we'd be honored to have you two." They shook hands. "Oh, and before you go…" David crept in closer. "The missus caught wind of what happened in the market a few minutes ago. Cashier gossip. I have to commend you for making the right choice."

"I made the only choice any married man would make, right?"

"You would think. Two married guys already went to the single mom's buffet if you know what I mean. Their wives are spilling the tea to my wife, and it's a little messy."

"That's what happens when you're married to the best psychologist in town."

"Yeah, it can have its downfalls. She's always in the middle of the mess, and I don't like it, but she loves helping people. Anyway, I know you just got here and things are moving pretty fast, but I don't want you to be intimidated by the drama that goes around here. Some of these spouses could have been spies in another life."

Jake smiled trying to hold back his laughter. "I don't have much to worry about with you in my corner."

David gave a flattered grin. "I won't steer you wrong. Let me know about next weekend," he said, walking away. "It won't be the same without out you guys."

"Will-do ."

* * *

Jake pulled up to a modern two-story home surrounded by woods. There were no other houses for miles. It was secluded and quiet, the way the *Wilkinsons* liked it. He came to the front door with some of the groceries. While searching for the right key, he noticed the door slightly ajar. His heart sank to his feet as he steamrolled through the door. The groceries crashed to the floor as Jake went on a hunt.

"Honey?!" he called. No response. "Are you home?" He went through the living room and the kitchen. There was no sign of Zasha. "Zasha—"He turned around and found a knife mere inches from his neck.

"Who is this Zasha and how long have you been seeing her ?" Zasha asked with a playful smile. Her hair was now a rich auburn color, and wrapped in a braided ponytail.

Jake exhaled deeply and pushed the knife away. "That's not funny."

"I wasn't trying to be. What's going on?"

Jake took a second to collect his thoughts. "I thought, the door, it was open and—"

"—I just came from my run. I probably didn't close it all the way ."

"I just got worried, that's all."

Zasha ran her fingers through his beard and pressed her warm lips against his. She held his face so he could look into her eyes. "Hey, we're okay. We covered our tracks. We did everything possible to delete our pasts. It's been eight months. You can loosen up just a little bit."

"What about The Catalogue?" Jake whispered.

"What about it? You destroyed it, remember? The world is secretly in your debt."

"What if there's another one out there?" Jake said. "It's possible."

"If we spend the rest of this life worrying about that, then we might as well kill ourselves and get it over with. Right now, I just want to be Mrs. Diana Wilkinson who's happy with her sometimes-estranged husband Mr. Nicholas Wilkinson. Can we agree on that?"

Jake sighed as he walked to pick up the groceries. "Yeah. That's one thing we can agree on at least."

Zasha rolled her eyes. "What's that supposed to mean?"

"You know what it means."

"Again, with this? Look, this was the best place to defect to. It's completely off the grid."

"Maybe a little too off the grid. You ever heard of hiding in plain sight?"

"Have you ever heard of rubbing elbows with the locals?"

"Places like this are too small, Zasha. This community has grown together through generations. There hasn't been a new family in this town since 1975. Us being here makes us stand out more than we think."

"We'll blend in eventually. Unless you're living underground, part of defecting is building a new life. You should listen to your wife. Especially since I have more experience than you at this kind of thing. I think I'm more qualified to make the call."

"And what brings you to that conclusion?"

Zasha shrugged her shoulders. "Let's see, I've been a covert agent longer than you have. I've been in hiding longer than you. I have done almost double the missions that you have. And my specialty is finding people. I think I know little something about the reverse process."

"You couldn't find The Wraith."

"That's because I wasn't looking for The Wraith," she said in a mocking voice.

"And that's just how good The Wraith was. He was right under your nose, and you didn't even know it. That, my wife, is how you defect."

Zasha scoffed. "What about the fact that you still think my real name is Zasha?"

Jake chuckled, but Zasha gave him an indifferent stare. "Yeah right. Then what is it? Jane Bond?"

She brought her face within inches of Jake's. "Like I

said, I'm not trying to be funny." A seductive kiss had Jake buckling at the knees. "But what I am trying to do is take a nice shower with my husband. You think you can handle that?" She gave him another, longer kiss.

His mind went blank when he felt her warmth. "Ye-yeah," he stuttered. "I just have a couple more bags in the car. I'll be right up."

"Don't leave me waiting," Zasha said as she strolled up the stairs.

"Hey, you were just joking about the name, right ?"

No response.

"Zasha?"

"I don't know who that person is!" she yelled from upstairs. "Certainly no one here goes by that name ."

Jake chuckled with uncertainty.

Jake opened the back of his car to retrieve the last grocery bag. As he reached in, he felt the cold barrel of an M-16 touch the back of his neck, followed by the bolt racking.

"Stand up, slowly," a distorted voice said.

Jake gradually did as he was told. "I don't know what you want, but you won't find it here." He saw a fleet of men dressed in black ops gear coming from the woods. They all formed a line and entered the house with their weapons drawn. Jake ran after them but was tackled by two other men.

"If you touch her, I'll kill you!"

"This will be a lot easier if you don't resist," the distorted voice said.

A single gunshot from the house had everyone on hold. "Zasha!" Jake yelled.

Everyone waiting outside charged into the house. Jake was escorted in behind the pack. When he came in, he saw a trail of blood leading to the living room. The closer they approached, the more unsteady his legs became as he dreaded the potential outcome. He got to the living room and saw Zasha sitting on the couch in her robe. The blood led to an agent lying on the floor. He'd been shot in the leg.

"What the hell happened here?" the distorted voice asked.

"She shot me, that's what happened," the wounded agent replied.

Jake sat next to Zasha on the couch and asked if she was okay. She nodded, making sure not to say a word.

Jake looked at the agent who'd escorted him in. "What the hell do you want?"

The escorting agent took off his helmet and balaclava to reveal his face. He was a young black man with a thick mustache.

"Who the hell are you?" Jake asked.

"My name is Malik Samson," he said with his regular voice. "I have orders to bring you both in alive, with pending instructions."

"No," Jake said. "We're not going anywhere."

Malik handed his gun to another agent and signaled for everyone to leave the room. "The people I work for don't want to hurt you. You can trust us."

Jake scoffed. "You have no idea how hollow that statement is."

"Look, we know you both have been through a lot. As much as I hate to admit it, we need your help."

"With what?" Zasha asked.

Malik sighed. "You two are the last few of your kind, with your special skill set, left on the planet. We want to utilize those skills to find someone of your…ilk."

"Who are you?" Jake asked.

"That will be explained to you when we get to headquarters."

"For what?"

"Asking twenty-one questions right now isn't going to get you any closer to the information you want."

Jake grabbed Zasha and pulled her close. "You said you wanted us to help find someone like us. Who's the other person?"

Malik chuckled in disbelief. "You don't know, do you?" Jake and Zasha looked back at him, confused. "I assumed you did. Why else would you two be in such deep hiding?"

"Would you cut the crap and answer his question?" Zasha demanded.

"While you two have been honeymooning in the woods, there's been a high-level threat stacking his chips from the beginning. If you thought what you went through was hell...you were just at the doorstep."

"This high-level threat...does he know we're alive?"

"Yes," Malik replied. "Luckily for you, we're building a team. We're going after him and taking him down, for good this time."

"Are you asking us what I think you're asking us?"

Malik nodded. "We're asking you to help us take down Do Shen and the organization he has growing as we speak. This isn't V.E.N.O.M. This is something far worse."

Jake and Zasha looked at each other, then back to Malik. Jake grabbed her hand and asked, "When do we leave?"

WORDS FROM THE AUTHOR

First and foremost, I want to thank God for blessing me with the patience to be a writer. It takes a toll on you mentally and emotionally to write anything creatively and put it out in the world for people to judge. So, for anyone who is in the process or on their creative journey, I wish you the best of luck. Writing V.E.N.O.M. was challenging for me both creatively and personally. I had to dig deep to build this story and connect with these characters on a personal level. This was a huge project for me and I couldn't have done it alone.

First, I would like to thank my beautiful wife, Alessandra, for not only putting up with my craziness, but also giving me my two greatest accomplishments...my children, Julian and Elena. My family is my biggest motivation.

Special thanks to family and friends who have supported my dreams from the beginning, specifically Benjamin Martin. Every time I would see him, he would ask how the book was going. He wanted to be one of the first to read it. Thanks Ben, for keeping me on my toes.

To my unexpected writing mentor, Richard Rumple, for some reason you saw something in me and decided to guide me through the rough terrain of writing. Whether it was critiquing my work, suggesting reading material, or just keeping a stern foot in my butt to keep me writing, you were always there to make sure I didn't lose focus. Thank you.

Last but not least, I must thank you, the reader. I am an independent authorpreneur and your reading this book means that it was more than a mere chance that it landed in your hands…it was destiny. My company *Red Rope Press* is about building personal relationships with my readers, and growing a community where people can come together to enjoy these stories, dissect them, put them back together, and start a dialogue about what they think and feel. A writer is nothing without his readers, so again, I thank you all for putting your trust in me and picking up this book and making my dreams come true. I want to hear from all of you! Please leave your comments on Amazon, Goodreads and other reading platforms so I can know how you feel about the book. I love you all and God bless.

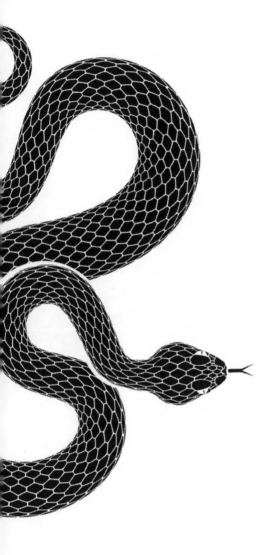

If you loved this book and would love to receive FREE short stories from the V.E.N.O.M. universe—and updates about the sequel to this book—please join our mailing list at www.tymitchellbook.com

A Sneak Peek at
Operation Nightfall

Operation Nightfall

Trapani, Sicily

The night was humid, but the ocean breeze cleared up the thickness in the air. The waves crashing on the rocks below put Jake in serene state of mind. Hearing the swooshing in real life was way better than listening to a recording. Add that to his handmade cigarette, and it was the closest thing to heaven Jake was willing to get near. His suit was custom-made, his hair gelled back and his face as smooth as porcelain. The overall effect was almost reminiscent of someone he once knew. A ghost of redemption, and his window to the other side that he might have been on . He took his last drag of the cigarette and flicked it into the ocean, then walked into the dark bar called *I Corti*.

Inside, there were a few locals and the bartender. Jake sat right at the bar and took a hard swallow at the assortment of alcohol displayed on the wall. His daze was interrupted when the bartender stepped in front of him.

"Preggo," the bartender said.

"Nastro Azzurro,"

Jake replied. The bartender cracked open a beer and handed it to him.

"Grazie." He took the bottle and let it sit under his nose. The smell of the pale lager brought back every drunken memory he could recall, and it made his stomach turn. He took a sip of the beer, and after almost a year of no drinking, the taste in his mouth made the ocean breeze feel like a smack in the face. Jake flashed his tobacco and rolling papers, and the bartender gave him an approving nod. Jake rolled his cigarette, and took a puff after he sipped his beer.

"Do you have enough for one more?" a voice said in Italian.

Jake turned around to see a heavyset man with hairy forearms standing right behind him. He took one look at the man and said in Italian, "Of course, my friend." He offered him a seat and rolled him a cigarette. The burly man spoke to the bartender in Sicilian. Jake's Italian was fluent, but his Sicilian was a little rusty. He could only pick up parts of the conversation. The bartender brought over two shot glasses of Grappa.

"For your troubles," the burly man said.

"It was no trouble at all."

"Salute!" They downed the shot glasses and Jake felt the burn from his throat to his stomach. "Americano?"

"Si," Jake said.

"I can tell. Your Italian is decent, but your accent gave you away. How did you learn?"

"I had a Sicilian girlfriend. I learned a lot from her... and occasionally she'd teach me Italian."

"I know exactly what you mean," the burly man said, laughing through a cough. "Is that why you are here? To forget about this ex-lover?"

"No. I'm actually here to meet someone."

"What is the name of this person? I come here every night. I know everyone who walks through that door." He winked at the bartender, and the bartender winked back with a smile.

"The man I'm looking for doesn't necessarily have a name. He's a myth more than anything."

"It sounds like you're in the wrong place. Like I said, I know everyone who walks through that door. Everyone, except you." The burly man studied Jake up and down before he said in broken English, "What is your name, friend?"

Jake was surprised that he knew English. He felt the whole bar get quiet waiting for his response. When he walked in, he'd counted three men plus the bartender, whose hand went under the bar and stayed there. Add the burly man to the mix, and it made for an interesting predicament.

"You speak English," Jake said, exhaling smoke. "Where did you learn?"

"Tourists. They come all the time. I guess I just…picked it up."

Jake chuckled. "Does he know that I'm here?"

"Does it matter?"

Jake took a long pull of his cigarette. "It did…for you."

He flicked the remainder of his cigarette in the face of the bartender and smashed the beer bottle over the burly man's head. Two men from the table behind Jake stood, but Jake kicked a stool into one's groin and rushed at the other with swift punches to the face. The third man sat with his hands up. He was no threat. The sound of a shotgun racking made everyone still.

Jake turned to see the bartender aiming and ready to destroy anything in his sight. The burly man came from Jake's right side and landed a punch the leveled him. Jake was carried to the bar and his head was held to the dried wood as the barrel of the shotgun was pressed against his ear .

"You should have never come here," the burly man said in Sicilian.

"Basta!" a voice shouted from the door. It was a voice Jake knew all-too-well from a life he left behind. The footsteps were slow, and echoed against the floor like any expensive shoe would. The mystery man stood over Jake.

Through his peripheral, Jake saw an older man with an even tan, a pencil mustache. His smile was genuine and troubling at the same time. "Do my eyes deceive me," the mystery man said in English, "or is this really Jacob Penny in one of my bars?"

"No need for glasses yet, old man."

The mystery man smirked. "I should have killed you when I had the chance. Then you wouldn't be able to make such smart remarks. But you had so much promise that you made me break mine. Never let a student better than me graduate alive. You were the exception. And the biggest regret of my life."

"Given your situation," Jake said, "that can't possibly be true. But I can change that. I'm here to make an offer."

The mystery man chuckled. "Chico." He signaled for the bartender to hand him the shotgun. "Now, why would I take anything from you if it means I have to pass up on my promise twice?" The mystery man placed his finger on the trigger and lodged the barrel deeper in Jake's ear. Jake had the answer, but he didn't know if it was good enough to keep him alive.

Made in the USA
Columbia, SC
16 April 2019